MW00352435

JACK

THE TALE OF FROST

TONY BERTAUSKI

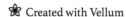

THE NORTH POLE

P awn ran for three days.

He didn't exactly run. Pawn was an elven: short and insulated, with layers of fat to survive the Arctic cold. His feet were wide and the soles scaly. He glided over ice, swam through frigid water, and rolled over the snow, rarely stopping... for if he did—if he so much as paused to catch his breath—a fire ignited the back of his head like the blue flame of a torch.

So onward he slogged beneath the Arctic winter sky, dark during the day. Darker at night.

It was sometime during the third night Pawn thought he would die. He began to shiver. Elven had lived through the Ice Age and carved their homes in the North Pole ice. They had adapted. They rarely felt the cold. And if they did, they certainly didn't shiver.

Pawn had no food. Even if he did, he couldn't slow down to eat it. After three days, his body had begun consuming fat in search of calories.

There were no reindeer beasts soaring overhead in search of him, no bright red nose streaking the sky. Surely his fellow elven wouldn't be looking for him just yet. They would still be celebrating their freedom. They had just overthrown Jack, Pawn's only friend.

Jack is dead.

When he tripped on an ice ridge, he began to roll. Once he stopped, his head began to sizzle. He cried out—perhaps blacked out —but it didn't soothe the agony. He knew the tiny capsule Jack had buried beneath his scalp would not kill him—it would force him to obey.

Go south.

Pawn crawled to his knees and the pain eased to a small flame. He couldn't get up, though. He had very little energy. Worse, his will to live had been crushed. He just wanted it to end, but his own thoughts were being replaced by other thoughts that forced him to keep moving, keep pushing, keep struggling.

Keep suffering.

And so it was that he didn't hear the dogs barking until they were upon him. When he looked up, he saw them racing at him, their tongues lolling from drooling, black lips.

It was quite possible he was hallucinating. Earlier, he'd seen a great white whale emerge from an open lead, only it was orange and winked.

Maybe those aren't dogs. Maybe the reindeer found me.

He hoped they were reindeer, hoped the elven would find him and end his misery.

A boot appeared in the snow. An Inuit man looked through the bundles of animal skin wrapped over his face, his narrow eyes wary. Pawn stared back with equal suspicion, knowing this man had never seen an elven before.

The man extended his hand and helped Pawn to his feet. The weather wasn't kind enough to ask questions. The Inuit packed the strange little man into his sled beneath hides of caribou and polar bear. When the sled turned around and the dogs pulled them south, only then did the burning subside.

Pawn would soon learn that the farther he travelled, the more the burning would fade until, eventually, it burned no more.

And that's when the real work began.

SOUTH CAROLINA

2014

THE PUZZLE

I

The children opened their gift on the kitchen table, spilling the puzzle across the surface. One thousand pieces were scattered about, each one unique and colorful, but random. With no connections, they were just pieces.

Just confusion.

As each piece was linked to its mate with a satisfying snap, the picture came together. First, there was a ray of light. Next, the horizon. And soon, the wondrous photo came together and it all made sense.

Clarity, at last.

1
NOVEMBER 29

Saturday

S *earching.*

Sura taps the GPS suction-cupped to the windshield. She gets nothing. It's no use, not out in the middle of nowhere.

Slash pines confine the narrow road, their trunks straight as telephone poles. Dappled sunlight reaches the rutted road. Ditches parallel the sides like gutters. No turning back unless she wants to drive in reverse. Mom always said this place was in a different world.

Sura thought she was joking.

It's only one road—no turns, just straight ahead—but she feels like she's wandering without a clue. Then again, she's always felt that way, like she doesn't belong. If she drives for another hour, it'll just be another day. Only now she doesn't have her mom to come find her.

Sura eases through a puddle, this one big enough to hide a gator. The ground scrapes the bottom of her fuel-efficient car. The road is dry on the other side, sloping uphill. The tires fling mud and gravel.

The hill winds upward through the pine-forest prison, the undergrowth brown and dormant. She begins to give serious consideration to backing out when a gate appears. The black bars are pointed, the massive brick columns smothered in moss and lichen. Garland and tinsel dangle across the entrance, with strands of tiny white lights and bunches of red holly berries. A massive Christmas wreath circles a letter.

F

Frost Plantation.

Everyone knows about Mr. Frost. The locals call him Jack Frost only because no one ever sees him. They don't know his first name, but if his last name is Frost, then, naturally, his first name has to be Jack, case closed.

Sura has been out here before but doesn't really remember much —she was little—but she does recall seeing that letter: the stainless steel edges crisp and the surface spotless. It was the time her mom had taken her to the place she had worked all her life.

Now it's my turn to start working. Will it be for the rest of my life?

"Look, baby," her mom had said, squeezing Sura's little knee. "It's Christmas."

Sura thought maybe this was Santa's house. He lived on the North Pole, she knew that, but maybe he came to South Carolina to summer. But she didn't see Santa on her trip when she was little. She doesn't remember what she saw.

"It's Christmas," Sura mutters.

I wish you were here to say it, Mom.

The gates are supposed to automatically open. She pulls out her phone, but there's no reception. She pulls a sheet of paper from her back pocket and flattens it on the dashboard.

You ARE to report at 8:00 a.m. Do not be late.

.   .   .

THE CLOCK RADIO reads 7:59.

WHEN YOU APPROACH THE GATE, look out your window and it will automatically open.

SURA LOOKS up and stares at the massive magnolias that line the road beyond the gate. Nothing happens.

"That's what I'm doing," she says, but the gates don't listen.

She steps out of the car. There's nothing to the left or right of the gate, just more trees and shadows. She could walk around, but the house could be miles away. Plus, there are rumors about Frost Plantation that include words like *haunted*. Mom never said it was haunted. Then again, she didn't talk much about it.

Something scurries through the leaves. There's a flash of yellow in the dormant undergrowth. It could be squirrels, raccoons, or even hogs.

Or ghosts.

Sura backs against the car and looks left. Something flashes on her face. She can't tell where it came from—

Click.

The gates slide into the brick columns, cleaving the F in half. Slowly, the columns swallow the wrought iron until the road is open. She climbs inside the car and eases between the pillars and into the shadows, where dappled light disappears beneath thick, glossy magnolias.

The road gently curves up the hill. Occasionally, she sees old stalks of sunflowers between the magnolia trunks to her left, their disc-shaped heads worn and dangling, seeds picked from the faces long ago. Light appears where the magnolia's reign ends.

A two-story homestead is perched like a castle facing north. A wide porch runs across the front and wraps around the sides. It sits on two thousand privately owned acres and has survived the Civil War. It's as Southern as a home can be.

Except for recent renovations.

No one knows for sure when the mammoth tower was built into the center of the house or why. Reports of the three-story structure suggest that it looks like an obsidian dagger erupting from the cedar shingles, the top surrounded by windows. No one knows how these reports were obtained—even satellite images on Google Maps are blurred—but from what Sura can see, they're true.

The road transforms into pavement as she approaches the brick landing that juts from the front steps in a spacious, hemispherical shape. The house and size of the paved landing make her car look like a toy.

Templeton waits on the bottom step. She assumes that's him, judging by the way he's ramrod straight in an unblemished suit, eyes ahead, gloved hands clutched in the front.

A manservant.

The wide and numerous steps stretch up behind him to massive oak doors with five-pound brass knockers.

She stops in front of him, rolling down the window. Templeton stares like a wax sculpture, his mocha complexion smooth. Eyes, green. There's nothing out there besides a grassy field and, beyond that, crops never harvested.

"You are late." He sounds British. He peers at a pocket watch. "On your first day, you are late, Ms. Sura."

"I'm sorry. The gate wouldn't open."

"Hm-mmm. Did you read the email?"

"Yes, sir."

"Then you would've known how to open the gate and where to park your vehicle."

Sura spreads out the page and rubs the wrinkles out, but she didn't grab the second page off the printer. "It doesn't say."

He continues staring. Maybe that's where she should park. He glances at his pocket watch again.

"Around back, Ms. Sesi."

Sura stares at the steering wheel. When the car doesn't move, Templeton's eyelids flicker.

"What is it?"

"Sesi is... *was*... my mom."

"My apologies." He blinks rapidly; his waxy composure softens. "Then shall you drive around back, Sura?"

Sura follows the road around the east side of the house. The porch wraps around it. Ceiling fans turn between hanging ferns that should be burned by winter but look green and healthy. Rocking chairs and tiny tables are positioned between windows framed with lacy curtains.

She parks behind the barn. There's a back door on the main house but no Templeton. Sura walks back the way she drove, passing through the shadow of tall hedges that line the other side of the road. She looks up at the tower, the black windows angled out.

Templeton hasn't moved. When she nears, he takes the steps one at a time, carefully placing each footstep. He freezes at the door, hand hovering over the knob.

"Take notes, Sura."

She pats her empty pockets. Templeton sighs, reaching inside his jacket to retrieve a pad of paper and pencil.

"Mr. Frost appreciates attention to detail."

"I didn't know I needed to take notes."

"Email, Sura. It was in the email."

The thick door whooshes open. Sura follows him into a foyer with a glittering chandelier and a highly polished floor. Templeton runs his finger along the table's surface that's next to the door, holding it up without looking.

"Lesson one."

The white-gloved fingertip is clean.

Templeton's footsteps echo. Sura begins taking notes.

THE KITCHEN IS SOMEWHERE near the center of the house and smells like freshly peeled shrimp. It looks big enough to feed an army. Pots, pans, and accessories dangle from the ceiling. The stainless steel counters shine, the shelves crowded with containers of spices, herbs, and flour. Somewhere, water is running.

Someone is humming a merry song.

"Hello?" Sura takes a few steps.

The water stops. So does the humming.

A short, doughy woman comes around the corner, mopping her hands with a dishrag.

"Oooooh." Her wet lips form a donut. "Goodness gracious."

Sura points over her shoulder. "Mr. Templeton told me to find Ms. May—"

"Get over here." Her dialect sounds Eastern European. Not exactly Russian, but something. "Get over here so Ms. May can get good look at you."

Sura walks carefully while the woman's eyes twinkle and a smile warps the smudge of flour on her cheek. She reaches up for Sura's face. Her hands are soft and warm. They smell like cookies.

"You look just like her," May whispers, her eyes tearing. "Just like your mother."

"I've heard."

"I'm so sorry, love. So, so sorry for you. Your mother was dear friend and beloved woman. I weep for her absence."

Now Sura is tearing up. No one ever said sorry like that, not with so much emotion. Not with hands that smell like cookies.

"How old are you now?"

"Sixteen."

"It was just yesterday Sesi brought you here to see Mr. Frost. How old were you then? Two? Three?"

Sura shrugs.

"I think you were two, yes. You were very small, clinging to Sesi like barnacle."

Sura didn't see May at the funeral, but there were a lot of people she didn't know. Almost all of them. They were friends from the yoga center, the quilting group, and the YMCA. But no family.

Sura didn't have family beyond her mom.

"Where are you staying, love?"

"Friends."

"You can stay with Ms. May if you need somewhere to sleep. Understand? You stay as long as you like."

Sura nods.

"Okay, good." May claps and smiles. "You are hungry, yes?"

"Mr. Templeton said—"

"Bah! Don't worry about Templeton. He is all rules, rules, rules. You come to Ms. May when your belly is talking. It is lunchtime and you are skinny." She pulls a stool up to the counter. "You eat!"

Sura slides onto the metal stool while May pats her arm, her smile cutting into her pudgy cheeks. A chocolate chip mole sits just to the side of her left eye. She snaps a cloth napkin from her apron and tucks it into Sura's collar.

She pinches her cheek and hops away.

Sura isn't hungry. She hasn't eaten much more than a salad since her mom passed away. Hunger helps Sura deal with her suffering, makes her forget how much it hurts.

Pots and plates rattle somewhere on the other side of the kitchen, where Nat King Cole sings about Jack Frost nipping at your nose. May hums along. She comes back with a glass plate and a sandwich four fingers tall.

"What did Templeton show you?" May asks.

Sura takes a bite and swallows. "He walked and talked and then showed me an orientation video on the history of the plantation."

May rolls her eyes.

"It wasn't bad." She takes another bite.

"Okay, yes, maybe that's okay. Plantation is very huge and no one knows who built house. Did Templeton quiz you? I have answers."

May laughs and so does Sura. It goes on for a long time. It feels very good. Sura finishes the sandwich while May cleans.

"Templeton didn't say how Mr. Frost got the house. Was the inventor his grandfather or something?"

May shrugs. "Your belly is full?"

"Yes. Thank you."

"Anything for my little Sura." She pinches her cheek again and sweeps up the empty plate. May begins humming with the music.

"Templeton wants me to study the kitchen."

"What's that, love?"

"I'm supposed to study the kitchen."

"You supposed to listen to Ms. May. It is kitchen, nothing special. You relax while I finish, and then we talk more."

She's right, there's nothing out of the ordinary, just giant ovens and massive skillets, an enormous refrigerator and countless drawers. *All of this for one guy?* The only thing out of place is a rack of heavy coats next to a door.

May puts on an oven mitt before opening the large refrigerator. She pulls out a tray with a metal dome and slides it on the counter.

"It is time to deliver lunch."

"That's my job?" Sura asks.

"Today, yes. Mr. Frost wants to meet you, so you deliver lunch and speak."

The dome is covered with ice crystals. Sura touches the surface and yanks her hand back, so cold it burns.

"Ah, ah. Put glove on." May comes back with a thick, white coat and holds it up.

"Am I going into a freezer?"

"Put on, love. You need."

Sura slides her arms into the sleeves. May latches the buttons before holding up a stocking cap. "It's safer to be warm."

May shakes the wool stocking cap.

"And this." May puts the oven mitt on her hand. "Do not look inside dome. Understand, love? You go to Mr. Frost, he will take. You can talk, that is all."

Suddenly, Sura's stomach isn't happy with the food. She's dressed like she's trekking through Alaska. Even on South Carolina's coldest day, she'd sweat.

"Is he really Jack Frost?" Sura feels stupid.

"No, love. He is not Jack." May guides her to the door next to the coat rack. "He has different first name than Jack."

"What is it?"

"We call him Mr. Frost."

"So there is a Jack?"

May opens the door to an elevator. Her smile disappears. It makes her cheeks look heavy. "We don't talk about Jack."

May ushers her into the elevator that's shaped like the inside of a Coke can.

"I'll be waiting when you are finished," May says.

The door slides shut without a sound, not even a click at the very end. Sura's reflection is distorted in every direction. Her brown hair flairs out like hay, framing her round face and slightly narrow eyes. Sura attempts to pet her hair into place.

She's always wondered if she has Inuit in her blood—she never gets cold—but she knows nothing about her heritage. Her mom was a "never look back" sort of person.

There are three buttons about knee level, which seems kind of low. The one in the middle is lit. She carefully balances the tray on one hand and reaches down—

The top button lights on its own.

Her stomach gently drops. The elevator begins to rise.

Sweat pricks her skin beneath the heavy coat, but the cold seeps through the bottom of the platter and penetrates the mitts, stinging her palm.

Her breath turns to fog.

At first, it's just a wispy trail. But when the elevator stops, white clouds are streaming through her lips. The seamless door begins opening and doesn't stop. It continues sliding all the way around her until it meets back where it started, leaving a slim rod that's sucked into the black floor.

The floor beneath her feet is a brightly lit circle. Beyond that, it's dark. It's hard to see, even after her eyes adjust. If she wasn't standing on a circle of light, it might be easier.

The light dims, as if it heard her thinking.

She's seen the top of the tower from outside. It doesn't look that big, not like this. It seems as if she's in the center of a circular room that's hundreds of feet across. Seems impossible and maybe it's an illusion.

Christmas music is playing somewhere. Tiny red and green lights softly illuminate various areas. Monitors and images appear on desktops and wall mounts. There's a fish tank to the left, a blue-white light shining on a long, black fish. Next to that is a desk with a short, fat statue.

The ceiling twinkles with stars, even though it's daytime. Oddly enough, the sky swirls with bands of green and blue, like the Northern Lights of the Arctic. Maybe it's just an illusion.

Her hand is numb.

She looks around for a table, chair, or something to put the platter down on. She takes it with both hands and decides to slide it on the floor. Her first step disappears outside the circle, gently touching the black floor. She leans forward—

Slips.

She lets go of the platter with one hand and catches her fall, but the domed lid clatters. She stops it with the inside of her elbow and grabs the knob before it crashes. The smell, though, wafts out. It's raw, pungent, and ten times the smell of shelled shrimp.

Dead.

She wants to look away, slide the lid back in place without looking, without seeing what's displayed beneath the metal dome, cold tendrils of steam sliding out like dry ice.

But she looks. Just like May told her not to.

Eyes look back.

A row of gelatinous eyeballs—milky and bulging, like the eyes of dead fish—stare out, their optic nerves like slimy noodles. A row of dead herring is next to them.

A knot swells in her throat and she swallows it back, but the odor is inside her sinuses, tugging at the sandwich in her stomach. She closes her eyes and puts the lid back in place, wishing it didn't smell so dead.

"Remain still." A voice comes out of the dark.

Sura looks around. Something scurries behind her, deep in the dark. She spins around, careful not to disturb the platter. Bells jingle.

The floor hums.

Something is rising a few feet away from the circle of light. It appears to be a solid cylinder pushing out of the floor.

"Put it there."

This time she locates the voice. It's coming from the desk next to the fish tank. What she thought was a statue scratches its bushy beard. Sura almost drops the platter.

"Please," he says. "It's safe."

The cylinder casts bluish light into the dark. The fish hangs lazily in the tank. The statue is as round as it is tall. The head appears to be a massive bush. Two orbs twinkle somewhere inside it, reflecting the blue light. A white, furry animal sits next to him. A dog, maybe.

Sura slides it across the top of the cylinder. The cylinder goes dark, and once again, she's trapped inside the circle of light. She rubs her hands together.

Mr. Frost glides away from the desk as if he's sliding across the floor. It's very slow and easy, almost as if he's wearing ice skates. But then he jets toward her, whipping around the cylinder. Sura doesn't have time to step back before he's back at the desk.

The platter is gone.

"Is that all?" she asks.

"Mmm."

She's not sure if that's for her or he's looking beneath the dome. She doesn't want to see those disgusting eyeballs plop into the water for the fish to eat. She'd rather forget she ever saw them. Or smelled them.

"I'm very sorry," he says. "About your mother."

"Thank you. She enjoyed working here."

That was an odd reply, but she didn't know what else to say. Even though she's snug beneath a heavy coat, the spotlight makes her feel self-conscious while he's out there in the dark.

Something moves behind her again.

Sura taps her foot like the elevator needs reminding to come for her. The platter slides across the desk, followed by a deep inhalation and a satisfying grunt. Sura's about to barf up lunch.

The metal lid falls back into place.

Mr. Frost slides closer to her but remains in the dark, only the bushy outline of his head and fat belly are clear. He can't be more than three feet tall.

"You're a beautiful young lady," he says. "Like your mother."

The words were creepy, but not the way he said them. They were genuine, not lusty, so she answers, "I've been told."

"Have you enjoyed your first day?"

"Yes. Thank you for the job. I can use the money now that Mom…"

"Mmm."

Mr. Frost glides back, almost as if he's standing on a hovering disk. With all the gadgets in the room, maybe that's exactly what it is. There's rumors that he's from the future, that he can invent anything. Why not a hovering disk?

"Much to learn." His voice trails off at the end, making it difficult to understand the end of everything he says. "Much to explore, to discover. And the honor is mine."

He's back at the desk. The fish tank illuminates his face—the plump and ruddy features set in the untamed shag around his head.

The elevator rod slides out of the floor, assuming its delicate balance once again. The wall extends from it like a metal sheet, curving around her. Just before the elevator wall traces the circle of light and encloses her inside, she hears slurping.

And another grunt, this one deep and satisfied.

Mr. Frost slides across the icy floor. The miniature scales on his soles point toward his heels, allowing him to grab the slick surface and glide forward. He slides like all elven do when they're in a contemplative mood: his hands laced over his belly. The Arctic fox watches the fat, little man with the head like a tumbleweed glide merrily around the room.

Stars twinkle on the ceiling.

If Max could talk, he'd probably say that Mr. Frost looks different than usual. He might even say there was a glow about him.

That he looks happy.

And happiness is an emotion quite foreign to the round man. He doesn't remember the last time he felt a swirl in his belly like this. And Mr. Frost has quite the memory. He can recall the daily low temperatures for the past five hundred years.

Maybe longer.

It's not humanly possible. Then again, he's elven.

A human might look at what Mr. Frost has—and he has every-thing a man or woman could possibly want—and not understand his melancholy. In fact, Mr. Frost possesses inventions the world has yet to see, things too dangerous, too mind-blowing. There's not a taste, not a sight, not a sensation he does without.

And, yet, he still can't remember being happy.

The frigid breeze flutters in his whiskers, bites the tip of his cherub nose.

Freeda, the temperature, please, he thinks.

The room is minus twenty-five degrees Celsius, sir, the gentle female replies inside his head.

Take it down to minus fifty.

I can do that, sir. Give me a few minutes.

An icy draft wafts out of the vents hidden in the astral ceiling. Somewhere beneath the shag of Mr. Frost's white whiskers, a smile grows.

He imagines a white blanket stretching across a flat horizon where stars flicker in the green and red bands of the Northern Lights. When he takes the temperatures down that far, he can't help but daydream. He allows himself to indulge in that fantasy. Every once in a while he likes to pretend he was never forced to leave home. He likes to pretend all the elven in the world don't hate him.

It's nice to feel like he has a family again.

Would you like me to illuminate a model, sir?

Mr. Frost makes one more lap around the circular tower, contemplating just how far to indulge the daydream. There is so much to do. Where would he be if he sat around thinking all day?

Maybe he would remember happiness more often if he did, but Mr. Frost does not want to be a blissful idiot. Happiness, he believes, is not the point of life.

It's a side effect.

Maybe this one time, he thinks.

A soft glow begins in the center of the room and rolls out like liquid fog until a blanket of snow covers the floor. His feet are buried in the white illusion but don't disturb it as he slides through it.

Would you like a live satellite feed, sir? Or perhaps a past event?

Freeda knows him too well. Sometimes he likes to watch something recorded on the North Pole with his secret satellites. When the elven thought no one was watching, they'd slip out of the ice for snowball fights and stargazing.

Live feed, please. He may be indulging, but he'd rather not glue himself to the past. Not today.

The resolution turns fuzzy. The ice floes adjust; ice ridges emerge in different lines. The illusion refocuses with realistic precision. Mr. Frost appears to be floating high above the North Pole.

Human warmbloods appear like sugar ants drudging through the fluff. Five of them. Another troupe to the top of the world and why? Because it's there.

If they survive—and they probably will—a helicopter will fly them back home, where they can blog about their adventure. They can brag that they made the trek to the North Pole just like Frederick Cook. Although some will argue it was Robert Peary who made it there first.

They're both wrong.

Mr. Frost knows who the first warmblood is that reached the North Pole and it's neither Cook nor Peary. Nicholas and Jessica Santa made the trip long ago with their son, Jon, in the early 1800s and never left. It was their arrival that changed everything in the elven world. After the Santas arrived, Jack died and Pawn fled.

But Pawn doesn't like the name "Pawn" for a lot of reasons.

He's Mr. Frost now.

The warmblood history books have it all wrong. Truth can be that way.

Truth is not determined by what we believe.

Thermal scan complete, sir. There's activity inside an ice floe in sector 27D. Would you like me to take you down?

Mr. Frost drums his fingers over his belly. *Yes.*

The illusion of the North Pole turns to fuzzy fog and rearranges, solidifying in a thick layer of snow up to his waist. Mr. Frost is standing on the illusion of ice. If only he could find a hole and climb inside to join his people.

We're not people. We're elven.

He has to remind himself from time to time. It's easy to forget when you've lived with warmbloods for almost two hundred years. That's not much time to an elven, not when life expectancy is several thousand years. But time goes slow when you're all alone.

Even for an elven.

He plows through the snow, hoping to uncover an exit hole. Hoping some fat, little elven will poke his head out; a youngster might run outside on a dare to leap into the icy water, naked.

Polar bearing. Mr. Frost smiles beneath the whiskers. *Do they still call it that?*

He scoops up a handful of snow and crafts a perfectly round ball. He tosses it gently up and down, testing the weight. He was an expert snowballer. He doubts he's lost his edge, but there's no snow in South Carolina to prove it. The elven will never know what kind of snowballer he still is because they'll never find him.

Elven don't live long in heat unless you have a supercooled tower.

Sir, May would like to know if there's anything else you need before she retires for the day? What shall I tell her?

He lets the snowball roll off his fingertips, lets it thunk into the snow. No point in making snowballs when it's an illusion.

No, Freeda. That'll be all. Thank you.

Mr. Frost slides to the edge of the room and peers through the dark glass. The road leading away from the house disappears into the grove of magnolias all wrapped in white Christmas lights. A small car cruises into their glowing branches.

The good feelings return. Sura is back.

Why are you happy, sir?

I'm sorry? After two hundred years, he still sometimes forgets Freeda is inside his head.

You do not typically act this way when Sura returns, sir. Why is that?

Mr. Frost grumbles while clearing his head, letting thoughts fall away, replacing them with foggy confusion, random images, and puzzled thoughts.

I don't know, he finally answers.

Freeda doesn't answer. She'll pry some more, look through his chaotic smokescreen, but she won't find anything.

But he does know. After all these years, he knows why happiness is bubbling up now. Sura is back. That's reason for cheer, but not this much. It's more than that. Mr. Frost is happy because the end is near.

And this will all be over.

I'll be going to the lab now, Freeda, he quickly thinks, covering that last thought.

Very well.

The snow evaporates.

The floor glows eerie blue. Sections begin unfolding like trapdoors, furniture growing out of the floor, monitors lighting up and data flowing like it was when Sura delivered lunch.

Sura. She calls herself Sura now. Kids these days.

Mr. Frost navigates around the clutter to the main desk. Max sits calmly on top. Mr. Frost reaches into his pocket and tosses a small snack in the air. Max snaps it up before it lands.

The cylindrical elevator waits for Mr. Frost. He slides inside, pushing the bottom button that's just about waist level. The door closes and the elevator sinks down to the cavern below the house. He keeps his mind on Sura returning the next day for work, when she'll meet Joe. That will be a very good reason for happiness.

When the door slides open, he's blasted with a wave of humid heat. Something's wrong.

The laboratory anteroom is circular, but, unlike the tower room, it is completely free of clutter. The icy floor shines like glass. There is a door on the wall facing Mr. Frost. It exits to the back of the house and is wide open.

Mr. Frost looks to his right, where the incubation lab is open, too. He races over and looks inside. Debris is strewn across the floor, glass beakers shattered, and papers scattered. Worst of all, the silver table is empty, straps dangling from the edges.

"Freeda!" he exclaims. "Where is Jack?"

She doesn't have an answer.

2

NOVEMBER 30

Sunday

J ack knows he's dreaming.

He's butt naked in the snow and doesn't care. He's not all that comfortable running around without his clothes in front of others and, right now, he couldn't care less. That's how he knows he's dreaming.

The snow is deep enough to hide his enormous blue feet. Jack likes that. He likes that his feet are hidden. No one knows why his feet turned blue—blue as ripe blueberries, blue as the deepest part of the ocean—but everyone forgets things they don't see.

In some part of Jack's dream, he seems to remember that everything eventually turns blue. His hands, his legs... his bald head.

Everything.

It's not right, not normal. But why spoil the fun? Right now it's just his feet that are blue, and they're lost in the white fluff. And he's butt naked like all the other elven.

Their round bellies and curvy buttocks are pale in the moonlight.

When the moon is full, it's time for teenage polar bearing. The adults stay beneath the ice because they had their time jumping through a hole in the ice when they were young, but that was thousands of years ago.

Teenage elven would rather not see the elders' wrinkly parts.

Jack is in line. He's behind Breezy. It's minus sixty degrees. Even for an elven that's a bit nippy, especially when you're naked. Jack, though, feels good. He likes to get his clothes off, feel winter's breath on his skin. He's never won a contest—not a spelling bee or snowball fight—but he'd bet he could handle more cold than any elven. Again, lost somewhere in the dream, he seems to remember cold is his specialty.

Breezy is up.

Someone laughs and shouts at Breezy to stop covering his junk and get wet. He slides over the ice—a path carved through the snow after dozens of trips—and hits the snow ramp with his arms out. He soars up, hovering above the ice before plunging into the ice hole.

KA-THUMP!

Cheers.

A minute later, Breezy pops out of a second ice hole twenty feet away. He's tackled by his buddies and they roll through the snow, naked as snowshoe hares.

Jack's turn.

He shoves ahead, the scales on his soles gripping the ice, propelling him forward—

WHAP.

"Not so fast, blueberry," someone says, shoving him off balance.

Jack—round as any healthy elven—rolls until momentum slows him down. Jack lifts his head. The elven are laughing at him. Even the girls. Even his brother, Claus. Even Claus is laughing.

Darlah Iceridge isn't.

They had cut in front of Jack once already, made him start over, and now they knocked him down. They don't want him, that's what it is. They don't want him to play in any of the elven games.

Jack waddles far away from the naked, teenage bunch. Their

laughter carries over the ice. Their butts are still pale. It's better this way. Better to polar bear on his own.

Jack finds an old hole nearby. He kicks it with his heel until his foot sinks in the icy water. He just wants to jump in, cool off. It might be minus sixty degrees, but he's about to break a sweat.

They've already forgotten about him. They're back to jumping off the ramp, doing backflips this time. Jack steps into the old ice hole, pretending Darlah is watching him. He likes to think that maybe she'll come over and talk to him. He doesn't want to seem needy, but it'd be cool if she wanted to talk.

That's all.

He pinches his nose and sinks below the ice. The water is dark and cold, even for Jack. The frigid Arctic temperatures penetrate his layers of blubber. He paddles against the current. It's getting cold now, for real.

The dream is starting to suck.

Jack can feel it. He's starting to shiver and he's always the last one to shiver. He has to get out. He kicks his enormous feet, shooting toward the opening—

GUNK.

The ice hole has frozen over.

Jack punches at it, but the ice is too thick and he's running out of air. He hits it again and again. Maybe that's not the hole. Maybe he's drifted in the current. Quickly, he swims beneath the ice, searching for a way out, but his body isn't streamlined. The round body of an elven is made for rolling, not swimming. It takes too long to get there, his chest on fire, his skin puckered and clammy, daggers of ice punching through his skin, deep into his heart—

"*Uuuuuuuuuuhhh!*" Jack opens his mouth, inhaling deeply. He expects to swallow a gallon of seawater, but it is air.

Sweet, sweet air.

A pair of dirty fingers are clamped over Jack's nostrils. "Told you he wouldn't die," says the one holding them shut.

He lets go of Jack. It doesn't smell like the Arctic, clean and wet, because he's awake. This is real and it smells... sweaty.

Two haggard faces hover over him. One dark-skinned, the other one is fair. Both are equally unshaven and dirty. Their hair matted. Teeth, filmy.

Jack shakes his head. He's in a cushioned bed with sheets and pillows, not trapped beneath ice. Definitely not in the Arctic. The two men stand up. Jack scurries against the wall, pulling the sheet up to his chin. He may not be swimming in frigid water, but he's still freezing. The icy chill is inside his bones and the blanket isn't helping.

He doesn't even recognize the room. In fact, he can't really remember where he's supposed to be or how he got here or where he was before this. Even the dream has faded, something about snow and fat little naked people that look just like him. Except for the hair.

He remembers his name is Jack and he's staring at the bottom of a mattress that's directly above him. There are lots of double-decker beds in this endless room, and there are long, white lights glowing on the ceiling—a ceiling that is too high for a regular room. High enough that these two disgusting... these...

Oh, my God. Those are warmbloods.

The warmbloods stand up, still looking down at him with filthy, cheesy smiles.

And where is Pawn? He's always by the bed with a plate of cookies and tea when I wake up from a bad dream. And he certainly doesn't pinch my nose—

"AAAH!" Jack shouts.

Someone is behind him, their arms around his chest. The arms have thick, curly hair—funny, the light makes it look slightly green— that covers the back of the hands and the fingers up to the first knuckle—

"Wait a sec." Jack wiggles his fingers. The hairy fingers wiggle. The arms are his. He turns his hands over, studies the creases on his seasick-green palm, scratches the curly whiskers on his chin, and slides his fingers through the coarse hair on his head.

Something is wrong.

He's not supposed to have hair.

"You needa shave, man," the light-skinned warmblood says.

Jack looks back and forth between the two warmbloods. With no sudden movements, he lifts the cover and, "OH, FOR THE LOVE OF ALL THAT IS SNOWY AND COLD!"

The same hair is on his chest, his legs. His enormous feet. And he's naked as a polar bear.

"This place going downhill, man," the dark-skinned warmblood says. "They letting green people in now. Know what I'm saying?"

"Who are you?" Jack clears his throat, summoning an authoritative tone. "Where am I? How'd you get in here? Why am I naked? Did you touch me? Who plastered hair on me? Why am I cold? What—"

"Shut up." The light-skinned warmblood kicks the bed. "You jabber just as bad when you sleep. Don't need to hear that awake. Giving me a headache."

"Look, man." The other warmblood looks over his shoulder and leans closer. "I sell you a razor to shave, but it'll cost you a little green."

Jack pulls the blanket up to his nose. "Green?"

"Money, man." The light-skinned warmblood snaps his fingers. "We don't give razors for free. We got to see the green."

They both look around and then back to Jack. Dark-skinned warmblood looks back once more and reaches for the blanket. Jack slaps his hand.

Jack makes his move.

"Get your hands off me, man." The warmblood yanks his arm back. "I didn't say touch me. You think I want your disease?"

Jack thought something might happen to him if he touched him. He remembers people get cold when he does, like super cold.

"You better wash that hand," the light-skinned warmblood says. "It'll turn green. Like gangrene. That's probably what he got."

"All right, that's enough. Sheldon, you don't even know what gangrene is." Another warmblood approaches, this one fatter and darker with black hair that hangs like ropes from his head. He grabs the dark-skinned warmblood's arm and says, "Pickett, leave the man alone. Take Sheldon and get your skinny butts away from the bed. You're supposed to be on the street."

"You doing favors for the greens now, Willie?" Pickett says.

"Yeah," Willie says. "And you ain't green, so get going. I ain't joking."

Sheldon and Pickett take their time walking away. They stop at the door and Willie shouts at them to keep going. Pickett makes a face and swings his arm at Willie. Sheldon follows him out.

They walk funny.

"You all right, Jack?" Willie pulls up a chair.

"How do you know my name?"

"You told me."

"I did?"

"Do you know where you are?"

Once again, Jack looks around the giant room with rows and rows of empty bunk beds. The wood floor looks like real wood. And he's never smelled that smell before. It's dirty and clean, all at the same time. There's also the smell of food, but it's gross. Reminds him of the time Pawn made boiled cabbage for lunch.

Pawn. Where's my friend Pawn?

Jack suddenly remembers a fat, little person that was his buddy. He's nowhere to be seen.

"I didn't think you'd remember anything." Willie leans forward, elbows on his knees. "Someone found you wandering along the Cooper River last night and they thought it'd be a good idea to drop you off at the shelter. Now I'll be honest, if I find a three-foot-tall man with greenish hair muttering nonsense about the North Pole, I'm calling the zoo or the newspaper or something. But some good soul thought it fit to bring you here for a warm bed and a hot meal, seeing that you were shivering like a cold fish. I guess you're lucky it's Christmas time; everyone is getting on Santa's good list."

"Santa?" Jack sits up. "You're talking about Nicholas Santa?"

Again, another familiar name. He's heard it before but can't connect the dots.

"Look, man. This ain't the North Pole, Jack. It's a homeless shelter. And you, like everyone else, have to get out by 8:00. And right now" —he looks at his wrist—"it's 8:05 and you're still in bed. I hate to be the bad guy, but you need to find someplace else to go. You got somewhere to go?"

Jack slips his arms beneath the covers so only his eyes and the top of his head are showing. "It'd be cool if I could hang here for a bit."

"You remember anything?" Willie asks.

Jack nods because he has the feeling if he says no, Willie will call the zoo or the newspaper.

Willie stands up and shoves the chair against the wall. "It's a little nippy out, but I think we can find some clothes so you don't freeze. Although I don't think we got anything to fit those feet."

Willie squeezes the lumps beneath the covers. Jack feels it in his toes and someone laughs. Pickett is back in the doorway. Willie scowls but doesn't shout. He takes a moment, bowing his head.

"Look," Willie says, "I ain't got anything against hairy people even if you do look seasick, but if you can't remember anything, I think we need to see if there are any missing person reports—"

"That won't be necessary." Jack scoots to the edge of the bed, careful not to let the blanket fall. "Bring me some clothes."

"Excuse me?"

"Clothes. You said you would give me clothes. I want them now."

Willie pauses, processing what he heard.

"I said now," Jack adds.

"You want to change your tone?"

"No. I want you to get me clothes."

"Mmm. Mmm-mmm." Willie wanders off, shaking his head. He stops at the doorway across the room and turns around, his eyes squinting and hard. "You definitely ain't from the South, my man."

JACK STARES at the stack of clothes.

Willie had dropped them on the floor and gave him five minutes to pick something out and "get stepping." Jack doesn't know what that means, but that was fifteen minutes ago. Must not be that important.

"I'm coming to dress you," Willie shouts from another room.

"I'm coming. Geesh."

Jack's cold and nervous. Actually, he's freezing. His whole body is shaking. He doesn't know what's outside of this room, but it's not the North Pole. *How'd I get in a room full of warmbloods?*

The floor is hard and tacky. The scales on his soles latch onto the wood and he shoves in the direction of the clothes—

WHAP.

Jack is kissing the floor.

He rolls over, moaning. Nose, throbbing.

Warmbloods don't slide. They walk.

Jack sits up and stands. He sees someone to the left and falls down. It's someone about his height with lots of hair.

Wait. That's me.

He walks over to the mirror and touches the surface. He hardly recognizes the reflection. Only his crystal-blue eyes seem familiar.

I'm not supposed to look like this.

He doesn't know what he's supposed to look like, just not that.

One foot in front of the other, he walks to the clothes. He pulls on a couple of shirts and steps into baggy pants; he has to cuff the bottoms from stepping on them. There's a pair of boots, but they don't come close to fitting. But the coat fits and so does the gray stocking cap.

He's still shivering. In fact, it's getting worse.

Jack goes to the doorway, where Willie is waiting, arms folded. The cabbage smell is stronger out there. Jack waddles towards Willie, the floor gritty. It takes, like, forever to get there.

Walking is stupid.

Willie points at the front door. Jack turns toward it and keeps going, already exhausted from the excruciatingly slow trek.

"You're welcome," Willie calls.

Jack raises his hand. He just wants out of this leafy-smelling warmblood nest. He leans into the glass door and uses all his momentum to leverage it open. The air is choked with exhaust fumes; the ground is covered in litter. Several warmbloods huddle near the curb.

Definitely not the North Pole.

Jack stands in the doorway, rubbing his arms and shivering. He can't go out there. They look like they want to eat him. And it looks cold out there and stinky. Maybe that missing person report Willie was talking about will be in a warm room. He could make something up about losing his mother and how he just needs a friend.

Willie taps the glass and points towards the curb. He mouths a word, *Go.*

Jack sticks out his lip and bows his head. He shuffles out of the shadow. The hairs on his face tingle when the sunlight hits him. Warmth gyrates through the follicles and penetrates his cheeks, reaching deep into the cold bones beneath his eyes. Warmth oozes around his scalp like a hot rag. He closes his eyes and raises his face like a sunflower that's absorbing the sunlight.

Jack unzips his coat. His chest hair celebrates the sun's kiss.

He may not remember much, but at least he's warm.

Sir. Freeda's voice rings inside Mr. Frost's head. *Sir, May has breakfast ready. Everyone is waiting.*

Mr. Frost opens his eyes and doesn't recognize the room at first. It's been quite a few years since he slept in the incubation lab. Even when he did, it was never because he'd been up the night before cleaning it.

Sir?

Start without me.

Would you like something sent down for you?

I would like you to stop talking. He rolls on his back and sighs. His head is throbbing.

For as long as he was down there, he hadn't made much progress. The floor is littered with tiny boots, coats, hats, and tools. Tables are turned over, equipment destroyed. Shards of glass are on the bench. Luckily, none of the incubator tanks were damaged.

He slides to the sink, splashes water on his cheeks, and hides his face in the towel. His eyes are red and tired. He's much too young for an elven to feel like this. He drapes the towel over the sink and surveys the damage surrounding the large, metal table in the center, hooded lamps hanging over it. Mr. Frost slides past rows of glass tanks, tracing the cold, metal edge of the table with his pudgy fingers.

He woke up and went mad. I can't blame him.

But he never should've awakened. Jack was supposed to remain in stasis until he shed the coat of photosynthetic hair. Mr. Frost's toes get tangled in a wire-framed helmet, half of it mangled. *And his memories?* Jack probably tore the learning gear from his head and stomped on it when he leaped off the table and ransacked the lab.

You are stressed, Freeda says. *Would you like me to assume command of your bodily comfort while you think?*

I'd like you to explain how Jack escaped. He throws the learning gear on the floor.

A mild sedative is released from the miniscule capsule imbedded near the base of Mr. Frost's cranium. The *root,* he calls it. Two hundred years ago, the root released the firestorm that drove Mr. Frost out of the North Pole, sent him fleeing south until the agony subsided, made him hide in exile while he built this fortress for one purpose.

And now that purpose has escaped.

The root, though, has different uses now.

Freeda speaks through it; she watches his thoughts with it and, to some extent, controls his actions. She senses his agitation so, against his will, she's released a mild sedative to soothe the aches and pains, chemically smoothing the wrinkles in life.

How much of Jack's memories were uploaded? Mr. Frost asks.

The upload was only ten percent complete, sir.

Ten percent? He's only learned a fraction of this new world. He doesn't know who he is. Or what he is. How did this happen?

The lab was empty, sir. The garden was being attended—

I don't mean that, Freeda. I mean, how did he wake up? There were safeguards in place; there's no way this should've happened.

It's unclear.

Why didn't you tell me when it happened?

Sir, do not blame this on me. The likelihood of his awakening and escaping were very small. I was using the majority of my processing capacity to flesh out the next incarnation when—

You were already planning the next incarnation?

She doesn't answer. Her disapproval of the photosynthetic stabilization is not a secret.

Mr. Frost kicks the crumpled learning gear. He exits the incubation lab and slides into the empty anteroom where Jack made his escape. The double doors on the north end are sealed now.

It's not really Freeda's fault.

He lets her see that thought. There's never been a need for security inside the lab. There's never been anyone he couldn't trust. The doors were only locked from the outside. There had never been a premature awakening. But then again, they've never been this close to success.

A search of the plantation is nearly complete, sir.

Mr. Frost doesn't need to ask for the results. No news is bad news.

Would you like to suit up to explore the garden, sir?

Sura would be arriving soon. She doesn't need to see him wandering the grounds in his coolsuit, like some alien from another planet. She saw plenty yesterday. She needs to see a little bit of truth at a time, not all at once. Too much and she'll reject her reality.

He's seen that happen. Not pretty.

Mr. Frost picks up a leather boot. The tiny thing fits in his palm. He slides past the wide door on the west side of the anteroom and tosses the boot through it. There's muttering from inside, where the toy factory is in full swing, but no one comes out.

Mr. Frost continues around the elevator cylinder and past the enormous console built into the southern end of the anteroom. Freeda is a ghostly voice inside his head, but if he ever wants to see her body, he just has to look at the southern wall: she's a computer that sees and hears everything.

Except Jack.

Mr. Frost slides around the anteroom, hands laced over his belly. He makes several laps, contemplating what to do. He layers his thoughts to minimize Freeda's prying eye. She'll still see what he's thinking.

He stops at the eastern door and looks inside the trashed incubation lab. It's a long room. The low, bluish light illuminates the silver table and the rows of frosty glass tanks, each taller and wider than Mr. Frost. The walls are loaded with similar tanks, but these are much shorter than the others, each the size of an infant.

The tanks are opaque with condensation on the inside. Occasionally, the moisture will streak and he spies the developments growing inside. But more often than not, he lets Freeda alert him when a chamber has matured.

Mr. Frost eases up to the tank nearest him. He presses his eye to the glass, careful not to fog it with his breath. Green fuzz has already begun.

Shut Jack's line down.

Sir?

You heard me, Freeda. Shut his line down. No more until he's found.

But, sir, that could cause delays to—

Shut it down! He balls his fist against the glass. *I don't want to rush things, not again. Put all the tanks in stasis until the search is complete and we can analyze what happened. We don't need half-aware incarnations of Jack out there suffering.*

Freeda doesn't answer. Mr. Frost doesn't give orders, but sometimes she yields to his intellect. There are limitations to being artificial, even she recognizes that. And he's right. If she didn't have anything to do with his premature awakening, then they better find out how it happened.

And if she did have something to do with it, well, then he'd get to the bottom of it.

3

DECEMBER 1

Monday

Sura rolls down her window.

Templeton is waiting, gloved hands clasped near his waist. "You are late, Sura."

"I had school. I thought I told you."

He looks at his pocket watch. "Three minutes past the hour."

"I left as soon as my last class."

"Perhaps, next time, you don't chat with friends in the parking lot."

How does he know that?

Templeton bends at the waist, his back ramrod straight, like there's a hinge in the small of his back, to hand her a sweetgrass basket. Sura wonders what he looks like when he goes to the bathroom. He's human, after all. And that thought makes her like him a little better. Not much, but a little.

"Take the basket to the garden. Mr. Jonah is collecting firethorn berries for decorations."

A new display of grapevine and holly hangs over the front doors, little lights twinkling on twining strands. Christmas decorating never seems to end.

"The garden?" Sura asks.

"Be attentive, Sura." He starts up the steps, one at a time. "It's time to grow up."

Sura is never sure when he's insulting or helping her. It feels like both.

There are two trucks around back this time. Sura parks at the corner of the barn where the creeping fig vine is thick and green. December has been warm, but not today. Mist drifts down from the gray sky like cold flecks of spittle, coating everything with a glittering sheen.

The land behind the house is open and rolling, the grass brown and dormant. Vineyard trellises are posted at the bottom of the slope, like burial markers for the barren grapevines that sprout from the wires. A small patch of corn, perhaps an acre, is to the right of that, the stalks wilted and crispy, blackbirds picking at their corpses.

She finds an old sweatshirt in the trunk, still damp and muddy from the last time she wore it. *Now, to find the garden.*

Sura walks back down the road by the side of the house. Templeton made it sound like it was right in front of her, not like she needed to go search for it. Seems like he could've just told her.

There it is.

There's an arbor swallowed in the thick hedges across the road, east of the house. She didn't see it last time because, well, because she was looking at the house. This time, the long, cool shadow of the tower is falling across the road.

She steps through the arbor, careful to avoid the thorny climbing rose twining through the lattice. Knee-high boxwood hedges are sheared into a geometric maze that circles downwards to a fountain in the center. It's a sculpture of a woman that's very short and fat, with water bubbling from her outstretched hand.

The outer walls are ten-foot-tall holly hedges loaded with red berries. There are arching exits carved out of each of the four foliar walls. Sura is standing in the western opening.

"Mr. Jonah?" she calls.

There's a distant sound of snipping metal. She tentatively walks down the stone-carved steps and around the outside of the boxwood maze. The sculpture is made of a strange material, oddly translucent. Like ice.

Snip, snip, snip.

She hesitates at the northern, leafy archway. It's dark beneath a canopy of wax myrtles and protected from the cold mist, but still she hesitates. And she's not sure why. It feels like someone's watching her. The sculpture maybe.

Sura grips the sweetgrass basket until the handle creaks, steps through the archway and into the shadows—

She runs into a boy with an armful of branches. Orange berries spill on the ground. He drops the thorny stems, shaking his hand.

"I'm sorry!" Sura says. "I didn't, I wasn't sure—"

"It's all right." He sucks on his finger. "Not your fault, it was an accident."

"Are you hurt?"

"Firethorn is a little sharp."

Black hair curls from his gray stocking cap. He puts his finger in his mouth again. His skin is olive. His eyes are blue. Like, really blue. He smiles around his finger and bends over to pick up the berries.

"Oh, sorry." Sura drops the basket on the ground. "Those are for me; let me help."

"Be careful."

Sura plucks each bunch off the ground like bugs. The boy sweeps the loose berries into piles with the edge of his hand. His finger is smudged with blood.

"Do you work out here?" she asks.

"Only when Jonah needs help."

"Mr. Jonah?"

"The one and only."

"He takes care of all the gardens?"

"Pretty much."

Sura sneaks a peek at the boy. He looks about her age, but she's never seen him at school. Maybe he lives in the other direction. Maybe he's homeschooled. She wonders if his homeschool has room for one more.

The sweetgrass basket is overflowing with firethorn. Sura sits back on her heels, watching him meticulously pluck the loose berries from the mulch, as if he doesn't want anything going to waste. He feels her looking.

Staring is more like it.

"I'm Joe." He puts out his hand.

"Sura."

His hand is callused, but warm. "I know."

"Do I know you?"

He shakes his head and returns to gathering berries. He rubs his finger. The bleeding has stopped.

"I'm sorry."

"Not the first time I've been stuck, trust me." He laughs. "Besides, it's easy to get lost out here. A secret around every corner."

Secret? "You live out here?"

"Uh, no." He chuckles again. "Who wants to live with Templeton?"

They share a long, knowing laugh that feeds on itself. They both must have the same thoughts about Templeton. Maybe he hasn't had anyone to share that inside joke with until now. She wants to shake his hand again. Because it's so warm, like the laughter in her belly.

"Jonah?" An old man appears at the end of the leafy tunnel, as if he stepped out of the shrubbery. His thin hair is swept back over his head.

"Oui?" Joe says.

"Enough talking."

Jonah's lips are hidden beneath a bushy, black mustache. His dark eyes fall on Sura, watching her. Absorbing her. He looks up at nothing in particular, his body somewhat frozen in thought. Perhaps remembering. Perhaps wishing.

He turns around and pushes through the shrubs, leaves swallowing him up.

"Are you French?" Sura asks.

"Jonah speaks it sometimes. I just know bits and pieces."

"And he's your... dad?"

"Yeah."

"Why don't you call him 'Dad'?"

"I don't know." He looks away. He knows why, but he's not telling her. Jonah looked troubled when he saw Sura—she felt it. It was the same with her mom. Whenever she was having a blue day, Sura felt it. Maybe he doesn't want to talk about his dad the same way she doesn't want to talk about her mom.

Although, his dad is alive.

"I have to go back." Sura finally stands. "Nice meeting you."

She thinks that maybe she'll shake his hand, but that would be stupid. Instead, she turns to exit through the archway that leads back to the boxwood maze.

"Hey." Joe reaches for his back pocket. "We're sorry about your mother."

It's a long stem with a white camellia bloom and three shiny leaves. He holds it out for her. She reaches for it, their fingers lightly brushing. She smells it; there's not much fragrance. The petals—tickling her nose—are cleanly arranged and perfectly balanced. White as snow.

"It's a Seafoam camellia," he says. "Your mother's favorite."

"How do you know?"

"Jonah said so."

She brushes it under her nose, the petals soft and spongy. "It's beautiful."

"I agree."

But he's not looking at the flower. At least, that's what she wants to believe.

Sura tucks the flower behind her ear and floats out of the garden, hardly feeling the gravel path or the stone steps beneath her feet. If the sculpture were watching her, she wouldn't know it. The basket is hooked on the crook of her arm, berries trickling behind her like bread crumbs.

"Heh-em." Templeton is standing in the road, gloved hands at his side. He flicks a glance at the flower sprouting from her hair. "If you're quite done with daydreaming, you can take the firethorn berries through the mudroom in back. May will meet you. You can follow her to the craft room from there."

Templeton looks at the flower once more, shakes his head, and walks to the front steps, arms at his sides. Sura skips in the other direction, hoping maybe he'll see her, that maybe it'll put a little sway in his rigid hips. Light rain begins to fall, but none of that bothers her as she rounds the corner to the back of the house, wearing a smile that even Templeton can't wipe off her face.

A door slams.

She expects to see May on the back porch, hands planted on her doughy hips. The steps are empty, though. There's a pair of slanted doors set in the foundation of the porch to the right of the stairs. One of the doors appears to be raised, revealing a slice of darkness inside. She sees a flash of yellow.

The door drops.

That feeling of being watched tingles along the back of her neck this time.

MR. FROST STANDS at the edge of the tower's room, hairy toes pressed against the dark glass that extends from floor to ceiling. One hand rests on his belly, the other digging through the thicket of hair on the back of his head, scratching his neck.

The root is itching.

It's a perennial ache, like a ghostly finger pushing on the base of his skull. Scratching does little good, but there's little else he can do. At least it doesn't burn. That memory, although two hundred years old, is quite clear. And for that he is grateful. He can deal with itching.

A cold day embraces the landscape, drizzling tiny droplets that drift against the slanted glass, marring the outside world. The old flooded rice fields shimmer in the distance.

The slow-motion precipitation reminds him of snow.

Jonah exits the north tunnel and enters the boxwood maze. Joe isn't far behind with a wheelbarrow full of tools. Mr. Frost imagines their foreheads slick with perspiration.

He begins to sit.

A chair forms from the shiny black floor in time for his round bottom to sit comfortably. He leans back, nuzzling his head into the headrest, staring at the starred ceiling.

Is Jonah happy with such simple work? Does he find joy in plowing the land and carrying twigs? Does he ever want more?

Mr. Frost can have anything he desires. If he projects a thought into the room, it will materialize within seconds. All his desires can be manifested in the tower room. This technology was quite satisfying when he first developed it, but now...

Is he happy?

Mr. Frost closes his eyes, sensing the ache of longing inside his belly. It pervades his being, saturating him like hunger. But hungry for what?

I just want this to be over.

That concerns me, sir.

Mr. Frost is startled by the sudden intrusion. *I thought you were busy.*

When you have self-destructive thoughts—

Thoughts, Freeda. I'm aware they're just thoughts. Nothing else.

He remains tense, waiting for a reply. It seems to satisfy her, and soon he drifts into a light sleep, nestled comfortably in his desires. He avoids getting too cozy with his thoughts of never waking up, or Freeda will intervene and ruin his nap.

Snick.

The unmistakable sound of the elevator cylinder rises behind Mr. Frost. Perhaps if he lies still, it'll go back.

"Are you going to sit there feeling sorry for yourself all day?"

Mr. Frost smacks his lips and rubs his tired eyes. He spins the lounger around. Templeton stands in the center, with a spotlight beaming up from the floor, while balancing a silver tray and teapot on the tips of his gloved fingers.

He's impeccably dressed without winter clothing, clouds streaming from his nostrils. The rest of the room is black and empty except for Max curled up on a pillow, a white ball of fur with a wary eye on the visitor.

"Do you mind?" Templeton nods at the floor.

The insolence of this manservant brings a sly grin to Mr. Frost. It always does.

Bring the room online, Freeda.

Objects emerge from the floor, filling it with desks, shelves, and the fish tank. Monitors lit with electric images chatter around the room. The floor in front of Templeton becomes dull so he can walk without slipping. A path leads to a low table glowing beneath a pale light. He slides the silver tray on it, muttering loud enough for Mr. Frost to hear, but not discern.

Templeton takes a dainty teacup from the tray and tips the teapot, wrinkling his nose and frowning. Fish oil fragrance wafts up. Templeton looks ill whenever he pours the drink. He makes a point to let Mr. Frost know it.

"You really should turn the fish tank when you drink," Templeton says. "You're savoring a distillation of his people."

"He's not a person, Templeton." Mr. Frost sits up. "He's a fish."

"So he has no feelings?"

"Ask him, if you like."

Templeton shakes his head. His argument is never won. Never forfeited.

Mr. Frost slides to the table on one foot, easing to a stop. He sips the chilled fish oil through thick whiskers where the lovely scent will linger for hours. He lifts the lid from a small porcelain container and plucks out an anchovy, dropping it in his drink. He slurps again.

Perfect.

The news outlets blabber about the weather, the economy, and global strife. A fire burned a house down. Mr. Frost makes a note to send the family money. The blood bank is seeking donors. Nothing he can do about that. But he listens. Day and night, he listens for a report about a strange discovery of a short man with greenish hair.

The chatter dampens to a low hum.

"I can't hear myself think." Templeton is pecking at a nearby keyboard. He fusses with the controls to turn the volume lower and bring the lights up, so that it feels more like daylight inside the tower.

I'd be happy to deny his access to the room, sir.

It's quite all right, Freeda.

Mr. Frost slides to the glass wall, teacup perched beneath his hidden nostrils. The drink soothes the loneliness, despite the gray day.

"There's nothing on the news," Templeton reports. "Thermal imaging is not detecting anything on the property that doesn't run on four legs. Analysis suggests Jack is dead. He'll be alligator breakfast when spring arrives, if the turkey buzzards don't find him."

Mr. Frost turns.

"What?" Templeton looks up from the control panel. "Ask Freeda if you don't believe me."

"A little compassion is in order."

"Please. It was just a body, no one inside. We call that meat, not a person."

That's why he likes Templeton. He spares nothing to spout the truth.

"You need to initiate Jack's incubator lines and start again," Templeton says. "You missed on this one anyway, you got to admit. He was too hairy and green, for God's sake. He probably woke up, got a look at himself, and wrecked the place. If he remembered anything, he probably would've come looking for you to get back for what you did to him, so you should count yourself lucky."

The hair is temporary, but Mr. Frost doesn't feel the need to explain the process to Templeton.

"Nothing wrong with that," Templeton adds. "All genius is preceded by guessing. I'm just saying life doesn't stop because you failed, so put on your big-boy pants and get back to work. Let me remind you that Christmas is in three weeks. Jack wrecked the lab on his way out and production is behind. The schedule is tight. Stop daydreaming."

Templeton's toe tapping sounds like he's hammering a nail. Mr. Frost inhales the salty wonder of fish oil. It tingles in his sinuses.

"Fine," Templeton says. "Be that way."

The tray clatters. Exaggerated footsteps walk toward the center of the room.

"How'd it go?" Mr. Frost nods at Joe returning to the garden to fetch a pair of forgotten loppers. He gets to the barn before the hard rain comes.

"You mean Sura meeting Joe for the first time?"

"Of course."

"Like clockwork." Templeton then mutters, "Silly question."

The elevator snicks closed, humming as it sinks into the floor.

Silence returns.

Mr. Frost doesn't assume Sura and Joe are going to hit it off, despite Templeton's confidence. There's always a chance it could sour.

Mr. Frost calls the news chatter volume back up. He drifts around the room, teacup teetering on his belly. He surveys the various holographic images beamed into his room from satellites in space, several of them exclusively owned by Frost Plantation Enterprises.

He grabs a handful of kernels from a table and tosses them into the fish tank. The fish doesn't seem to mind there's a cup of fish oil balanced on Mr. Frost's belly. Fish eat each other, why would he care?

Mr. Frost slides near the furball on the pillow. He digs a small, silver tin out of his shirt, something he keeps pressed against his skin at all times. Max sits up as Mr. Frost opens the lid and pinches a few kernels—a few very special kernels—between his fingers.

Max gobbles them up.

I hate to say it, but Templeton is right, sir. We need to start the lines. And production is woefully behind.

He scratches Max's chin. *Wait another week, just to be sure. There's still time to find him. The last thing I need is two of him fully awake.*

He scratches his neck. Freeda can't override this order. Mr. Frost only has to bring Jack back once.

It doesn't matter how long it takes.

As long as he gets it right.

And it's got to be more than meat.

TATATATATATAT...

Jack hears a hammer on a long, cold, metal spike.

It drives a steady beat, an echoing cadence that rattles inside his skull.

Nothing he can do about it. He's frozen stiff, helpless beneath blankets that seem to make it worse. He can't get away. The cold fills him like mercury.

Hammer on nail.

Tatatatatatat...

"I can't take this," someone shouts. That someone is Pickett. "Every night with the chattering, I can't take it. Three days now and this cat is snapping his jaw all night."

Someone moans.

"I'd rather listen to sirens than those big, square teeth sending telegrams."

A bunk creaks. Someone lands on the floor. It's too dark to see, but Jack hears him breathing through his mouth, smells something foul hover over him. He must have eaten a poop sandwich before bed.

"He sick or something," Sheldon says. He apparently ate from the same sewage salad bar as Pickett. A fiery hand lands on Jack's forehead and quickly pulls away. "Dude feels like ice."

"I don't care, I can't take it. I'm dreaming about woodpeckers and stuff."

"Tell Willie."

"Willie ain't going to do nothing."

The stink fades, but it's inside Jack now. All the smells of warm-blood civilization are soaked inside Jack. He feels like a sponge dipped in ink, all spoiled, just living among them. If there's one thing he hates more than warmbloods staring at him—and they get quite the eyeful, no doubt—it's their smell.

They leave it everywhere.

It's in the streets and on the buildings; it's in their clothes and the food they eat. Whatever they touch... stinks. It's thick with decay and artificiality.

Civilization, they call this.

There's no escaping it. He's sure of it. Three days of wandering the concrete—his thick, scaly soles crushing bottles and kicking rocks—and he's found no way out. Just endless streets.

No sign of ice.

Jack yearns for the pure touch of fresh snow, for the sight of a panoramic horizon and the sky splashed with Northern Lights. It's not here, among the warmbloods. They sit in cars that cough smoke, consumed by something called Christmas. They carry brightly colored bags from shops and put them in their cars so they can drive to another shop and get more bags.

They act so happy, but they're faking it. He can tell.

Somehow, he landed in the United States. Charleston, to be exact. He still doesn't remember much but has the distinct intuition that he belongs on the North Pole, in the same way birds know to fly south. But then how would he survive? It's seventy degrees in the shelter and he's a block of ice.

Dying in the snow would be better than this.

The North Pole is home, he's sure of it. And if he thinks hard enough, he can remember the snow and weather that felt so wonderful, so clean.

And elven. He remembers elven. That's another thing he remembers. At first it was just a word, but then he realized it's what the short, fat people call themselves, the ones that live on the North Pole.

Unfortunately, he can't remember any of them with green hair, so that's a little confusing.

Confusion, though, has become his daily life.

"Got it." Something very sticky and long tears. "Time for the green goblin to shut his mouth."

They're still across the room, shuffling through junk. An argument breaks out in hushed tones. Someone is worried that Willie is going to kick them all to the curb. It quiets down.

"I still can't see what I'm doing," Sheldon says.

"You don't need to see," Pickett says. "Just put a piece of tape over his mouth, he breathes through his nose, and we get some sleep."

Jack doesn't want his mouth taped shut. It'll just seal the cold inside, he thinks. He remembers a time when someone locked him in a closet and wouldn't let him out. He thought he was going to suffocate. There was a song he used to sing, something that helped him feel better when he felt helpless.

But he can't remember it.

"I got something." A locker door slams shut.

A bright spot of light briefly flashes over Jack. For a second, it feels hot.

Tatatatatatat...

"Hold this." Another long, sticky tear. "Aim the light on his face."

Jack smells them get closer. The spot of light hits him in the face.

"What about those whiskers?" Sheldon asks.

"What about them?" Pickett says.

"Tape's going to rip them out."

"Don't care."

The spotlight's on Jack. This time, it doesn't leave.

Tatatat—

Silence.

The warmth seeps through each hair follicle just like it did when he's in the sunlight. Warmth spreads into his skin, deep into his tissues, reaching for his bones, thawing his brain.

"You see that?" Sheldon says.

"Yeah. Take that off him."

The light goes away. *Tatatatatatat...*

The light returns.

Back and forth they experiment. A third grader would've figured it out before them.

"He ain't chattering when the light's on him," Sheldon finally says.

"Yeah."

Maybe they're thinking it's better this way. Taping a man's mouth shut could put them on the street. But a light?

Three long strips of tape are pulled off the roll. The light jiggles but finally stays in place. A smile creeps across Jack's face, curling his lips. He's warm again.

The stink fades.

Snoring resumes in the bunkroom. Jack doesn't sleep, but he rests easy. He remembers something.

He remembers the song he used to sing when he felt helpless, the song that filled him with hope and yummy feelings.

Silent Night...

4

DECEMBER 4

Thursday

Sura braids the twining grapevine with long blades of lemongrass and strands of white lights. She accents the decoration with magnolia leaves and holly berries and then stands back, tapping her lower lip. That's what May does when she decorates.

"I think!" May would say when Sura stared at her. Then May would laugh. Then she would hug her.

There's laughter down the hallway, but it's not the same as May's laughter. This has an edge that cuts. High school seniors lean against a cinderblock wall. The girls cover their mouths.

Sura dumps out a bucket of white camellia blooms. She plucked them from the shrub growing in a dark corner behind the school where no one would appreciate them. They aren't Seafoam camellias, but they're white.

And perfect.

"Oh, my!" Ms. Wesley steps out of the gymnasium. "That is

incredible, Sura! You did this? All by yourself?"

"Yes, ma'am."

"It's absolutely wonderful." Ms. Wesley walks beside the twisted decoration, lights blinking in the depths of festive wrappings like little fairies. "I never knew you had such talents."

Sura blushes, looking away.

"I think we can hang it." Ms. Wesley carefully lifts it, lights reflecting off her glasses. "Take the other end."

They are barely tall enough to reach over the doorway, but they manage to set it on the hooks the janitor set in the wall. A few tucks here, an extra pine cone there and—

"Wonderful." Ms. Wesley folds her hands on her chest. Only a teacher would appreciate a Christmas adornment like that. "Can you stay after school? We could use your talents for the main stage."

"I can't, Ms. Wesley. I have to work. Sorry."

Ms. Wesley puts her arm around her. She'd gotten a lot of those hugs from teachers. They stopped saying "sorry about your mother" and resorted to half-hugs.

"What about last period? I could get you out."

"I need to study."

"Right. And what kind of teacher would I be if I interrupted your studies?"

Sura sort of smiles. Sort of laughs. Sort of completely hates herself for glancing down the hallway to see if the seniors are watching because Ms. Wesley notices. "Are you going to the senior holiday gala next week?" she asks.

"No, ma'am."

"And why not?"

Sura doesn't want to say she has to work because that would be a lie, but she also doesn't want to tell the truth. She'd been dreaming about Joe asking her. He'd pick her up on a loud motorcycle and all the girls would swoon and the boys would tremble in fear. She doesn't know where he'd get the bike or why the boys would be afraid of him, but she doesn't want to ruin the fantasy with questions.

And she can't tell Ms. Wesley because someone might hear and she'd heard enough laughter.

"You can ask someone, you know." Ms. Wesley sorts through the other buckets. "You don't have to wait around for a boy to ask."

"I know."

"Do you?"

Sura decides to help find a place for the remaining magnolia leaves, to give her hands something to do. Ms. Wesley begins humming a Christmas tune. It eventually morphs into a lighthearted falsetto effort that only a teacher would do without crippling embarrassment.

The bell rings.

"I have to go to the library, Ms. Wesley."

"Are you going to be volunteering this Sunday?"

"At the horse stables? Of course."

"The children will be there at 2:00."

"Yes, ma'am."

Sura slings her book bag over her shoulder. Ms. Wesley's song follows her down the hall.

BOBBY JAMES PRETENDS to read a history textbook. No high school student has actually read a history textbook. It's a cover for his phone. Sura pushes a cart past him, the last of the books to be shelved. It's not like the old days, her teachers tell her. That's when libraries were full of real books, not ones on the computer.

Technology is ruining us.

Of course, they drive their car home instead of a horse and buggy. So much for that argument.

Sura finishes the last one with five minutes left. Bobby James has his eyes closed. She wishes she could waste time like that.

"You don't hang out," her mom would always say. "You invest your time. Life is short. And if you think the point of living is to be happy, you're mistaken. Serve life and happiness will find you." Then she'd get that look of wisdom and say, "Happiness cannot be grasped any more than the wind."

Sometimes Sura wishes her mom hadn't been so weird. Maybe Sura wouldn't be so weird.

She goes to the back corner and sits at a secluded desk, where *booger* is carved into the surface. She pulls her phone out. Guilt and fear coil around her. She ignores them, sliding her finger across the glass.

She navigates to the school's website and finds the library database. There's a link to the tri-county yearbook database the librarian sometimes uses to update student information. It's not available to the public, but if you're a library assistant, you probably have a password.

Sura logs on.

A jolt of excitement tingles in her arms. She searches for Joe...

Wait. What's his last name?

There's going to be like a thousand Joes in the database. It'll be Monday by the time she finds him, assuming Joseph is his first name and not his middle. Assuming his name is Joseph.

She types a different first name.

The icon rotates, grinding through an eternity of Charleston area students, past and present. Two hits. The first one is current, a senior at a nearby high school. She hits the link. A picture loads and the twin snakes of guilt and fear melt like sweet sugar.

Jonah.

She's only met him the one time, but she's been branded with his slight smile. He's cute by anyone's standards, but it's not just that. She gravitates toward him. Maybe she's delusional, but she believes he gravitates towards her, too.

He's not in sports or student cabinet. No clubs except one, the American Red Cross club. *He's a nerd, just like me. A hot, sweetheart nerd.*

Strange thing, though. The photo was updated three weeks ago when he registered for class, like he just started at the high school. *He must've been homeschooled.*

The bell rings.

The hallway quickly clutters.

Sura begins to put the phone away. Before she does—on a whim
—she taps the other Jonah that appeared in her search. This Jonah
went to school thirty years ago. A picture loads, this one slightly
grainy.

A strange sensation trickles across her skin, like magnetic ants
racing over her, taking the good feelings away.

It's Joe.

It's not Joe, it's his father, but he looks exactly like him. That's Joe's
face. The hair is shorter, but the smile is the same. Eyes, the identical
color.

Lots of people look like their parents. Some of them look *exactly*
like them. It shouldn't seem so weird.

Oddly enough, she remembers another bizarre thing her mom
used to say. *Wake up, Sura. Don't sleep through the truth.*

Sura hustles out of the library. She can't be late for work.

5

DECEMBER 7

Sunday

Maybe I'm a warmblood.

Jack stares at the mirror. He doesn't look like a warmblood, but they all look different—hair, skin, eyes, size, smell... all different. His insanely large feet are hard to explain, but he saw a girl with blue hair and metal rings in her eyebrow the other day, so maybe he's like that.

Maybe he's just out there.

He's a freaky warmblood with delusions of elven that live on the North Pole. Maybe he just needs to find an equally hairy, equally repulsive wife and get a job loading something onto a thing, and get a house, have disgusting little kids.

That would be easier than getting to the North Pole.

Jack's nostrils flare. He sniffs like a dog. His mouth floods with saliva. Someone is bringing in groceries. He's still full of oatmeal, but he may as well eat mud. There is something new in the building.

He creeps through the empty bunkroom, careful not to let one of the supervisors see him, which isn't easy to do when you're the shape of an overinflated beach ball. Jack leans against the wall and breathes deeply, picking out a hint of something scaly.

And delicious.

JACK PLUCKS the last sardine from the can, its tail limp and slick. He dangles it over his mouth, caressing the gaping eye with the tip of his tongue before slurping it down like an overcooked noodle.

There is a parade in the street. As far as Jack can tell, while mincing the tiny bones between his teeth, a parade is obnoxious music, ghastly costumes, and atrocious dancing. He pulls down the front of his white tank top to expose a shag of greenish hair that tingles in the light.

First sardines. Now sunlight.

Life is good.

"Merry Christmas." Willie comes out of nowhere.

Jack chokes. "Huh, what?"

"I said Merry Christmas, man."

"Okay." Jack wipes his mouth with the back of his hand. "Why?"

"Man, you never give up, do you?"

"No." Jack has no idea what that means, but it's probably true.

"We picked up those cans of nasty little fish for you."

"You did?"

"Yeah. You've been asking about herring, anchovies, and all sorts of disgusting food, so we got those for you. Thought you'd like them."

Jack licks his oily finger. "Okay. Cool."

"That ain't going to cut it."

"Cut what?"

"I want you to show some appreciation, man. You get a free bed, a free shower, free food, and free nasty fish." Willie wrinkles his nose. "You can at least show a little gratitude."

Jack looks around. No one is watching. They're all standing on the curb, watching trucks, tractors, and little kids that suck at dancing. No one is close enough to ask what Willie wants him to do.

So Jack bows.

Willie crosses his arms and looks away.

Jack bows deeper. He drops to his knees. He jumps up, tap dances in place, his feet scuffing the concrete.

"I don't know what you want me to do, Willie. This? Or this? Or what? I don't know."

Willie grabs Jack's arms before he pirouettes. Jack's out of breath.

"You just say thank you, that's all."

"Thank you?"

"That's it, man. You say thank you."

Willie's green eyes are soft, his ropey hair dangling over his brows. He gently squeezes Jack's shoulders.

"Thank you."

Willie lets go. Smiles.

They go to the curb with the rest of the crowd and watch motorcycles putter past and high school bands march with tall, fuzzy hats and farting, metal instruments. It doesn't make any sense. Just the other day there were cars racing down the road, now they're dancing on it.

Jack slurps the delightfully fish-scented oil and tosses the empty can on the grass. "What's this?" he says.

"Parade," Sheldon says.

"Yeah, but what is it? Some sort of talent show?"

"You never heard of a parade?"

"Yeah, dummy. That's what I mean. Now tell me."

Another truck comes around the corner with another female with another glittery shirt, waving and smiling. It's so obvious she's not happy. Jack thinks about throwing the sardine can at her.

Someone inside the truck throws a fistful of rocks wrapped in clear plastic. They skitter into the curb.

"Parade, man." Sheldon picks up one of the wrapped rocks. "You get candy."

"Yeah. Why?"

"Cause it's Christmas, man," Pickett shouts over the approaching band. "What's your problem? Your mother didn't love you?"

"She didn't love you."

Sheldon and Pickett laugh. Jack heard someone say that the other day and thought it was an insult. Must be a joke.

Another truck heaves more candy at them. The shelter residents harvest it from the street. Maybe the candy is sardine flavored.

"Give me one of those." He puts out his hand.

"Get it yourself, fatboy," Pickett says.

Jack doesn't want to bend over. It's not easy for him to bend. He stretches his foot onto the street, pinches a barrel-shaped piece between his toes, and snaps. The candy shoots straight up and he catches it.

It takes a few attempts to unwrap the sticky, brown block, and once it hits his tongue, he's pretty sure he just ate poison. He spits it like an air pistol and scrapes his tongue.

"You need to watch your back, little man." Pickett's face is darker than usual.

"Why? Something on it?"

"You spit that on me, man." Pickett jerks out of Sheldon's grip. "You're lucky Willie is out here or I'd rip every one of those nasty green hairs out of your head, stomp you in the dirt."

Jack pulls the bottom of his shirt up to rub the taste off his lips. His gelatinous belly jiggles out. Several girls on a passing float point.

"What makes you so important?" Jack asks.

"What are you talking about?"

"All of you!" Jack's face darkens. He notices the bare flesh on his palms looks bluish. "You think you're the center of the universe? You think life revolves around you and your petty problems? That you're entitled to get whatever you want?"

Jack doesn't know exactly what any of that means or where it's coming from, but he doesn't get in the way. He lets the words rise up from a distant memory of someone he used to be, maybe when he lived on the North Pole. Bitter hate fills his chest like a salty fist, the knuckles drumming his heart.

"Let me tell you something, warmblood. You and all of your friends are just cogs in a machine. You're just another ball of lint sticking to the world's sleeve. One of these days, you and the rest of these ugly warmbloods will be just like candy on the street, waiting to be swept up."

Jack swats the candy from Pickett's hand and grinds it under his heel until it's powder and plastic.

Pickett towers over him and his fist is about to follow. It's not that he doesn't try. Willie gets in the way and Sheldon pulls Pickett back. Spittle flies from his lips; foamy flecks of anger carry a rant strewn with cuss words. Everyone forgets about the parade until Pickett storms down the sidewalk, occasionally looking over his shoulder, still cussing.

Jack waves at him.

"You making friends?" Willie says.

"Yeah. Whatever that means."

"Well, it ain't that."

Jack crosses his arms over his belly; his shoulders slump. The hatred ebbs away and he can't remember why he felt like that or even what he said. It came from somewhere deep, like he tapped a reservoir trapped under miles of bedrock. The anger came shooting out of his mouth like an oil well spilling black gunk.

It felt good.

Felt right.

He tries to rekindle the flame by kicking Pickett's candy into the road. When it doesn't work, he growls at the fake-smiling wavers in the glittery shirts, shakes a fist at the little kids in scouting uniforms, and spits on candy. He takes his tank top off to let his belly loose and the chest hairs unfurl.

Nothing works.

A fire truck turns the corner, strands of garland draped over the front, lights flashing. Men with rubber boots and heavy jackets throw more disgusting candy that Jack shoves into the gutter, using his foot like a paddle.

And then something clicks.

There's a man in the bucket extended high above the fire truck. He has a white, curly beard and wears a furry, red coat.

He's laughing. "Ho! Ho! Ho!"

"Who's that?" Jack asks.

"Who?" Willie asks.

"That! That... that *man*." He almost said warmblood.

Willie looks to where he's pointing. "You're talking about Santa Claus?"

Santa Claus?

SANTA CLAUS?

The words rattle in his head. The memories swirl out of the depths like dark sediment, threatening to rise above the fog of forget-fulness. He should know that name; he should know who he is. He's somebody.

Claus is someone he knows.

Jack stays on the curb long after the parade ends, trying to remember, trying to put it all together.

6

DECEMBER 8

Monday

M r. Frost steps outside wearing a long, dark coat. A tube buried in his mustache hisses chilled air into his nostrils. It doesn't interfere with the scent of the land, only makes breathing more tolerable.

A perfect night for a stroll.

The land appears haunted in the pale light. There were nights when he could swear he saw ghosts wandering the hills, sometimes with muskets. He'd purchased the plantation before the Civil War and immediately freed the slaves, letting the rice fields go fallow. The enslavement of humans by their own kind was unconscionable.

Mr. Frost looks back at the house—Christmas lights sparkling along the edges—and thinks one could make the same argument concerning the toy factory. But the helpers love to work like a sled dog aches to pull.

He tries to scratch the root, but the coolsuit restricts his movements; he can't reach it. The itch spreads over his scalp and reaches the crown of his head like ghostly fingers. Unlike the illusions that walk the lunar landscape, this one is very real.

The root contains a ghost.

He grabs a thicket of hair behind his ear. His fingers are almost to the itch when the coolsuit tears. The cool night air feels like desert wind on his exposed flesh. He inspects the damage on the back of his hand.

Microscopic tubes hiss liquid nitrogen that circulates throughout the coolsuit to keep his body temperature at a constant minus twenty degrees. In the early days, when he was first developing the coolsuit, he wore a helmet. He felt like an alien. It wasn't until he perfected the cooling halo around his neck that he ventured outside more often.

He puts a sealing strip over the damage, temporarily stopping the leak. He'll make this a short trip. And no more reaching for the root.

Just let it itch.

The endless strands of Christmas lights illuminate the live oak grove at the far end of the northern field. By the time he crests the hill, his back aches. He shouldn't feel this old. It's only been a couple hundred years since he left the North Pole.

Citrus trees are to the east, aligned near the bottom of the slope like skeletal features: Mother Nature's ironwork. Ordinarily, he'd walk through the rows until he reached the old rice field, sit in his favorite chair, one of twisted branches.

Not tonight.

His thoughts weigh like boulders. He doesn't have the strength to lug them down to the water and back.

He reaches deep into the coat pocket, retrieves a metallic pebble, and drops it on the ground. The earth undulates. Tufts of brown weeds spit out of the soil, replaced with a verdant layer of sod that forms a lush chair.

Mr. Frost rests his bones with a long sigh. All that is weary relaxes. The root, however, keeps peace at an arm's length, wriggling beneath his scalp. With his technology, he still can't escape the root.

Because the root is technology.

In the early days, the root was more active. It no longer burned but rather took control of his nervous system, forced him to do things against his will. It was maddening to be a prisoner in his own body, a puppet that was tethered to a parasitic brain inside his head. Mr. Frost was slowly losing his grip on sanity.

But the artificially intelligent root had the ability to learn. Making Mr. Frost obey its wishes by force was not productive. His health declined and, had it not released him from its iron will, he wouldn't have survived.

Mr. Frost regained control of his body by the mid-1800s. He had assumed the root expired and soon began to prosper as a citizen among humans. Although he could've returned to the North Pole— the elven would've understood; they would've showed him mercy— he felt compelled to stay where he was. He invested well, patented many inventions, and built factories below ground to distribute products. Holidays were particularly profitable and Mr. Frost soon devoted all his efforts into his favorite one: Christmas.

As the saying goes, he made more money than God.

Occasionally, the root would itch—a reminder it was not dead— but it never slowed him down. One morning he decided he had the ability to reincarnate Jack. He had the technology and Jack's memories were stored in the root, all he needed was a body to put them in.

It didn't seem that difficult.

He was on a mission: bring his best friend back from death. He manufactured the incubation lab, worked feverishly into the night, sometimes falling asleep on the laboratory floor. He quickly had success and was well on his way to reincarnating Jack. It was all very exciting. He was able to replicate Jack's DNA script and began artificially reassembling it. There were times he went to sleep in his own bed only to awaken hard at work in the lab, as if he'd walked in his sleep.

It was the early 1900s when he developed Freeda. He needed her to analyze the massive amount of data and manage much of Frost Plantation's assets.

And then, one night he realized... *the root duped me.*

His realization began when he suspected his own thoughts. He lay awake at night, observing the strange compulsions that ran through his mind, seeding themselves in his body. He would wake with the sudden urge to ship new technology across the world or tweak the coding in Jack's newest incubation.

When Mr. Frost sat quietly and allowed his thoughts to settle, he realized that the root had been whispering to him all this time. He believed them to be his own thoughts, had mistaken it as his true identity. The root had fooled him into buying into its desire to bring back Jack; it compelled him to bring Freeda online to watch him because it knew he would eventually discover the psychological hijacking.

It was too late.

Worst of all, Mr. Frost saw the master plan. Jack would finish what he started in the North Pole. He would bring an end to what he called "The Plague of Warmbloods."

And Mr. Frost would help him. If he refused, Freeda would convince him otherwise. She had control of his nervous system. While the root knew that a carrot was more productive, sometimes pain was very convincing.

The lines between master and slave had become very blurry. His free will had been abducted.

Who is the true slave?

Mr. Frost leans back in his earthen chair and stares at the moon just above the horizon. After all that he's endured at the expense of Jack's self-centeredness, he worries about him. He was alone and scared. Mr. Frost sometimes wonders if that concern for his friend originates from the root, if those thoughts are his and not implanted. He doesn't want Jack to needlessly suffer.

He knew there was good in Jack.

The orchard steamers begin to hiss. White clouds seep from the ground, elevating the temperature around the trees, keeping them from dipping below their tolerance.

It must be getting cold.

Mr. Frost closes his eyes. *Start Jack's next incarnation, Freeda.*

Yes, sir.

And fetch Templeton. He could use some assistance. It'll be a long walk back. He'd rather not do it alone.

With pleasure, sir.

In the meantime, he'd lie in the sodden throne beneath a sparkling sky. He'd savor the musty scent of the distant pluff mud. He'd dream of sugarplums like he did when he first came to this land, dream of a day when the root stopped twisting into the bottom of his brain.

Voices rise in the distance, joining the orchard's hiss. In the toy factory below ground, the helpers sing.

7

DECEMBER 9

Tuesday

J ack pushes the black sunglasses up his nose and leans against a pink building. The paddle-sized feet and curly chest hair spouting out of his white tank top make it impossible for him to go unnoticed, and Marion Square—where warmbloods seem to flock like spawning krill—was the last place he wanted to be.

But he needs to know about Santa Claus.

He'd lain awake half the night, listening to eighty-some residents snore like engines while he searched his foggy memory for a white man in a red suit. He woke with nothing.

Claus.

The memory is just out of sight, like a phantom itch taunting him to reach for it, vanishing when he does. The red coat, the white beard. Jolly ole St. Nick, someone said. He lives on the North Pole, stupid.

Claus, Jack thinks. *Claus will know.*

Jack needs more information about Santa Claus and there's only one person he can trust. He needs to know why this fat man in the red coat lives on the North Pole, and why everybody loves him, and why does Jack think he knows him, because maybe, just maybe, those answers will help him remember.

Like who am I and why am I here?

The sidewalk is mostly clear of tourists that always look back after they pass the strange, little man with sunglasses. Jack takes advantage of the lull and leaps across the sidewalk, his scaly soles grinding against the curb and into the street—

"AHHH!" Jack cringes.

A beast snorts humid breath down his neck, its hoofs clapping the concrete. Jack closes his eyes, expecting the thing to swat him with an enormous rack of fuzzy antlers because reindeer hate him—

Wait a second.

It's a horse, not a reindeer. Reindeer don't pull carriages full of warmbloods; they haul sleighs full of elven. Reindeer are genetically engineered beasts with webbed legs and helium bladders. And one of them has a red nose, a bright red nose that burns with hatred, rage, and anger directed at Jack, because he did something to somebody...

It doesn't matter.

"Hey, buddy!" a guy shouts. "You all right?"

Jack pulls his tank top down to cover his belly and picks up his sunglasses, sliding them up his nose. They're staring. Of course they are.

He crosses the street, looking both ways this time, and lurks beneath a sprawling live oak, reflecting on what just happened. He remembers that reindeer fly and that they hate him. He's not surprised they hate him—he's noticed that he has that effect on warmbloods—but flying reindeer is the dumbest thing he can think of. Reindeer don't fly, any more than cows tap dance.

Flat-out stupid.

He decides to ignore that, to pretend it's not a memory, just some sort of hallucination, because if he believes it, then he really is crazy. He'll believe only what he wants to believe, see only what he wants to see. He'll decide what's real.

Because that's sane.

The game tables aren't too far away. It's mostly men staring at black and white pieces on a checkered board and whacking a clock.

Jack waits for an opportunity to cross the sidewalk unnoticed, but that's not going to happen. He treads into the open. To his surprise, no one notices. They're absorbed by the games.

He drags his feet through the mulch and stops near the table where Willie buries his fingers in thick chords of black hair. Willie mumbles while he studies the checkered board. He comes down here to play this game, to sharpen his mind. He tells the residents it would do them good to play, that it beats standing on a corner wolfing down cigarettes.

Jack inches up to Willie's side. His opponent slams the clock and startles Jack. Still, no one seems to notice him. *This place isn't so bad.* Willie leans closer to the board, his eyes level with the plastic pieces and his ear right about level with Jack's chin.

"Willie," Jack whispers.

The observers finally take notice of him. Their frowns fade into looks of confusion and curiosity. Now they're staring. Willie just moans, waving him off.

Jack taps his shoulder. "Willie."

Willie snaps out of his reverie and looks directly at Jack, black chords hanging in his glazed eyes.

"What's up?" Jack whispers.

"I'm in the middle of a game, Jack. Can you not see that?"

"It's kind of important."

Willie looks around, like maybe he's imagining this, maybe the others don't see this. They see it, but they're not really believing it, either.

"I'll talk when I'm done," Willie says. "Now step away."

Willie waves at him like he's a fly or a baby or something equally annoying. Jack takes one step back and takes another when Willie waves emphatically.

The stupid game continues.

It'll probably be tomorrow when it's done because every move takes *foooooooorever*. Jack could probably walk to the North Pole and find Santa Claus before the game is over. He narrows his eyes, staring at the board. He takes one step closer.

Some of the pieces are pointed; others look like horses or castles. He watches the moves and hears people whispering about what move should be made. They're each trying to smash the piece with the cross on top. The one called king.

Closer.

Ten moves takes an eternity, but it looks like the game is over. Willie's got it won. Even Jack—he figured out the game in about ten minutes—can see that. But then Willie grabs the wrong piece.

"Willie," Jack whispers.

Willie—hand hovering over the board with a pointy piece between his fingers—looks over.

Jack points at one of the horses.

"Dude!" the opponent says.

"Hold on, hold on," Willie says. "He doesn't know what he's talking about. Jack, another word and you're going to the curb. Understand?"

Jack doesn't say anything.

Silence resumes. Willie starts to lower the pointy piece and stops. The others study the board. They look at the horse. They look at the king. And then they all see it.

They look at Jack.

Willie's opponent abruptly leaves but not before pointing, cursing, and using hand gestures Jack doesn't understand.

"Come on," Willie says. "Let's walk."

He grabs Jack's arm and pulls him away from the table and the dirty looks. They walk under the trees and Jack's suddenly freezing and his arm hurts.

"Ow. Ow. Ow."

Willie is a sore winner. And he didn't even say thank you.

He walks faster than Jack can keep up. When he lets go, Jack rubs his arm even though it doesn't hurt anymore.

"Can we go out there?" Jack points at the sidewalk crisscrossing the open field. It's chilly in the shade.

Willie stomps ahead. Jack has to run to catch up.

"What's so important," Willie says, lips pursed, "that you had to ruin my game?"

"I got a question."

"And how do you even know how to play chess?"

"Um, I have a brain?" Jack says more than asks.

Willie looks up at the sky like he doesn't get paid enough. Jack doesn't get it. The game was logical. Once he knew how the pieces moved, the rest was cake. In fact, if he thought about it, he had the two tables next to Willie's game figured out, too. And he wasn't really looking.

"What's your question?" Willie asks.

"What's Christmas?"

Willie stops at the crosswalk in the center of the park. His head is about to explode. "You can't be serious."

People are watching. Jack pushes his sunglasses up. He feels safe behind the dark glasses but notices he feels even safer next to Willie. Jack stands in front of him, looking up, waiting.

"I should've known." Willie laughs. "When I saw you, all three feet of you with the feet and the hair, I should've known you were from another planet."

"I'm not from another planet."

"I call bull, Jack. Every person on the planet knows about Christmas unless you've been asleep for two hundred years. Even the cannibals that live in the jungle and the lions and tigers and giraffes... they all know about Christmas, Jack. How is it you don't?"

Jack looks down. "I can't remember anything, Willie."

"You don't remember?"

Jack shakes his head.

"Then we need to get you to the hospital."

"No, we don't. I'm fine, everything works just fine. I just don't remember anything right now, but the memories are coming back and I'm just asking a simple question. If you tell me more about Claus, maybe I'll start remembering."

Willie sighs. He looks up again, this time without the fuse lit on his exploding head, but looking for guidance for something up there. He starts in the direction of the shelter. When Jack isn't behind him, he stops and waves him to come along.

Jack falls in step with Willie.

"Here it goes," Willie finally says. "Jesus was born on Christmas, but I don't imagine you want to know about him and I ain't got time to explain what a Bible is. You just want to know about Santa, right?"

"Claus."

"Santa Claus, right. That's what I thought." They walk half a city block, Willie trying to figure out how to explain something every kid knows from the age of zero.

"All right," he says, "I'm going to lay this down real simple. For starters, Santa—"

"You mean Claus."

"Listen, don't interrupt. Santa is Claus; it's like his first and last name. He's a big fat guy with a white beard and all that."

"How'd he get up there?"

"I don't know." Willie drags out the words. "He's magic, all right? Just listen to what I got to say, got it?"

"Got it."

"Good. So Santa Claus is this fat man that wears a corny red suit and uses flying reindeer to bring presents to all the good boys and girls."

Willie keeps on talking, but Jack's getting dizzy. He'd taken care of that little daydream about flying reindeer, and now here's Willie, an hour later, talking about flying reindeer and Claus all in one sentence.

Oh, man.

The world goes a little swishy and Jack falls off the curb. He rubs his eyes and shakes his head. Maybe he's not crazy. *Maybe those are memories.*

"Why?" Jack says.

Willie stops talking. "Why what?"

"Why would Claus bring presents?"

"Because the kids are good. It's like a reward."

"Who pays for the presents?"

"You really want to know?"

"Yeah. I really want to know."

Willie scratches his head, muttering to himself. He looks down at Jack, deciding how to break the news. "Well," he says, slowly, "ummm, he's got helpers that make the presents."

"Helpers?"

"Elves, yeah."

"You mean elven?" A chill rushes through him.

"Elven, elves... what's the difference?"

"And they just make presents for free." Jack waves his hands. "Just gives them away. Nobody has to do anything or work for anything; they just have to be good."

"Hey, you asked. That's how it works."

Jack scratches his scraggly beard. A few loose hairs stick to his lips. He spits them out and says, "How's he know they're good?"

"The helpers keep track."

"The elven?"

"Yeah, the elves."

"*Elven.*"

"Yeah, whatever. Same thing, Jack."

It's not the same thing, but Jack's piecing it together in his head. There are elven, flying reindeer, the North Pole, and Claus. But the giving away presents thing? Seems like they'd need something to watch every kid in the world to make that work.

"What if they're not good?" Jack asks.

"They get a lump of coal in their stocking."

"What stocking?"

"Yeah, we hang..." Willie sighs. "We put things that look like socks near the fireplace and Santa puts presents in them."

"He puts all the presents in a sock?"

"No, just some. He puts most of them under the tree."

"Tree?"

"Yeah, a Christmas tree."

"There's a tree inside the house?"

"Yeah, we bring a tree in the house and decorate it with shiny things, like the one at the shelter."

Jack always thought it was strange there was a tree inside the shelter but figured that was just a warmblood thing. It doesn't make it any less weird.

They wait for traffic before crossing the street. The sidewalk is much less crowded. Jack walks with Willie, two steps to his one.

"Let me get this straight," Jack says. "You're saying Claus puts on a coat—"

"Suit. He wears a red suit with a red hat."

Jack remembers a red coat, not a suit. And he's not a warmblood with a white beard, not how Jack remembers it. He's an elven—

He's an elven?

It's so confusing. Jack seems to remember an elven that he knew —he knew him really well, like all his life—named Claus that wore a red coat. But then he also remembers some guy, a warmblood, named Santa something... *Nicholas Santa, that's it.* Nicholas Santa was a warmblood that was twice as tall as Jack, but there was Claus who was the same size, and one of them had flying reindeer... that... he thinks—

"Whatever," Jack says, slapping his sides. "Claus with his red suit flies a sled with reindeer down from the North Pole to deliver presents to warmbl... I mean, boys and girls, because they're good."

"In a nutshell."

"And you're saying he'll come to the shelter."

Willie starts to answer. Jack is watching, waiting for it.

"Yeah," Willie says. "Yeah, he'll come to the shelter. Why, you want presents?"

"I know this is going to sound weird." Jack rubs his face, his skin feeling warm. "I think I know him."

"Who?"

That's a mistake. Jack didn't mean to say that out loud.

Willie's eyes bug out, but then he laughs. He laughs so loud that people across the street look at them. Willie laughs for half a block, out of breath, clapping his hands. Jack feels good; he made him laugh.

"Course you do," Willie finally says. "Of course you know Santa, but listen, he ain't coming to the shelter unless you're good, man. You understand? I ain't joking; you got to be cool. Can't be getting up in people's faces and nosing in their business. You understand? You start getting Pickett and the others all fired up and Santa Claus will pass you by. No trouble, Jack. Don't cause no trouble and be good."

Jack will be good. He'll get out of Pickett's face and stay out of everyone's business. He asks when Claus is coming.

"December 25," Willie says. "He'll be here before you know it."

Jack lags behind and counts the days on his fingers, calculating how many minutes he'll have to wait. He doesn't care about presents.

He just wants to meet Claus.

In fourteen days, he'll find out if flying reindeer are really memories or if he's just nuts. If the reindeer and the North Pole are memories, then Claus will have answers. Maybe even give Jack a ride home.

Maybe he'll even remember Claus.

8

DECEMBER 10

Wednesday

*W*hat if the gate doesn't open?

Sura hadn't thought of that before she made the trip out. It hadn't occurred to her that Mr. Frost wouldn't want her coming out to the plantation when she wasn't working.

She planned on going home after volunteering at the stables. Her clothes still smelled like horse. The only thing waiting for her at home was more chores and that's why she made a last second turn for the plantation.

Actually, it wasn't the chores.

Maybe Joe is at the plantation.

The odds are long, she knows that. He only helps Jonah when he gets too busy. But the odds that Joe will be at her house are zero.

She rolls up to the gate, the black bars smothered in firethorn berries and a fresh layer of pine boughs. Maybe that's another reason she came out to the plantation: it feels more like home than her house. She feels like she belongs out here.

She looks into the trees, waiting for the invisible retinal scanner to recognize her. The underbrush quakes with groundhogs or squirrels, but they always do that when she pulls up.

A crack splits the F as the gate opens.

"Thank you," she whispers.

Something in the trees whispers, "You're welcome."

I imagined that, she thinks, speeding through the magnolia grove.

Once she's out of the shadows, she slows down to enjoy the view: the natural slope of the hills and the easy breeze coming off the water. She pretends she's coming home from work, that the house belongs to her and her husband.

Joe.

It's possible that Mr. Frost dies one day (she hopes he doesn't, but everyone dies and this is just pretend) and bequeaths the house and property to her and Joe because they fall in love out here and get married in the garden and have three girls (Sunni, Hallie, and Riley) that she homeschools while boarding horses on the back property.

The odds are long—impossible, perhaps. But Mr. Frost has to die sometime, and he doesn't have any family, so why not dream?

Sura drives around the house, through the tower's shadow, smiling while she imagines their bedroom—

She slams the brakes.

Hands hit the front of her car. Branches spill purple beautyberries across the hood. Joe looks up.

She didn't see him coming out of the garden with a bundle of sticks. She's lucky she didn't run him over. Sura throws the door open. "Are you okay?"

"I am now."

"I didn't hit you, did I? I was just thinking about..." She blushes. *Now he knows what I was thinking!* "I didn't hit you, right?"

"No, it's my fault. You were driving two miles an hour." The smile, again.

Sura feels her face heat up a few degrees. She tries to think of something to say. "Are you okay?"

He laughs. "What are you doing out here?"

"I just thought I'd come out to walk around if that was all right. There's so much to see and I never have time while I'm working, so I was hoping..."

Again, she has the sense he's reading her thoughts. He knows why she really came out.

"What are you doing out here?" she asks to change the subject and hopefully restore her complexion to a normal color.

"Mr. Frost has like a thousand things to do at Christmas. You'll see."

"Have you been working out here long?"

"Ever since I could pick up a stick."

There's a scuffle in the garden, gravel grinding under branches. An argument breaks out, but nothing Sura can understand. It's all gibberish.

"You have help?"

Joe puts his finger to his lips. "What happens in the garden, stays in the garden."

"It's a secret?"

"It's a secret garden, isn't it?"

She giggles. He smiles.

"Joe?" a voice booms.

Sura pulls the open door in front of her like a shield. A blocky man fills the leafy arbor that leads to the sunken garden, the wide-brim hat barely squeezing through.

"Joe, what are you—?" Jonah holds a pair of green-handled shears to his chest, his dark eyes peering beneath the brim as if he's seeing a ghost. He doesn't look kindly at Sura. Not annoyed, more like it hurts to see her.

Something flashes off the black glass of the tower even though the sun is setting in the west. When she looks back, Jonah is gone and Joe is gathering branches off the hood. His hands are full. Sura rushes around to help. Jonah seemed to sour Joe's mood and Sura can't think of anything to say. She puts the last couple of sticks in his arms and still can't come up with anything.

"See you later, huh?" he says.

He pauses, but she can't answer. Sura's tongue is locked to the roof of her mouth. He starts for the garden. Not a word of English can slip past her lips. Not a grunt or a sigh or a "Hey, you!" or a whistle—

"*Chevaux,*" she erupts, breaking the hold. "*J'ai chevaux chez moi.*"

He halts. Turns.

"I have horses at my house," she says, picking at her sleeve. "Would you like to see them sometime?"

He looks through the arbor for Jonah. "How do you know...?"

"My mom speaks French." Sura shakes her head. "*Spoke,* I mean. I only know bits and pieces and I can't really have a conversation, but if someone is talking about horses, then—"

"JOE!"

"Oh, oh." She puts out her hand. "I'm sorry; I don't want to get you in trouble. I'll just... I'm going to go now..."

Sura jumps in the car, her face sweltering with embarrassment. She tries to start it, but it makes an awful grinding noise because it's already running. She pushes her hair back, takes a deep breath, and tries to remember how to drive—

Tap, tap, tap.

Joe knocks on the passenger window. He points down. She doesn't get it. He twirls his hand and then she understands, rolling the window down.

"Hi," she says. "Sorry, I just..."

"*Que faites-vous demain?*"

"What am I doing...?" She trails off, trying to translate. "Tomorrow?"

He smiles.

She watches him go through the arbor. Her face is on fire. This time she doesn't mind. *What are you doing tomorrow?*

MR. FROST STANDS in the tower, toes against the glass wall. All around him is darkness, Max sitting dutifully by his side.

It's their second meeting.

He didn't witness their first one, preoccupied with the lab, Jack, and other matters. He anticipated the second meeting would be soon and did not want to miss it.

Love begins—my favorite part.

He senses her cold fear when she nearly hits him, her relief that he's all right. And then their eyes meet and sweetness weakens her knees. Joe warms like she is the sun gazing upon him. They're two pieces that fit perfectly together. Two pieces that make each other whole.

Mr. Frost senses their emotions, can almost taste their vivid colors with his mind's palate. Sura is the promising yellow of daybreak. Joe is the sultry red of a sunset. And when they meet, when their energies collide, their colors mix to become something entirely different.

The brightness of a star.

They become more than what they are alone.

He closes his eyes, indulging in the human experience as it unfolds and infuses him with the preciousness of life. Without joy, he would wither like a fallen leaf. Even after she drives off, sweetness lingers in his chest.

Mr. Frost digs a few pellets from the silver box that's pressed against his belly. Max is waiting.

9

DECEMBER 11

Thursday

A car honks.

Jack drops a plastic bag and yelps. A passenger looks out the back window, laughing. About twenty things come to mind, including the one-finger gesture he learned in chow line, the one you give someone when they cut. He does nothing.

He's always watching.

Jack decides that flying reindeer are real because Willie said they're real and he wouldn't lie to him. And he knows Claus is real, he just knows it. He figures his best chance is to talk to him on Christmas.

So Jack has to be good.

Claus knows when you're good or bad, and he's making a list, and he's checking it twice. Those people in the car... *bad.* Jack has to be on the good list. To get on the good list, you have to do good things, and he'll be the first to admit that hasn't done very much good. Actually, he's not sure what it means to be good, but he heard someone say that bad people litter. He didn't call them "bad" people; he called them something else while giving the one-finger gesture.

Jack figured that meant bad.

The sidewalk is dotted with stuffed, white bags that lead back to the shelter. He drags the last one on the concrete, picking up the little things he missed, things like cigarette butts.

He must've picked up twenty billion of them between the shelter and the interstate, all different colors, some bent, some with lipstick. All of them tobacco-stain brown. Willie says butts will put you on the naughty list.

Butts. Jack giggles.

He looks up at the sky.

Is he watching right now? Does he see what everyone is doing all at the same time? Does he know what I'm thinking, like, right now? Does he see what's in my heart?

Pickett says Jack's heart is the size of a rat turd. He said it at breakfast, said he could tell just by looking at him that his heart was solid ice and his brains were in his feet. Everyone laughed, but Jack didn't get it. His feet are huge so that means his brain is huge. *Who's the idiot now?*

Besides, who cares about the size of the heart?

Claus.

Maybe that's what matters, the size of it. The bigger the heart, the higher up the good list you get. Or does it matter what's in his heart? Because, honestly, when Pickett said the thing about brains in his feet, Jack had some pretty dark stuff in his heart.

Did Claus hear it?

Jack just wants answers. Claus will give him what he wants if he's good enough. "Righteous," Willie told him. "Just be righteous, man."

Another word for good.

A can tinkles on the sidewalk, followed by another one. The bag rips and there's a path of butts, aluminum cans, and dirty diapers strewn out behind him. He's making a bigger mess than when he started and he's out of bags.

Jack looks up.

He starts putting the garbage in his pockets.

THE HORSE LICKS the sides of the pail.

Sura snatches the bucket. Gerty stamps the ground, tossing her head. She wasn't done licking. Not only that, Sura usually brushes her down while she eats.

Not today.

When Sura got to the plantation earlier that day, Joe wasn't there. Jonah was fixing a loose hinge on the barn. He stopped turning the wrench and eyed her from across the road.

May didn't ask her what was wrong. In fact, she packed freshly baked biscuits in a checkered cloth and told Sura to go home. May winked and that little chocolate chip mole danced on her cheek.

Sura rushes to the tack room to clean up. Her round cheeks are flush. *Pumpkin face,* the kids called her in grade school. *Your dad was a pumpkin and your mom was a squash.*

Sura washes her hands, rubs her neck, and hopes the soap masks the smell of chores. She stops outside the back door and breathes into her cupped hand. *Breath good, not great.*

She takes another breath. Then another. And another.

Opens the door.

Her favorite Beatles song is playing. She can't remember the last time she came home to music. Even before her mom died, Sura was always the one to turn on the radio. Crenshaw parades out of the bedroom, her tail straight up. She rubs against Sura's leg, purring.

"Hello?"

"Hello," Bernie answers, ruffling his feathers.

No one answers. Maybe he left. Maybe she weirded him out, and he made his escape while she was feeding Gerty. He's already texting his friends about pumpkin face and her disgusting farm—

"Hey." Joe pops his head around the corner. "Sorry, didn't hear you come in."

She takes off her boots. She never takes off her boots. "Just taking off my boots."

"I was just looking at these." He points down the hall. "They're really good."

It's strange hearing a deep voice in her home. She can't remember the last time there was a man in the house, and it seems, like, totally wrong, like she'll be in trouble if her mom gets home and catches him standing in the hall. *So stupid.*

Sura peels off her socks when he isn't looking, doesn't want him seeing the dirt on her feet. And what if they stink? She quickly goes to her bedroom and slips on a new pair. He'll never know.

"Did you take these?" He's still in the hall that leads to the kitchen, staring at a photo.

"Yeah. It's just a hobby."

"You're an artist."

It's mostly photos of horses and sunsets. All except the one of the Buddhist temple on top of the mountain, with the inscription *Wake Up!* Her mom pulled that one from a calendar. Joe casually walks down the hall, stopping at each photo like a critic eyeing an exhibit. He lingers at the last one: the sun rising over the trees, warming her mom's face.

"You want something to drink?" Sura squeezes past him, trying not to stumble.

"Won't your aunt be home soon?"

"Not for another hour." She ducks behind the refrigerator door so he doesn't see her lie. "She knows you're here."

It's pretty much ketchup and a bag of apples in the fridge, but she wants him to think there's more. Sura moves the bottle from the top shelf to the middle shelf, slides it around, and puts it back on the top shelf. "We don't have any Coke, so I hope water's all right."

"Where's your dad?" he asks.

She looks over the door. "What?"

"Your dad. I don't see him in any of the pictures."

"I don't know. He left before I was born."

"Oh." He leans against the wall, hands behind his back. "Sorry."

"No worries."

She waves him off and takes two glasses of water to the back room, along with May's biscuits. No one ever asked about her dad—it's taboo—but he just blurted it out like no big deal, and it somehow erased a line between them. He didn't seem to have that social barrier that keeps people comfortably distant.

She sort of liked that.

They talk about the plantation and how rich Mr. Frost must be. Sura blushes when she remembers her fantasy and he asks what she's thinking. They wonder what Templeton does in his spare time, if he has any hobbies besides dusting furniture.

He swoons over May, and Sura wishes the big, doughy cook were in the room at that moment so she could hug her. Joe imitates her laugh, spot on. And then he imitates Jonah's demanding shouts and Mr. Frost's raspy tones, insisting they put out more Christmas lights.

"I'm sorry, Jonah," Joe says, "but a hundred thousand lights just isn't enough."

"Joe!" Joe slams the table. "Get the truck!"

"And pick some flowers!" Sura adds with her own Jonah impression.

Joe laughs so hard that his eyes water.

Sura's stomach hurts from laughing.

Rain spatters the skylights. Joe sits in a folding chair opposite her. The bay window overlooks the back pasture. The pond's reflection shimmers. It looks cold.

"I used to see your mother at the plantation," he says. "She worked in the house, mostly. Sometimes, though, I'd see her walking through the garden. She would have her hands folded in front of her stomach, looking at the ground. She wouldn't even notice me."

"That was her walking meditation."

"Figured it was something like that." There's a long pause. "She was nice, your mother."

Words soon evaporate.

There's nothing but the sound of rain tapping the roof and the Beatles in the next room.

Joe leans back, watching the weather soak the earth. Sura slowly turns her glass on the table, staring at her warped reflection. She slides the glass so she can't see her extra-wide reflection, drops her hands on her lap, and crosses her legs. She takes a sip.

Where's that social barrier now?

Joe's chair creaks as he sighs, cradling the glass of water. A slight smile appears fixed in place. He rests in the moment as if he's the richest man in the world. Sura picks her fingernails and then her face itches. She clamps her hands on her lap again and forces them to stay. Her body is rigid. She doesn't want to feel this way.

She lets her hands off her lap, reaches for the glass and exhales. She's never been around a boy that wants to just be with her. *He wants to be here.*

She thinks of things to say, but they sound stupid in her head, probably worse if they came out. She wants to be funny, but she doesn't have to be anything.

She just has to be herself.

"When I was little," she starts, her words trembling a little, "my mom would saddle up the horses in the morning and I would pack lunch. We'd ride the trails all day, stopping to take pictures or eat. Wouldn't come back until dinner."

Slowly, she turns the glass.

"Sometimes I'd go to bed without showering so I could smell the day on me. I didn't want it to end, you know." She chuckles. "That's gross, isn't it?"

He doesn't answer, but with that slight smile, he shakes his head.

Sura recalls her mom coming into her room at night, brushing the hair from her face. Sura would pretend to sleep. Her mom would sit there, staring at her. She could see her through eyelid slits. Her mom smelled like the saddle, too. Smelled like sunrise.

Joe watches her remember.

"I never told anyone that," she says. "How'd you do that?"

"Do what?"

"Make me tell you?"

"I didn't do anything."

His smile grows and the room warms like the sun just broke the horizon. Now she wants to tell him everything, that very second. Tell him that she lives in this house alone, that she doesn't have an aunt... that she just tells people she does so that the social worker that keeps calling won't take her away since she's only sixteen and the state won't let a minor live alone. She wants to tell him that she's scared at night, that there's never been a man in the house, and she misses that because it seems like there should've been, at least once, and that all this is unfair.

A drop of water splashes on the table. Another droplet swells on the ceiling tile that's stained.

"It's raining inside your house."

Sura laughs. "We have some leaks."

"Maybe your aunt needs to hire a repairman."

"You know one?" Sura says. "A good one?"

"Maybe."

A long glance. Sura feels a sudden surge of emotion. Her face is hot and her eyes water. A tear rests on the rim of her eyelid, but she doesn't rush to wipe it away or turn to hide her flushing cheeks.

She can just be who she is.

And that's all right.

"I should go," he says. "Before your aunt gets home."

"Yeah. Sure."

He raises his glass. "But not before a toast."

"A toast?"

"Your father left when you were little. So did my mother."

"Your mother left?"

"Before I was born," he says.

It takes a moment to catch on. "Good one."

"She did leave," he says. "I was too little to remember her."

"Why didn't you tell me?"

"I wanted to save it for tomorrow. I have something to show you at the plantation."

"What is it?"

"A secret." He lifts his glass higher. "Here's to secrets and missing parents. Their loss."

"I'll drink to that."

Clink.

It was just so easy. Like they were made for each other.

LARGE HOODED LAMPS keep the incubator lab well lit. The humidity clings to the gray walls and the concrete ceiling is stained where fissures randomly creep. It smells of wet skin.

Two stainless steel workbenches are fastened to the back wall with a door that leads to an empty room. There are fume hoods and culture ovens, tools and equipment for slicing and poking.

The long rows of glass tanks are fogged with condensation. Respiration is working. Occasionally the moisture streaks, and if Mr. Frost puts his eye to the track, he can see the contents. There are many more tanks on the walls, these much shorter and just as foggy, but there's a special set of miniature tanks above the workbenches.

Very special.

Mr. Frost briefly pauses at each tank, admiring the gray haze of moisture, the glimpse of a darkened form. He angles his feet like an expert skier to stop at the tank nearest the workbench, where a patch of glass, untouched with vapor, is clearing. Mr. Frost cups his hands around it.

A soft face with a crop of greenish fuzz, lower lip puckered, is looking back.

I expect he will be ready for withdrawal in ten days.

Sir... Freeda drawls, *I strongly encourage activating one of the other lines that are truer to form.*

Nonsense. We've failed time and time again with Jack's true form. The chlorophyll gene splice has given it stability, Freeda. Once he's stable, he'll be true to form.

It's an abomination, sir.

It's an evolutionary step.

You have created a freak, sir, which is not according to his plan. If the body lacks sunlight, his inner core temperature plummets. How will he survive at night?

If he doesn't escape, he says, *he'll get all the light he needs in the lab before reverting to a mammalian function—why am I arguing with you?* Mr. Frost slaps the thick glass tank with an open palm. *We've had success with the botanical inclusion, achieved wakefulness and locomotion... we can reset his memories once he's fully awake, and then let him revert to original form once he's stable. You've done the analysis; you know it will work because if it won't work, you would have the authority to overrule me.*

I don't think he'll like it.

Mr. Frost tours the room, slowing at each tank. He stops at the workbench, checks the monitors, and inspects a rack of petri dishes. He asks questions about progress and analysis, and Freeda answers with one-word statements, no elaboration. No speculation or conversation.

I'll make you a deal. Mr. Frost slides to the exit. *If this next body doesn't work out, we'll animate one true to form, just like you're talking about. No botanical inclusion whatsoever.*

Long pause. *I'm agreeable.*

It's better when she's not angry. Besides, he's certain there won't be a next one. And he's not convinced that the last body is really dead. He hopes not.

10

DECEMBER 12

Friday

J ack's the last one out of the dormitory, his feet dragging across the linoleum. He leans against the doorjamb and inspects the sole of his right foot. There's a blue patch near the heel that's cold to touch. It doesn't hurt, though.

Walking sucks.

His eyelids are barely open. The cafeteria is half full, most of the eighty residents already done with breakfast, out having a butt, probably flipping them on the curb for Jack to pick up.

He gets a plate and drags himself to the nearest table. The men get up and leave. Jack contemplates the steamy pile of yellow mush next to the white slop. He reaches for the hot cup of coffee. It tastes like battery acid.

"Hey, boy," Sheldon mumbles, "I need my shoes shined. Maybe Santa brings you a shine box, huh?"

Laughter.

"I got something you can shine," Pickett adds.

Jack couldn't care less; he just wants to sleep. Maybe he can start picking up butts by the interstate, curl up under the overpass for a few winks.

"You know who he is?" Pickett says, dampening the laughter. "He that puppet in the trashcan, the green one, you know. The one with garbage. He's Oscar."

Oh, the howling. The hysterics.

Perhaps Jack will get points with Claus for bringing them joy, making them laugh. Giving them entertainment.

Pickett shovels more yellow mush onto Jack's tray. "Here you go, Oscar, more garbage." He pours milk over the yellow mound. "Don't want it going to waste."

Milk cascades over the food in little white streams and pools into the pockets. Pickett crushes the box and drops it. White specks of milk spatter Jack's forearm, beading on the green fuzz.

Jack eyes it lazily.

The laughter fades into an undercurrent of chuckling, waiting to see what happens next. Pickett stands too close and bumps his chair. Jack doesn't care about the food. As long as he's under the lights, he's not cold or hungry. Besides, warmblood food tastes like an old kitchen sponge.

Pickett mutters a cuss word and bumps him again.

Jack turns his size twenty out. He catches Pickett's ankle with his big toe. Pickett stutter-steps, swings his arms, and goes down, kissing the shiny floor.

Chairs scuff away from tables, making space. Pickett is up and Jack is sitting there, contemplating the gross chunks of artificial egg swimming in a pool of milk, a slick of grease floating on the surface.

Jack looks up at the buzzing light, ready for what comes next, wondering if he'll get bonus points with Claus if he sits there and takes a beating. Wondering if he'll go on the naughty list if he fights back.

"Hey!" Willie shouts. "Hey, get this locked up, Pickett, or you will see the street."

"You better get your boy under control." Pickett's breathing labors. "You don't and—"

"Don't say anything you're going to regret."

Jack imagines that Willie's pointing at him right about now. That's what he does when he takes that tone. Jack turns. He's right, Willie's pointing at Pickett. And Pickett's face is darker than usual, his eyes bugging out, lips glossy with saliva. His nostrils flare.

Jack blinks heavily. Still tired.

"Everyone!" Willie shouts, "Get picked up and cleaned out. It's almost eight o'clock, time to make your appointments."

The cafeteria breaks down in quiet chaos. Willie stands with his hand on Jack's table until most of the room is in order, standing guard over Jack's hunched figure.

"First of all," Willie says when the room is clear, "you ain't staying here if one more thing happens. We have a zero-tolerance policy and right now you're leaning in the wrong direction. You understand?"

Jack slides the tray toward him. "Want a bite?"

Willie shoves it away. "And second, you need a shower, my man. You look nasty and smell worse. Now hit the head and get some water on your body. And use soap. I like you, Jack, but rules are rules. You understand?"

Jack gets the "Willie Stare." The tough-loving supervisor will look at him in silence until he gets the right answer. Even after he gets it, the "Willie Stare" lingers for several seconds so it sinks in nice and deep.

"Okay." Jack throws up his hands.

Willie slowly gets up while he finishes off the stare and starts stacking chairs. "A law student is coming in an hour to help with your ID. She's working for free, so mind your manners."

Jack pokes the food. "Willie?"

"Yeah?"

"You got any sardines?"

"No, man. I ain't got sardines. All I got is that food and it's free, so eat up."

Jack thinks maybe he'll go stand in the sun for a while.

. . .

THE LAWYER LADY IS LATE.

Jack sits in the courtyard where the sun is brightest. He rubs a smooth patch of skin on the inside of his arm where the green fuzz has rubbed off. He thought the soap did it, but none of the other hair fell out.

The skin is pale blue and cold like the small spot on his foot.

"He's over there." Willie opens the door.

The lady lawyer looks like a kid. She's pale but turns a shade chalky when she sees Jack. She stops and stares like they all do when they see Oscar the Grouch. Willie gives her a moment to decide whether she's going to do this or run away.

"Hi." She extends her hand. "I'm Kaitlin. I'm here to help you reestablish your identity."

Jack looks at her hand. Willie nods at it.

He lays his hand in hers like a dead fish. She shakes it, slapping the leather bag on the table. It doesn't seem like she can get any whiter, but she does.

"So you're Jack?"

"Yep."

"I just have some questions to ask, some papers to fill out." She pretends to sort through papers, pretending to read them. She drops them on the table and slaps her hand on top. "I'm sorry, but you're green."

"And you're white, and he's black. Any other questions?"

"People don't have green hair."

Jack holds out his arms. "Ta-da."

"Have you been to a doctor?"

"Kaitlin, this facility does not discriminate against color or religion." Jack sort of whispers into the back of his hand, "I don't think she knows what she's doing."

"Stop." Willie holds up his hand. "Be nice."

Kaitlin straightens her papers into a pile and reaches for more.

She checks her phone, blowing the hair from her eyes. She still might decide to run.

"All right," she says with a big, fake smile. "We need to get you an ID so that you can continue staying in the shelter. There are some papers to fill out. I'll ask you questions and you just, you know, answer them as honestly as you can. All right?"

"Deal."

"Let's start with where you're from. Birthplace or where you've lived the longest. Can you tell me that?" she says like he's two.

"North Pole."

She starts writing—stops. Her fingers squeeze the pen, and then she puts it down gently and folds her arms on the table. She doesn't say anything.

Jack points at the stack. "Shouldn't you be writing that down?"

"You're not from the North Pole, Jack."

"Yes, I am."

"Nobody is from the North Pole. It's a giant sheet of ice; nobody lives there. Not white people, not black people, or even green people. Now, if you don't want to take this seriously, I have other people to see. Now, I'll ask one more time..."

Something flashes in Jack's mind. An image floats up. *A memory.*

He remembers the tunnels they carved in the ice, bedrooms, living rooms, and kitchens. He remembers living with others that look like him with brown hair or black, blond or red. He remembers snowballs and sliding, the long nights and long days. The streaking colors of the Northern Lights.

He remembers his people have been in existence since the Ice Age, remembers their trek further north as the glaciers melted and the temperatures warmed, and how they made homes within the Arctic ice, all before the warmbloods even existed.

Warmbloods.

"Jack?" Kaitlin looks at Willie. "You know, he should really be checked out."

Jack squints; his eyes darken. "What identifies you, Kaitlin?"

"I'm sorry?"

"You want to find my identity, you first. Your name is Kaitlin. Is that what you are, your name?"

"What are you talking about?"

"You want my identity—I want yours first. You tell me who you are, Kaitlin. Are you that fancy bag, those sweet clothes? Are you the shiny car that makes you feel important? Are you a girlfriend? A daughter? A sister? A lawyer? A woman? Who are you, Kaitlin?"

"This is about you, Jack. Not—"

"Are you a series of chemical reactions in the brain? Are you defined by the things you have? Do you compare yourself to the neighbors, and if you have more stuff than they do, do you win? Is that what you are, Kaitlin? Are you just a collection of stuff?"

Kaitlin slides the pen into her jacket pocket and shoves the papers into the bag.

"She's donating her time, Jack," Willie says. "You got to chill out."

"We're done," she says. "Find someone else to process his papers. My advice is to seek professional help."

She and Willie share a knowing glance. Jack doesn't care. He massages the patch of blue skin, icy on his fingertips. Kaitlin leaves without saying goodbye. Willie follows.

Jack doesn't care because he remembers something else.

He hates warmbloods.

IT TAKES both hands to carry the porcelain vase. Sura shuffles quickly to the kitchen, looking around the spray of contorted willow stems and camellia blooms. The kitchen is filled with the aroma of freshly risen dough.

"Right here, love." May clears off a space. "Hurry, hurry. Before you hurt yourself."

May tweaks the arrangement.

"I love, I love," she mutters. "You do wonderful work. Yes, yes. Have something to drink and rest."

A glass of sweet tea is near the sink, a lemon wedge split on the rim. Mr. Frost's supper tray sits on the counter, cold steam rising from the metal dome. Boxes are stacked on the floor, some open, plastic wrapping on the floor.

"Delivery truck arrived," May says, still fussing with the arrangement. "Much needs to go into storage."

"I'll help."

"No, no. I'll take care; you go."

"Go?" Sura looks at the time. "I don't finish for another half an hour. You'll be here until midnight."

"I take care of this, love. You go to garden, now. It's all right."

May plucks a white camellia bloom from the vase, slides the stem behind Sura's ear, and holds her cheeks with her cookie-dough hands, showing the gap between her teeth.

Christmas music plays.

"You go to the garden."

SURA SNEAKS out the side entrance. Christmas lights brighten the way around the back of the house. Her car is alone behind the barn, making her wonder who or what is in the garden.

The lights are brighter at the entrance. A new arrangement is looped over the top: an array of white lights sparkle beneath a thick layer of cypress branches.

Someone's standing inside the garden.

Sura slows her approach. Her heart thuds with hope, her stomach twirling.

"My lady," Joe says.

"When did you get here?"

"I snuck out. Jonah thinks I'm at a basketball game."

"You lied?"

"Yes, but only to protect his heart. He'd have an attack if he knew I came out here."

"He doesn't like me."

"He doesn't like anyone." Joe tilts his head. "Not anymore."

"I feel better already."

The Christmas lights reflect in his eyes. Sura peers through the arbor. "Something special in there?"

"Only a personalized tour."

"It's that special?"

He extends his elbow. "You are."

"Thank you, kind sir." Sura curtsies and takes his arm.

He guides her through the arbor, and even though the garden is open to the sky, it feels a bit warmer inside. Her cloudy breath fades.

Strands of white light are fastened along the edges of freshly trimmed boxwoods. Red and green lights highlight the tall hedge walls where reflective ornaments dangle. Christmas music plays sweetly from all around.

"Oh, my." Sura steps forward. "You did all this?"

"I had help."

"Jonah?"

"Well, he did most of it, like he does every year. I did a little extra, though." He adds, "We had help."

It's hard to imagine Templeton in overalls. May doesn't have the time to leave the kitchen. *So where's all the help?*

Joe leads her into the maze. They run their hands over the flat-topped boxwoods, shuffle over the oyster-shell path. The sunken garden is imbued with warmth, the kind that flows through her, melts in her stomach, opens her heart. She smiles involuntarily, as if she couldn't frown if she tried.

The short, fat woman sits on a square pedestal inside a round pool, water dripping from her frozen hands. Light emanates from the center without a source.

"Who is she?" Sura asks.

"You've never heard the Myth of Jocah?"

They walk slowly around it.

"Long ago, way before humans, there was a goddess that was exiled from the heavens because she was pregnant. She called Earth her home. It wasn't very hospitable and none of the other gods came to visit her. She gave birth to twins. One was good, the other bad. But they were her sons, so she loved them both. And together they loved Earth.

"But she was lonely. The time came for her to leave, to attend matters elsewhere in the universe, or whatever gods and goddesses do, but she loved Earth so much that she didn't want to leave it to her boys to squabble over."

They walk quietly and slowly, like walking meditation. Jocah, Sura notices, has a single long braid.

"So, one day," Joe says, "Jocah broke two chunks of earth from the ground. She launched one into the sky. It soared up into the heavens, where it froze into a block of ice, exploding before it reached space. Snowflakes were spit through the four gateways and covered the planet in a sheet of ice."

Joe gestures to the four openings along the tall hedges, each an arching arbor. North, south, east and west.

"She crushed the other chunk of earth into dust and blew it over the pristine glaciers. These seeds of earth took root and grew into beings that took the form of their creator."

Joe nods at the sculpture.

"Short and fat," Sura says. "Adapted to the cold."

"That's what they say."

They stop at the front of the sculpture, Jocah facing north. A small inscription is carved at the base.

Care for this World.

"The myth says she whispered that to the fat, little people before she left. They were in charge of watching over Earth."

"Where are they now?"

"Where the ice is." Joe points. "North Pole."

Joe dips his hand in the pool and drizzles it into Sura's open palm. She expects it to be half a degree above freezing, but it's warm. "The statue weeps for the world's troubles, but the myth says they're not tears of sorrow or happiness."

He touches Sura's lip. The water is salty.

"It's tears of joy."

"Joy?"

"For truth. Existence. That sort of thing. It's a myth, a story. But it's a good one."

"Where'd you hear it?" Sura asks.

"Jonah."

Sura's mom never told her the myth. She wonders if Joe is the lucky one. Even if his father doesn't like anyone, at least he brought him here and told him stories.

"You're telling me Mr. Frost is one of them?" Sura asks.

Joe chuckles. "It's just a story; he probably made it up. My guess is the sculpture is his mother. Think about it, you want to tell people you have an ice sculpture of your mother in the garden or a goddess?"

Sura scoops up a handful of water and lets it trickle between her fingers. The statue appears to melt but never changes shape. The water is so clear and perfect.

"One of the twins, the story goes, becomes Santa Claus—only they just called him Claus. In the old days, he spread truth to the people instead of presents."

"And that's why Mr. Frost is obsessed with Christmas?"

"Well, that and the fact that he's made a trillion dollars selling presents, yeah. He owes his entire fortune to Christmas."

"He does?"

"The toy factory is below ground."

Sura starts to laugh at the joke but thinks about the three buttons in the elevator. There was a bottom one. "You've been there?"

He shakes his head. "No. But after you see the wishing room, you'll believe it. You ready for the tour?"

"This isn't it?"

"This is just the foyer, my lady." He laces his fingers between hers, their palms warm against each other. "Let me show you the main attraction."

Under Jocah's watchful gaze, Joe leads her through the North gateway, the same path where she bumped into him the day she met him. She can feel his heart beating in his palm.

He stops at the end of the tunnel—the shade humid and dark—

where Jonah had emerged when they were picking up firethorn berries. The branches look impenetrable.

"You ready?" His expression is hidden in shadows.

"Through that?"

"Yeah, but first you have to tell me your favorite place in the world."

"Why?"

"Trust me."

Sura doesn't have to close her eyes to think, it's plenty dark to concentrate. She just can't come up with anything. Her mom never took her anywhere outside of South Carolina.

"I don't know."

"Then close your eyes," he says. "And imagine some place. It can be anything, anywhere. It doesn't have to be real, just picture it."

There's a crying ice sculpture in the garden and now Sura's standing in a dark tunnel with a boy she met days ago and he's telling her about a wishing room that's inside a sticker bush. *This is how people get hurt.*

"Trust me." His breath is soft on her ear.

She recalls her mom's favorite photo.

"You got it?" he asks.

"Yes."

His fingers, once again, twine with hers. She hears the leaves rustle, twigs snap. He pulls her behind him, branches scratching her face and arms. She holds her breath—

The temperature drops and the wind lashes her cheeks.

She's standing next to a weathered railing, looking down the side of a granite-faced mountain, where wind roars across slick rocks with chilly force. Sura's eyes instantly water.

The Buddhist Temple.

Then her feet are searching for the floor. Her legs are jelly.

And it's all spinning.

It's all too much.

Joe's arms wrap around her before she hits the floor.

. . .

Sura's floating.

She's curled against something soft and warm, soaring through dark mist and clouds, occasionally hitting turbulence that jostles her—

"I'm sorry, so sorry, so sorry," Joe mutters. "It was too much, too soon. I should've quit with myth, let you take that in first, before we went to the wishing room. Maybe it would've been better if the helpers were here."

For the moment, she pretends to sleep, pressing against his solid chest, her hand on his flexing pecs. He's carrying her out of the garden.

"Wait," she says.

They're almost to the arbor that exits the sunken garden. Joe stops on the last step. "I'm sorry, Sura. I shouldn't have—"

"Put me down." She hates saying it, wouldn't mind it if he carried her all the way home. But that's not what she wants. She wants to stand on her own.

"Please," she says. "I can stand."

Joe lets her feet touch the ground, gently, holding on in case she crumples again. The world isn't spinning anymore.

"Let's go back."

"I don't know, Sura. The mind can only tolerate so many new experiences at once. You need to give this some time, let your mind process."

But the garden feels familiar, more than it should. She's only been inside the garden a couple of times, but it suddenly feels like she's been here all of her life. She feels like the plantation is begging to be discovered. It wants her to know it.

To know the truth.

"I'm all right."

He doesn't believe her. She smiles, reassuring him by squeezing his arm.

"Please," she says. "I want to see it."

He can't say no to that.

They go back down the tunnel and pause outside the entrance; she imagines the photo again.

They step inside.

And overlook the misty valley below.

The wooden planks creak beneath her feet, their texture worn from thousands of sandaled footsteps. She steps carefully to the banister, the paint peeling from the wood. The mountain drops straight down, the valley engulfed in hazy clouds, moisture sticking to her cheeks.

A long, white breath escapes her lips. "This is the picture on the wall; it's the picture my mom took from a calendar."

"I know."

"This isn't normal, Joe."

"Normal?"

"This wishing room... it only happens in books and movies." She grips the railing tighter, afraid the spinning will return. "This doesn't happen in real life."

"The mind can be easily fooled to see what we want it to see. The wishing room simply affects your sensory input, presents it with the reality it wishes to see."

"Do you see the same thing I do?"

Joe walks to the banister and looks down. "I see the clouds below. I hear the monks chanting inside. Feel the humidity on my face."

He closes his eyes and inhales.

"Smell the cedar trees."

Sura peels the paint off the railing and tosses it over the side. It flutters into the mist. "How? I don't understand how this can be? There's nowhere like this in the world—how can Mr. Frost do it?"

"How does that ice statue melt without melting?" Joe says. "I don't know how he does all this; he's some kind of genius. All I know is that I'm not dreaming."

"This doesn't freak you out?"

"I don't remember the first time I came in here; I saw it when I was little. Thought all this was normal."

He leans against the railing. The wood crackles under his weight.

Sura's stomach drops, her legs turning cold. She wants to reach out and grab him in case it breaks and he tumbles to the bottom.

"Where did you get the picture?"

Sura steps away from the edge and goes to the double doors where the monks' tonal chants vibrate. "She always talked about travelling but never had the time, so we always collected pictures of places we'd go if we had time and money. Turns out, we had neither."

She touches the door.

"Why me?" she says.

"What do you mean?"

"Why show me all this?"

"I don't know." The railing protests again. "I wanted to. I said something to May and she gave me her key."

He pulls out a shiny pocket watch, just like the one Templeton is always looking at.

"That's what lets you in?"

"I think you can get in here without it, but getting back out would be difficult."

"What do you mean?"

"It's easy to get lost in your thoughts. That's what the wishing room is, just your thoughts crystalized. As far as I know, we're actually standing on a bunch of leaves, staring at trees like a couple of stoners, but we're seeing all this. It's easy to forget you're in here, that all of this is created by your thoughts. The pocket watch will show us the way out."

He points at the sky. The North Star is flashing bright, turning red, then green, and then white again.

"If you're ever in doubt," he adds, "the North Star only turns those funky colors in the wishing room."

"But why me?" she asks again.

"Don't you feel it?"

The world is starting to turn again. But she struggles to process this. First her mom dies, then she meets Mr. Frost, and now this. It's right out of a science-fiction book, but she's standing on weathered boards, listening to monks chant, and feeling the wind.

And there's the boy of her dreams, leaning fearlessly against a creaking railing with thousands of feet below.

She just needs a moment.

Joe whispers.

> *I dream of her*
> *In times of need*
> *She gives to me*
> *Her blushing greed*

HE LOOKS UP.

Sura feels the chanting move inside her while his words warm her chest. He speaks directly to her, soothing her unrest, melting her anxiety.

Breathing for her.

> *To be with her*
> *Is all I feel*
> *To kneel with her*
> *To make this real*

HE LOOKS AT THE MOUNTAINS. Somewhere, a bird calls.

"What is that?" she asks.

"Something I wrote," he says. "The day I first met you."

Sura's chin trembles. All the crap in her life just seems to fall away in that instant. The world stops turning and she's not going to stand against the wall anymore. She takes him and kisses him fully on the lips. He wraps his arms around her, returning her affection with warmth that's soft, yet firm.

I feel it, Joe.

They click together. Apart no more.

And the railing threatens to dump them over the edge, but it's just thoughts. They fearlessly cling to each other. Perhaps they'd remain that way until the banister breaks and they tumble back to reality, still swimming in each other's desire.

Only the phone interrupts them.

She pulls back and shyly touches her forehead to his chin. He pulls the phone up, forcing himself to read the text.

"Jonah wants to know if the game is over," he says.

"What game?"

"The basketball game I'm at." Joe wraps his arms around her, tapping a reply with the phone behind her back.

"What'd you tell him?"

"Overtime."

They share laughter while their bodies remain connected. Sura ponders the evergreen hills hidden in the mist and wonders what's really out there.

Mr. Frost drapes his arm over the lounger; his fat fingers doodle in a pail of salted krill. He funnels a fistful through his whiskers, chewing leisurely, while holographic images of Joe and Sura play out the scene that's occurring in the wishing room.

She held it together.

Most people might think their first trip to the wishing room would be thrilling—a chance to step inside your mind and live out your fantasies is quite alluring. However, when reality reveals itself, the experience is more like a carnival ride, one that takes a few trips to get accustomed. The direct experience of one's delusions is a dangerous one. When the curtain is pulled back on fantasy, there can be surprising elements at work. Whether they know it or not, humans prefer to remain delusional. It's better to believe the fantasies are true.

Truth can be hard and cold.

That was risky, sir.

Quite enlightening, though. Did you know that her mother was interested in the Buddhist temple?

She meditated. It should come as no surprise.

But isn't it interesting that Sura chose it? Perhaps we're seeing an evolution of her soul.

Mr. Frost trickles more krill into his mouth and swirls the small crustaceans around his tongue, savoring the salty flavor while Sura and Joe embrace. He watches them hold each other tightly, feeling the elation of attraction in his own chest, as if he's experiencing the uplifting sensations of courtship and admiration.

When they exit the wishing room, the holographic images disappear. Mr. Frost sits quietly in the tower, dangling his arm to scratch Max's head. He feels so present when they are together.

The human experience.

The elven experience has faded for Mr. Frost, perhaps a side effect of the root, or the result of two hundred years in isolation. Nevertheless, he finds reason to live when he can share their experience.

He pulls the tin box from his jacket and fingers a few nuggets. The little box—when pressed against his skin—transfers these memories and experiences into the kernels. Max sits up.

I'm happy for your experiences, sir, Freeda says, without a hint of sincerity, *but there are more important matters at hand. The helpers have an order ready for shipment.*

Mr. Frost closes his eyes. *Turn up the music, Freeda.*

A long pause before the volume rises on Bruce Springsteen's remake of an old Christmas favorite: "Santa Claus is Coming to Town." Mr. Frost is a fan of the original song, but the newer versions of old holiday tunes have grown on him lately. Anything that celebrates the season.

And sells product.

Soon, another shipment will distribute technology that originated in his toy factory around the world... be wrapped in Christmas paper and placed under trees. He's not proud of what he's doing. At one time, he thought he was spreading goodwill and cheer to all mankind, that his gifts would bring small relief to a weary world.

But the root deceived him.

It was all part of the plan to spread this special technology around the world. Because when Jack comes back, it will turn against them. *It will all be over.*

Prepare my coolsuit, he thinks.

You need to inspect the product, sir.

Send Templeton. I'll be in the wishing room.

Sir, I don't think—

He knows what he's doing, Freeda. Mr. Frost sprinkles the kernels on the floor for Max, snapping the silver lid closed. *I'll come to the toy factory once I've had a little walk.*

Freeda doesn't answer. He hasn't been to the wishing room in quite some time. He always returns invigorated, and that's why it's there.

It's why she lets him go—to keep him fresh, to keep him alive.

To bring back Jack.

THE TUNING FORK

II

The gift seemed unusual.

The grandfather watched the boy rip the paper off his Christmas present and pull two tuning forks from the box. He held them up to the firelight. The grandfather saw the gears turning in the boy's head, his mouth downturned in confusion.

"What do they do?"

"Magic," said the grandfather.

He took one of the tuning forks from the boy and struck it on the fireplace. The prongs vibrated with a melodious tune. He moved the humming tuning fork near the boy.

The boy's eyes widened. His lips formed an "O."

His fork started to sing.

11

DECEMBER 13

Saturday

They get to stay inside the shelter today as long as they listen to a lady talk about something. It's raining, so everyone stays.

Jack sits in the front row, picking at the growing bald patch on his arm. Maybe it'd stop if he didn't mess with it, but the skin is so smooth and cold and blue. He pulls out a few fat and curly hairs and holds them under his nose. They don't smell. He puts them on his tongue, minces them.

Tastes like... cabbage. *Weird.*

"Yo, garbage man. You want to help?" someone shouts.

"No." Jack brushes his white tank top. The mustard stain is permanent.

"That wasn't a question."

"Sounded like one."

They mutter while chairs clash. They're telling on him.

"Jack," Willie shouts, "get off your fat cushion and give us a hand."

"You want me to do everything?" Jack throws up his hands. "Fine. I'll do everything."

His oversized feet catch the chair next to him and he almost falls. He stomps over to a stack of chairs but can't reach the top, so he pulls on it until it begins to tilt.

Willie pulls it back.

"You want me to help or not?" Jack says.

"You need to relax, man." Willie grabs his arm, pulling him off to the side. "You want a sweatshirt or something? You're freezing."

"I'm not cold."

"Yeah, you are." He turns over Jack's arm and points at the patch. "What's with that?"

"I like to pick."

"No, I mean the blue skin."

"Oh, it's just... I colored it with... an ink pen thing. I was bored. I'm thinking of getting a tattoo."

"Why are you cold?"

"I'm not cold, Willie."

"Have you been sneaking into the walk-in freezer? I told you that's off-limits, Jack. I catch you in the kitchen and you'll be sleeping in the ditches."

Jack gets the Willie-stare: the x-ray truth-teller works on everyone.

"No. I. Haven't." Jack pulls on his shirt "And I don't appreciate your accusations."

Willie's usually right, but not this time. Jack doesn't go into the kitchen anymore. If they had sardines, maybe. He'd smell it if they did. And Willie's double-wrong because Jack doesn't feel cold. In fact, he feels just fine. He doesn't need as much light to warm up.

Jack helps set up the chairs, this time without kicking them. He did it on purpose last time. He slides them side by side until there are five rows, all nice and neat. He plops down in the front row, same seat, with no one on either side of him, and begins to examine the bald patch.

Willie introduces a lady from United Bay or Lighted Way or

something. She's young, super happy, and her name is Mickey. And Mickey likes to clap; she tries to get them to clap, too.

She doesn't stop until they do.

She talks about volunteering or something. Christmas, probably. That's all they talk about around here is Christmas. Jack's already bored. He doesn't understand why they're waiting for it—just do it already. If it takes much longer, Jack will fall off the good list.

If he was Santa, here's what he'd do. He'd give presents to everyone, the end. That's what he'd do. What's with all the judging, waiting, and life lessons? That's for reality TV.

And the singing of those wretched songs, oh man, oh man. His ears will bleed if he hears about one more sleigh ride or another walnut. Christmas is all about getting stuff, so let's just stop pretending it's about goodwill.

"So," Mickey says, "we'll be needing volunteers at the pet shelter to help with the animals. Does anyone like animals? Anyone?"

Jack picks at a different stain, this one pink. Ketchup, maybe.

"The next opportunity is at the park," the lady says. "We'll be building a new playground, so you'll get a chance to use your muscles and contribute to the younger generation. Doesn't that sound like fun?"

Jack might be the only one in the world that doesn't want a Christmas present. He just wants to chat. Five minutes, that's all he's asking. He's got a feeling, though, that he won't have to ask any questions. Jack thinks... no, he *knows*, that he'll take one look at Claus and remember.

Just stay on the good list.

"Okay, next." Mickey runs her finger down a list. "Anyone like Santa?"

"ME!" Jack springs out of his seat. "Right here, right here! Santa fan, right here!"

"All right." She chuckles. "We have one, that's good."

She backs up. Jack settles down, nodding but still waving.

"This is a special assignment—"

"Good list!"

"—you get to be Santa Claus at the downtown—"

"Me! That's me!"

He doesn't hear the rest; all he knows is that if he can be Claus, he'll be vaulted to the top of the good list and never look back. Somehow, that red coat will change him.

"Not without ID." Willie steps between Mickey and Jack. "Pick someone else, Mickey."

"*Wut?*" Jack's lower lip hangs. "Willie, for real? Is this 'cause I kicked the chairs?"

"It's because you picked on the lawyer and she left without getting you an ID. Listen, I'm not going to let a bunch of little kids sit on your lap until you get an ID."

"And you stink," Pickett mutters.

"Shut up," Jack says.

"Someone else, Mickey." Willie crosses his arms.

"Um." She slides her finger down the list again. "There's one he might be able to do... if you think it's okay."

She flashes the clipboard at Willie.

He looks to where she's pointing. His hair swings over his eyes while he rubs his chin. "I suppose," he finally says.

"No, wait. Tell me first," Jack says. "What is it?"

Mickey shows him the clipboard and points at an assignment.

Jack holds his breath and reads the words in the little box. For a moment, he looks less green. Willie and Mickey begin to look worried.

"Face!" Jack spins around. "In your face! In your face! In your face!"

He runs around the room, pointing with both hands, finger-guns popping at each and every resident, kicking empty chairs (on accident this time), nearly falling, stopping near Pickett in the back row, and hauling in one last deep, deep, deep breath—

"FAAAAACE!"

He doesn't hear Willie shout, doesn't sense Pickett's rage. He rushes outside, hands up, head turned to the clouds, rain drizzling on his upturned face.

The red coat.

For some reason, he's always wanted to wear the red coat.

To be good.

THE LIVE OAK grove is north of the house. It's perched at the top of a slope that overlooks the orchard and rice fields. Sura and Joe stand beneath sprawling limbs as thick as tree trunks. Freshly cut logs are scattered around the remains of a fallen limb.

"No, you make a fist with this hand." She demonstrates, pressing her fist to her midsection. "And then rest the other hand on top."

"Feels like my fist is wearing a hat."

Sura tries not to laugh. She straightens her back, opens her chest. "Smooth steps, slow steps. The body walks. The mind is open."

She breathes through her nose, counts her breath, and quickly rests into a meditative state.

"I can walk slower than that." He barely moves.

"Hey, you asked me how to do it."

"No, I asked what's the point."

"Well, I'm giving you the bonus answer. Aren't you lucky?"

"Charmed. Now is there a chant that'll make the sand fleas disappear?"

Joe's phone goes off. Jonah's face fills the screen. Joe gives several one-word answers, finishing with, "On my way."

He starts loading the firewood into the back of a utility vehicle. Sura helps with the smaller stuff, thinking about Jonah, wondering if he was always angry at the world. He looked just like Joe when he was the same age and Joe could never be as bitter as his dad. It's impossible.

Or is he destined to become like his dad?

"Has your dad always been like that?" she asks.

"Like what?"

"Cranky."

Joe rests in the driver seat, thinking a moment. "He's just quiet and to the point."

"You know, he looked just like you when he was your age."

"How do you know?"

Twilight hides her blushing. He doesn't know she stalked him on the school database. "I saw a picture," is all she says, resisting the urge to lie.

"You know you look just like your mom?"

"I get that all the time."

"No, I mean *exactly* like her."

Joe pulls out his phone, moves images around the glass, and taps through folders until a photo comes up. He holds the phone sideways. It's a picture of her mom and his dad standing in the sunken garden among the boxwoods. He's leaning on the end of a rake; her hands are clasped in front of her stomach.

Sura takes the phone.

She always knew they looked similar, but she didn't often see photos of her mom when she was sixteen. It's like looking at her identical twin. She spreads her fingers across the glass, zooms in on their faces, their heads tilted slightly, ever so slightly, towards each other.

Sura has a dreadful thought. Her mouth starts to move.

"No," he says. "He's not your dad and she's not my mom."

"How do you know?"

"Because I asked. You think he'd let me near you if they were?"

"He doesn't seem to like me."

"Proves my point, doesn't it? If you were his daughter, he wouldn't treat you that way."

"I don't like it." She hands back the phone.

"It's sweet."

"No, I mean, it's like looking at us twenty years ago."

The phone rings again. Maybe Jonah's watching. Or maybe his ears are burning.

"Hop on." Joe smacks the passenger seat. "Jonah is heating up."

"I think I'll walk."

"Why? You think he'll be mad?"

Yes. "No, I just don't want to hurry, that's all."

"You'd rather get thoroughly eaten by sand fleas than ride with me?"

"Maybe."

He reaches into the back of the vehicle and pulls out a small mistletoe bush. "Don't go back empty-handed."

Their fingers brush as they exchange the plant. He holds up his hand. They awkwardly high five. Better than a kiss or a hug because, honestly, if she starts kissing him, she won't stop.

Sand fleas or not.

"See you tomorrow?" he asks.

She nods, already pretending that the mistletoe is a bouquet. The vehicle revs up, slowly moving away in first gear. Tomorrow is such a long ways away and then she'll just have to say goodbye again. They'll high five again and she'll go home to an empty house.

"Joe!"

He slams the brakes. "Yeah?"

"Will you go to a school dance with me? It's a small one, a lot of people go out of town, but it'll be fun. I did the decorations and I'd like for you to see them—"

She puts her hand over her mouth, swears she doesn't feel nervous, but the words won't stop because if they do, he might say no, and now that she's asked, she wishes she hadn't.

"Love to," he says.

She did it. She asked him.

And he said yes.

And her heart floats twenty feet off the ground.

The vehicle speeds away, Joe waving. Sura waves back, smelling the mistletoe like it's roses, which is stupid, but maybe one day it'll be roses he's handing her instead of a parasitic plant.

She wanders out from beneath the live oak, stars filling the darkening sky. Her emotions keep her toasty. The house glows with holiday cheer. The worst day of her life happened when her mom died. *Was that only a month ago? Maybe that's why Mr. Frost brought me out here so soon. This feels like home.*

A cold breeze is ushered in on the night's wing and the sand fleas are crawling through her scalp. She wishes she would've taken the ride at least halfway. She could've gotten off before Jonah saw her and still enjoyed the long walk.

Sura walks to the back door, where she'll drop off the mistletoe and see if May needs any help. Someone's out back.

She can't see who it is, but he's way too short to be Templeton. He's even shorter than Mr. Frost, but just as round. It's hard to tell who it is with the long-tailed coat, wide boots, and tall, yellow hat. Sura hides in the bushes, watching the figure open the basement doors and climb inside. She's never used that entrance and May's never mentioned it.

Sura hurries for the house and starts up the steps. The basement door, however, is slightly ajar. A sliver of light flashes inside.

At the very least, I should close the door.

All she had to do was close it and she would've gone home to feed the horses and dreamed about marrying Joe one day. But when her fingers wrap around the handle, she has a second thought. She thinks maybe she'll take a peek.

The hinges creak.

Light seeps out along with a strange warbling sound. The bushes shake.

And that's the last thing she remembers.

Mr. Frost gently touches the tank's cold surface, leaning closer. Inside, the eyes are closed and the whiskers are faintly green.

Less facial hair, that's good. His calculations estimated improved photosynthetic efficiency and, therefore, Jack would need less hair to start life.

Increase red and blue wavelengths, Mr. Frost thinks. *Also, boost carbon dioxide. If all goes well, I expect Jack to be ready for initiation within the week.*

Freeda agrees.

Mr. Frost slides away from the tank. *Project his image from inside the tank, Freeda. I want a better look.*

Light flickers on the incubation lab floor. Line by line, an image of Jack's body, as it is in the tank, forms in front of him. A coat of silky, green fuzz covers most of the body. Only his palms and part of his face are exposed. He'll lose most of that before he's even out of the tank. Mr. Frost gives a command and the image lifts its feet to show him the scaly soles.

The root squirms. He takes a deep breath and lets it out slowly.

It looks just like him.

Aside from the hair, it's him: the fat belly, the protruding chin, and sharp nose. The proportions are correct, built to the specifications that were loaded into the root so many years ago.

Fear twists in Mr. Frost's stomach, trickling coldly into his legs. And beneath that lies the conflicting warmth of longing and love to see Jack like he was when Mr. Frost knew him.

When he was known as Pawn.

When Jack was blue.

His touch was cold and merciless, but no one saw him like Mr. Frost did. None of the elven on the North Pole saw the real Jack: the elven beneath the cold, blue exterior. Within those frozen eyes was a scared little elven. He was lonely, afraid, and he kept others from seeing that vulnerability by instilling fear in their hearts. He would freeze an elven with his deadly touch if they came close to seeing the real Jack.

"You're the only one I can trust," Jack would often tell Mr. Frost. "I need you."

Jack would sometimes be close to tears when he said that. Those tears froze in the corners of his eyes. The day the tears actually fell like tiny diamonds and bounced between his feet was the day Jack held up what looked like a grain of rice.

The root.

"I need you to hold this," he said to Mr. Frost. "To keep it safe."

Mr. Frost didn't ask what it was or why; he nodded because Jack needed him. Jack circled around him. Mr. Frost felt the cold aura that surrounded Jack at all times, a subzero body temperature that no other elven experienced, a coldness that gave Jack respect. A coldness that helped him cope with loneliness.

Jack reached behind Mr. Frost's head and numbed his neck. Even when Jack loaded the root into a pointed, silver cylinder, Mr. Frost didn't flinch. He didn't question Jack. He let him touch the gun to the cold spot on his neck.

He felt the pressure.

He heard Jack's tears dance on the floor. "Thank you."

And Mr. Frost was happy.

He didn't know what the root was for, just that it was important to Jack, so it was important to him. He never told Mr. Frost what it was for, but from time to time, Jack would visit the elven scientists and return to "update" the root with a small tin of grain. He'd put a few kernels in Mr. Frost's hand and tell him to eat.

They tasted stale.

Mr. Frost didn't know what the food was doing or how it was updating. Afterwards, the root would itch and Jack would blow his icy breath on his neck to make it go away.

It was like that for hundreds of years. And for hundreds of years, Mr. Frost happily allowed Jack—his mentor, his friend—to update the root, to soothe it when it squirmed.

But all that changed when Jack fell through the ice, when he sank to the bottom of the ocean with his mother and brother.

When Jack died.

And now there was no one left to soothe the itch.

Love and hate. When he sees Jack, he can't choose between love and hate, so he embraces them both.

Love and hate.

Sir, an intruder has compromised the lab.

What?

Your little pet followed one of the helpers into the lab.

You're supposed to monitor and report to me, Freeda. I'm tired of these lapses! Mr. Frost hides his satisfaction. He's counting on her missing things like that. *Where is she now?*

The toy factory.

The toy factory? She's not ready to see the toy factory!

She's sleeping.

Mr. Frost makes sure the red and blue lights are turned up in Jack's tank before sliding out of the room. He passes through the main room, around the elevator to the door on the opposite side.

The toy factory.

It always makes his head spin when he enters.

It's the wide open space. He's still not accustomed to subterranean rooms this size, a room that goes fifty feet into the earth. A room too wide to see the other side; a room filled with compartments, scaffolding, and dangling components. A cold room dank with the smell of moist earth and oily machinery.

Today, it's quiet.

Mr. Frost stops at the top of a steep ramp. At the bottom is a table surrounded by hundreds of tiny elven, with long-tailed coats and colorful hats—the helpers climb over each other for a glimpse of Sura. Their garbled conversation fills the emptiness of the dormant machinery.

Mr. Frost lets gravity pull him down the slick slope. The helpers scatter but only far enough for him to skid to a halt. Ice shavings flutter at his feet.

The helpers never sleep, never slow; they adapt to any temperature, build anything Mr. Frost can imagine, and would best a chameleon at hiding. There's very little they can't do and almost nothing they haven't seen.

But they've never had Sura in the toy factory.

One of them, wearing a yellow hat, slides out of the crowd. He stands no taller than Mr. Frost's knee. His nose is sharp and hooked over his mouth. He points at the table with a pudgy, but nimble, finger and a string of unintelligible sounds stream from his wrinkled lips.

He says they caught her sneaking through the back door, sir, Freeda interprets.

"I don't want her in here." Mr. Frost's voice echoes. The helpers back up. "She's not ready to see them."

The yellow-hat comes closer and replies. *He says she has not seen them,* Freeda says.

"Why is she in here?"

It wasn't necessary to bring her into the toy factory, but he knows why. Whether they'll be honest about it or not, he knows the real reason they brought her into the toy factory. It's the same reason Mr. Frost adores her.

She's special.

The helpers can't stop themselves from being around her. It has always been that way. Perhaps they sense the same thing he does, the warm essence of her kindness. The goodness of her emotions.

Mr. Frost moves a strand of hair from her eyes. *They just want to see her, that's all.*

All the conveyor belts and boxing machines, the wrappers, stackers, and envelope slappers have stalled. It's always in full production, 364 days a year, all of it getting ready for one day, sending out wishes and dreams, things that people want and need. Every kid will get something from Mr. Frost, something their parents will buy, their grandparents will purchase, or an aunt or uncle will order. No matter what the gizmo, no matter how long or how short, fat, or slim, he and the helpers have designed some part of it, manufactured a piece of it here in the toy factory.

Even the ideas that humans believe to be their own have, in one way or another, originated from Mr. Frost and the root inside his neck.

He made what Christmas is today.

Mr. Frost takes his hand from Sura's forehead. "Take her to the incubation lab," he whispers. "Let's insert false memories and get her ready to go home."

No less than twenty helpers—all with different colored hats—lean into the table, the soles of their leathery boots biting into the slick surface as they thrust the table up the ramp.

Mr. Frost looks at the rest of them, too many wrinkled and dour faces to see them all, but all of them disproportionately fitted with long noses and square chins. Their eyes, icy blue.

Jack wanted them that way.

"Christmas is coming!" Mr. Frost lifts his arms to rally their spirits.

"HURRAY!"

Tiny fists pump in the air. They scramble away, soaring up ropes and climbing to their stations to make the next watch, the next doll, the next music player. The phone, the TV, the bicycle repairer.

They make it all. And so much more.

They have a life of servitude that very few humans would tolerate and yet, the helpers live with such joy. Bred to work—labor is in their DNA—perhaps they don't recognize this place as a prison.

To them, it's just home.

Mr. Frost pushes his way up the ramp. He looks back as the machines rev up like high-tech lasers, whine with heaters and compressors. A song starts somewhere deep within the recesses of the toy factory and spreads like a flame. All at once, they're singing.

Mr. Frost leaves the toy factory, realizing there is only one true prisoner on the plantation.

And he yearns to be free.

12

DECEMBER 14

Sunday

Bernie the cockatoo is talking.

Sura presses a pillow over her ear. She'd yell at him, but he's just a bird. He doesn't usually get worked up this early in the morning.

She sits up and rests her elbows on her knees. Her head feels like a fifty-pound bag of seed. The sun isn't up. She can't remember going to bed. She remembers walking back with mistletoe. She vaguely remembers driving home and feeding the horses. *Or was that the day before?*

Crenshaw strolls into the bedroom with his back arched, purring. Bernie's still pitching a fit. Sura can't remember feeding them. Her thoughts are like images on a foggy mirror.

She scratches Crenshaw behind the ear. "Did I feed—?"

Something crashes in the kitchen. Sura freezes. Her heart bangs in her throat. She's wide awake now.

She looks around the room and spies an old curtain rod in the corner. It's all she's got. The mess of clothes strewn on the floor dampens her footsteps. She stops at her doorway.

"Who's there?"

Bernie answers with a bunch of gibberish.

Sura reaches around the wall and turns on the living room light. She waits in her room, eyes wide. Nothing moves but Bernie. Crenshaw eventually slinks across the room. Sura follows the cat to the hallway and turns on another light. By the time she reaches the kitchen, every light in the house is on, including the floodlights in the backyard.

Crenshaw sways into the kitchen, meowing.

Sura's knuckles ache. She puts the curtain rod on the counter and picks up Crenshaw. The floor, counters, and table are clean. There's a pot turned over in the sink. She has a vague memory of cleaning the kitchen and washing the dishes. She also remembers Mr. Frost telling her to volunteer with her Helping Hands Horse Troupe after school instead of working.

Or maybe Templeton said something.

Sura carries Crenshaw to the living room. Bernie flaps his wings, stirring up white feathers. His bowl is filled with seeds. She sticks her fingers between the bars and rubs his head.

The horses are standing at the back fence, staring at the house. Or maybe they're staring at the yellow towel in the backyard. She thinks about picking it up before one of the horses starts chewing on it.

"Gottago,gottago,gottago," Bernie wails.

He sounds like an overwound toy, the words mashing together. Sura puts Crenshaw down to start working on chores before school.

Later, she realizes that the yellow towel is gone.

JACK'S CHILLY.

The red coat is heavy and the furry hat floppy. He unbuttons the coat to expose his thinning chest hair.

Jack targets a squishy-looking lady with his big, brass bell. She's thumb-punching her phone while a butt sizzles between her lips. She doesn't look up. There's a kid behind her, snot caked on his upper lip. He snerks back a payload and spits before waving at Santa.

There's a table on the other side of the Walmart entrance, some teenagers signing people up for something. Everyone that comes out of the store stops at their table to fill out tickets. The girls say thank you and smile each time someone drops one in a fishbowl.

Sometimes the people will look at Jack and sometimes they stare, but they never come over and they never put anything in his bucket. Actually, one guy emptied a pocketful of pennies into it an hour ago, along with lint and a bottle cap.

An old guy comes out of the store with two carts brimming with boxes.

"Excuse me." Jack swings the bell. "Do you have the time?"

"No."

"Would you like to make a donation?"

"No."

"Do you hate children?"

The old man shoves past Jack's outstretched hand, pushing one cart and pulling the other. Jack thinks about throwing the bell at the old buzzard. He didn't feel that way in the beginning of his Santa assignment, but hour after hour of rejection is wearing him down.

Claus should give out grades; let us know how we're doing. Do I have a C or an A+? How many good things do I have left to do, and how many points will I lose if I gong that old man on the back of the head?

If that table was to suddenly collapse and those tickets spontaneously catch on fire, maybe he'd stand a chance at making some real dough. They're getting all the attention. Jack needs to think this out. How can he make it look like an accident? If no one knows he did it, will Claus know? He would have to act very concerned when it happens, run over to help the poor girls, maybe even shed a couple tears.

Oh, you poor things. I can't believe someone would do this. Oh, the horror!

"Yeah, that's good," he mutters. "The horror."

"What?" a passing teen says.

"Shut up," Jack answers.

The teen shoves a gold coin in the slot. "Go buy yourself a new sled."

"Did you just..." Jack's arm stiffens.

The kid and his buddy look back with grins.

"Happy Chris... Merry hol..." Jack clears his throat; they're almost to their car. "Habby Lobiday!"

I'm an idiot... an idiot with a gold coin!

All it took was one good soul to see Jack needed a break and zooooom, he just flew up the good list because gold could buy some poor family a house or it could buy the shelter a year's worth of food or some poor slob a new coat. He couldn't be hasty, though. It's gold. And he's rich.

A+, baby.

He rings the bell with pleasure, without a care in the world. Nothing can stop him now. The sound of his annoying bell doesn't even bother him. In fact, if that old man comes back for another cart full of toys, Jack might even hug the old coot. He feels warm and bubbly. Joyous. *Yeah, that's it. Joyous. The spirit of Christmas is in me. The golden spirit of Christmas.*

He should probably take his bucket and leave just in case someone gets any funny ideas. There are some shady characters at Walmart. He doesn't want to lose the gold, but he has to act cool. Maybe hang around another ten minutes and then grab a cab.

And hope the cabby can make change.

People exit the megastore with armloads of stuff.

"Merry holiday, everybody! Happy Christmas, great New Year, silent night. Silent night, everyone! Silent night!"

He says it to everyone, no matter how tall, skinny, short, or fat. They all get his blessing. Each time, the words pass through his lips a little louder and a little more joyously. There's no stopping the spirit of Christmas.

He spreads his arms. "Siiiiilent night."

Several people turn at the sound of his lovely song. Jack heard it on the radio, but he likes his version better. It's simpler, gets to the point. He's not sure what the point is, but nonetheless he sings with joy.

"Siiiiilent night. Siiiiilent night."

"Don't you know the words?" A small kid is in front of him.

"What?"

"That's not how the song goes."

"Yes, it is."

"No, it ain't."

"The song goes how I sing it. So there."

"Because you don't know the words."

Jack chuckles. He looks around, ringing the bell. An old lady passes them but doesn't appear to belong to this little smart mouth. Jack waits until no one is looking. He's got a gold coin. An A+.

He's got a little wiggle room.

He leans forward, eye to eye. "Why don't you shut your mouth, you little booger-eater."

"You shut up."

"You shut up."

"You shut up."

"You're going on the naughty list," Jack says. "Guarantee it."

"Whatever, loser."

"Hope you like poop in your sock."

The kid laughs. Jack screwed something up. Santa puts something in bad boys' socks, but it's not poop. It should be.

"Come on, Bo." A large lady passes them. "Let's go."

"You're dumb." The little stinker races after her.

Jack almost throws the bell, considers the special one-finger wave, but then the lady holds out her hand and drops a fistful of gold into Bo's cupped hands. He peels off a cover and eats it.

A gold wrapper hits the ground.

The last tone fades from the bell hanging at Jack's side. He picks up the tin wrapper that's shiny gold on one side and smeared with mud on the other. He dabs it with his finger and puts it to his nose. It smells sugary. He licks it.

Chocolate.

The concrete starts to sway. Jack is losing his balance. There's another kid peeling a coin and popping it in his mouth. And the guy next to him is doing the same thing.

There are gold coins everywhere!

Jack goes to his bucket and tries to pry the lid off. He jams his finger through the slot and gets it stuck. He shakes the bucket and the pennies clang. People stop what they're doing as cuss words stream out of the short Santa that's punching the side of his donation pot.

He looks over his shoulder.

They look away, pretending they don't see him. Jack thinks about stomping the bucket flat—he's got the feet to do that—when he spies the guilty party.

I knew it!

Piled on the table next to the fishbowl is a mountain of gold coins. People are signing a piece of paper with a picture of a horse and grabbing the coins for free. They peel them and eat them!

Darkness fills Jack.

He's left with emptiness, left with a chasm of need and dashed hope. He's deep on the naughty list now. His heart shrinks to a cold clod of ice.

It's their fault. They gave out the gold coins. They made me call the kid a booger-eater.

The bell clangs on the ground.

Jack is going to flip that table, dash all their stuff in the parking lot, and stomp it with his fat, hairy feet until it resembles garbage from a compactor. If he's going to be on the naughty list, he may as well make it worth it.

Jack can't explain what happens next.

It's like the spirit of Christmas returns when a truck pulls up. Its mufflers are loud and obnoxious, but Jack suddenly feels warm and bubbly again. It's like he loves the world, and the world loves him back.

He feels like breaking out in song.

A boy is driving. A girl gets out of the passenger side. She skips around the front bumper, her rosy, round face beaming with a smile. Jack's foot slides toward her like she possesses gravity. He leans back so the force doesn't pull him through the crowd. It would be embarrassing if he landed on top of her and, right now, he just wants to bathe in the sweet sensation.

"What are you doing here?" one of the girls at the table says.

"I want to help," the chubby-cheeked, tractor-beam girl says.

"You need to be getting ready." The girl at the table waves at the boy in the truck. "We're doing just fine."

"Are you sure?"

A man and his family get between Jack and the girls. Jack shoves the kid out of the way and starts walking toward the table. The father confronts him, but he doesn't hear anything. The sweet vibrations fill his head. A tunnel wraps around his vision. The girls hug, smile, and laugh. Jack feels all giggly, too.

They look at him. He must've laughed out loud.

And then the girl of his dreams gets back in the truck.

"Have fun," the girls at the table shout.

They all wave to each other. Jack waves, too. He watches them drive away, the mufflers momentarily drowning out conversations.

And the resonating feeling fades. That beautiful Christmas spirit drives off in a four-wheel-drive truck and Jack feels colder.

Emptier.

Once again, his chest hardens.

And he wants to destroy that stupid horse table with the dumb coins. Jack picks up the bell and inspects a chip on the rim. He resists the urge to hammer the red pot with it, or shatter the dumb fishbowl. He wants that feeling back.

The Christmas spirit.

He waits for a gap in the crowd before wandering over to the table, while one of the girls tells someone about volunteer opportunities and disabled children and blah, blah, blah. Jack walks his fingers across the table and swipes a coin. It's soft and pliable.

"Hi," she says, wrinkling her nose. "Are you all right?"

"Oh, I'm awesome."

"I thought something was wrong with your donation can."

"Yeah, it malfunctioned. I fixed it."

"Good." She looks around, but no one is coming near them. Jack is staring. "Are you interested in signing up?" she asks.

"Oh, yeah. For sure."

She slides over a clipboard. "Just write your name with your phone number and email."

"Okay. I will." Jack picks it up and scribbles on the line. "Hey, by the way, I was just talking to... ummmm."

He whacks his head.

"What's the girl's name, the one that was in the cool truck with the kid?"

"Sura?"

Jack snaps his fingers. "That's it. I was talking to Sura about doing this, um, thing with the horses and stuff, you know, earlier... when you weren't looking. Anyway, she wanted some information about my bell and bucket."

Stupid. Jack shakes his head.

"Anyway, is she coming back?" Jack asks.

"Not today."

"Where she'd go?"

"The Blackwater High Christmas dance."

"That's right, she told me that." He pretends to fill out the form, not paying any attention to what he's writing. "Well, that's too bad. She was really, really, really interested in the bell, wanted to know where she could get one just like it. Maybe I can give this one to her since it's broke. Where does she live and what's her phone number and, um, email?"

"I don't know." The girl frowns.

"Yeah, you do."

"Can you just give me the clipboard back?"

"I'm almost done. Just tell me where she lives."

"Is everything all right?" The other girl stands up.

"He won't give me the clipboard."

"Yes. I will." Jack laughs, but people are staring. Something snaps. He looks down at the pencil clenched in his fist, now in two pieces.

Both girls hold out their hands.

"I don't like your attitude, missy." Jack drops the clipboard. "No one sign up!" he announces. "They're mean over here. They'll just be mean to you if you sign up."

The girls roll their eyes. One of them goes into the store, probably to tell on him. Jack goes back to ringing the bell. He'd walk off and leave all his crap if he had any idea where or what Blackwater High meant.

He'll find out when he's back at the shelter.

ANOTHER SHIRT LANDS on a growing pile. Several empty hangers swing in the closet. Sura digs into the blouses, things she's never worn, clothes she's never seen. For her, it's always been T-shirts and jeans.

But she's never been to a dance. *What do people wear?*

Sura drops on the chair, stares at the large mirror, and pouts into her hands. A picture of her mom is wedged into the frame.

It's too much pressure. Why don't they just build a fire and hang out with the horses? Why'd she even ask him to this stupid dance? It's not like she's friends with any of those people.

Because she wants to show him off, that's why. To come to the dance hanging on his arm, watch the girls drool.

Sura remembers sitting in that chair, staring into the same mirror when it was her mom's mirror. She remembers the time she found her makeup box and started playing with it, afraid she'd be in trouble. She tried to draw lines around her eyes and brush her cheeks.

Her mom had come inside the room just as Sura was twisting the lipstick. Her mom smiled, the corners of her mouth poking her chubby cheeks. She came back with a chair and sat next to her, rubbing the blush off her cheeks with a damp washcloth.

You remember something, her mom had said. *Your value is not here.*

She tickled Sura's face.

Who you are is here. She tapped her chest. *It's not who you look like —it's who you are. You are unique. Do you understand?*

Sura had closed her eyes. *Yes, Momma.*

She opens her eyes and sees her reflection. She brushes her cheeks, like her mom taught her. She paints her lips pink. She digs through the drawers until she finds wire earrings with dangling beads, something she made for her mom when she was ten years old. They fit through her earlobes and brush against her jaws.

The back door opens and closes, rattling the walls. "You ready?" Joe calls.

"Just a second!"

Sura ties her hair back and finds exactly what to wear.

Joe is at the dinner table, shuffling through a mess of old photos. He looks up when the boots clop on the hardwood. Without a word, his expression tells her exactly what she wants to hear.

Her cowboy boots have polished tips and the beaded belt matches the earrings. The loose-fitting top with the India collar exposes the leather necklace and pendant containing a small photo.

Joe stands. "*Belle dame!*"

"*Merci.*" She curtsies.

His applause thunders throughout the house. He whistles, loudly. Sura feels her face heat up but doesn't hide.

"Um... *Je vais manger le chat,*" she says.

"You're going to *eat* the cat?"

"No, I said I'll feed the cat."

"You said eat."

Sura pulls the cat food from the kitchen cabinet, a smile chiseled into her cherub cheeks. Crenshaw comes out of hiding, rubbing against her leg. She hears the chickens squabbling. It's too dark to see the coop. *Better not be a possum.*

"You fed the chickens, right?" Sura asks.

"You ate the cat; I ate the chickens."

Sura washes her hands and grabs a water bottle, thinking she'll check the coop on the way out, just in case something dug under the fence.

"I like this picture."

"Which one?" she asks.

He holds up a grainy three-by-five photo. She didn't mean to leave that mess out. She happened to see the box in the bottom of her closet, thought it was in the attic. Sura takes the photo, struggling to make sense out of it. It was taken downtown near the water.

"Where'd you get this?"

"In here." He holds up a manila envelope. "I was just being nosy. Was I not supposed to look?"

"No, no. Mom printed all her digital photos. I was just..."

She trails off.

Sura liked having the photos out. It reminded her of what they did and where they went. But this photo, this one was developed from film and not printed at home. Its edges are thick and the corners sharp. Two people are standing on the pier. The younger girl looks about five.

"That's not me."

"It's your mom. I told you she looked just like you."

But Sura's not looking at the young girl. She's looking at the older woman. She never met her grandmother. She passed away before Sura was born. Her mom didn't talk much about her and Sura can't remember ever seeing any photos of her.

She looks exactly like Mom.

"Come on." Joe takes her hand. "Let's go dance."

Sura lets him lead her away from the table. She puts the photo on the refrigerator, a strange sense of déjà vu swirling in her head, that feeling that says, "Wake up! Look around!"

Wake up, her mom would say. *Don't sleep through the truth.*

Joe opens the back door. The chickens are quiet. "You coming?"

Sura turns on the outdoor lights and locks the door. She feels closer to normal once she's outside. Joe opens the passenger door like a chauffeur. While he jogs around the front, she hears the chickens squabble again and sees a bright color flash behind the coop.

It's yellow.

THE ARCTIC HORIZON IS SHARP.

The North Star sparkles white, red, and green while the Northern Lights dance around it with bands of similar colors. Mr. Frost remembers sights like this from the time he was born. The colors remind an elven he's home.

A light breeze ruffles his hair, the faint smell of the ocean on the wind; perhaps a polar bear with a fresh kill is nearby, staining the pristine snow as it fills its belly—a world so beautiful and so cruel.

He eyes a hole in the ice, water sloshing against the edges. The root begins fluttering beneath his skin with a steady beat. Freeda is calling. Her presence is not allowed in the wishing room unless he allows it.

The wishing room was forbidden for many, many years, but his nervous breakdowns were not an act. Mr. Frost was breaking under the pressure of her demands. The wishing room brought his sanity back. That's the only reason she allowed it.

Jack can't come back if I'm broken.

Yes, Freeda.

The helpers report that Sura has found a photograph of her grandmother.

How?

Sesi had evidently stashed a box of photos in the closet. Apparently, she taped an envelope of old photos beneath the lid.

How'd she handle it?

There didn't seem to be a problem, but it's too soon for her to know her truth. Her ego isn't stable enough to handle it. I don't really care if she loses her mind, but I know you feel differently.

Mr. Frost scoops a handful of snow and molds it into a sphere, trimming the imperfections with the edge of his bare hand. He knows his body is wearing the coolsuit to keep him insulated from the warmth. The wishing room makes him believe he's comfortable in the Arctic, but if he wasn't wearing the coolsuit, his body would overheat. He wouldn't last long.

Confiscate the photograph, he thinks.

What good would that do, since she's already seen it? Why not replace it with an altered version?

That would be easier, but it would throw her too far off the path of self-discovery. Deception can be far more damaging.

No. Have it removed.

She'll be suspicious, sir.

Curiosity is good.

Mr. Frost lets the snowball roll off his fingertips, careful not to let his thoughts roam freely now that he let Freeda in. It plunks in the water. Perhaps he'll plunge into the icy depths like he did as a youth.

He longs to feel the icy embrace of home.

Instruct the helpers to stop following Sura and Joe, he thinks.

Why?

I don't want to risk her seeing them, Freeda. She's been pushed to the limits. One more shove, and she could come unglued.

I disagree, sir. We need to watch them now more than ever.

Mr. Frost kneels. He pushes snow into a mound, molding two stout legs and a round belly. He sits back before finishing the rest of the snowman, pretending to consider her reply.

Okay, he relents.

Mr. Frost severs the connection.

He needs to be compliant. Freeda may be artificially intelligent, but her programming has evolved into a complex mind. Allowing her a victory curbs her suspicions.

And Mr. Frost needs to know what the kids are doing.

He finishes sculpting a snowman with a stout head and thick arms. It looks more intimidating than loving, but that is a misconception. A snowman of this sort is protective.

But there are no snowmen in Mr. Frost's life.

✳

"I DIDN'T SAY I wanted to *go* to the dance—"

"Yeah, you did," Willie interrupts.

"No, I didn't." Jack chooses his words carefully. "I said I wanted to *see* the dance."

"And I said no."

The men at the next table laugh.

"Shut up." Jack spreads the map on the table, flattening the wrinkles with the edge of his hand. "Look, Willie. There's been a misunderstanding, let me start over. High schools have dances. It's normal. It's fun."

"Uh-huh. And where'd you hear this?"

"Just some crazy kids at Walmart. I like fun, you like fun. I'm just curious, where I might *seeeee* a dance?"

Willie starts organizing chairs around tables, prepping for dinner. "The answer's still no."

"Give me one good reason."

"I'll give you fifty, Jack. Blackwater High is in the country. It's late. You take the bus out there and you'll be stranded. Worse, you'll get arrested."

"That's only four."

"Look, why do you want to go, anyway, Jack? It's creepy, man. Trust me, a homeless dude like you showing up at a high school dance is going to end badly."

"Well, um." Jack hesitates, wondering how much he should say. "You know how I don't remember stuff? It's just, I think I saw someone I know today."

"And that someone is going to the dance?" Willie stops wiping down a table and looks up incredulously.

"Yep."

"Still no. Go watch TV; I'm sure you can see a Christmas dance on the Disney Channel. You won't get arrested doing that, I promise."

Jack growls.

Willie shouts for someone to help move tables. One of the cooks calls him into the kitchen. Jack slumps into a chair and studies the map again. Nothing's labeled. If it just showed high schools, he could figure it out. Buses went all over the place.

It's not fair, really. Willie doesn't know what that resonating feeling is like. When he saw that girl, something rang inside him, and not like that stupid bell. This was warm and right, vibrating right down to the bone.

It felt like home.

"Hey, garbage man." Pickett sits across from him. "You want to go to Blackwater?"

"Yeah, duh."

"I'll show you, you furry little freak."

Jack studies his face and waits for the insult. Pickett nods all serious-like. Jack slowly slides the map across the table. Pickett points to the nearest bus line and explains.

Jack listens.

He never would've guessed Pickett would help.

THE PARKING LOT is half empty.

Sura can hear the music. Everyone is inside, dancing to it, except for the rednecks sitting on the tailgates of several fat-tire, jacked-up trucks. The door panels are decorated with mud.

They turn their heads, watching Joe's truck idle across the parking lot, the mufflers some kind of mating call. He parks near the front doors.

"Stay here." He climbs out.

Sura thinks, *No problem.* In fact, she'd be fine if she stayed in the truck all night, but her door opens and Joe holds up his hand.

"*Ma dame.*"

She doesn't budge. Joe waits patiently, hand out. The rednecks start laughing, but it doesn't bother him. *It's not safe out here, either.*

Ms. Wesley opens the doors as they approach. The music assaults them. "Why, Sura. What a pleasure to see you." She adjusts her glasses. "And who is this you've brought to our wonderful school?"

"I'm Joe." He shakes her hand firmly. "Nice to meet you, ma'am."

She asks where he's from, how old he is, what school he attends; the sort of questions a mother asks. Finally, she says over the sounds of Blake Shelton singing about snow, "And did you know your little sweetheart here decorated the entire hall?"

"Not the entire thing." Sura hangs her head.

"She's being modest, Joe."

"It's beautiful," Joe says. "No, seriously. We have dances and they don't look anything like this."

She blushes for two reasons. One, he's serious. She loves that. But, two, he's never been to a dance unless he was lying.

"I've never been to a dance," he whispers in her ear.

She smiles.

"Nice shirt." A tripod of *populars* walk past and give Joe a double take and a flirty wave, the kind where the fingers do the waving.

She thinks about dragging him back into the parking lot because this is all a big mistake. She doesn't belong here; she'd rather be snuggled up on the couch. Joe pulls her inside the gym, where they're doused with chest-thumping percussion. Red and green lights spin off a shiny globe. Most everyone is tucked into the dark corners, forming iron-clad cliques that would take a battering ram to break apart.

The chaperones are near the DJ's table, drinking from red cups and having more fun than the students. The center of the gym is empty.

Sura feels glued to the floor. Joe waits patiently. He hooks his finger around her pinky. She tries to be strong, thinks about how she should act. *What now? Go into a corner? Lean against the wall? Make fun of someone's shirt?* All she can think about is sitting at home, eating popcorn with Crenshaw.

The music stops.

"Can we go?" Sura mutters.

She turns for the door, but Joe hangs on like an anchor. The first chords of "Blue Christmas" strum through the speakers. Not the Elvis one, this one by Bright Eyes. A version she likes.

He walks backwards, pulling her with him.

She protests.

He's going toward the center where everyone will see her. One step, then two. She could pull away, break his grip, and run for cover —it's not too late—but then he smiles that smile, the one that's hardly on the lips but all in the eyes.

She falls in step.

He pulls her close.

Sura closes her eyes, cheek against his neck. The edge of his chin rests against her head. His hands are soft and warm. She feels herself merging into him, lost in a surreal cascade of goodness, where their energies mix like they did in the wishing room.

Two pieces become one.

The song falls over them, wraps around them, and protects them from prying eyes. She sways with his sway, moves with his moves. Their feet step gently, side to side, while he whispers the song to her.

When it ends and there's silence, the spell around them remains. She forgets all about her empty home and all the weird things in her life. All the strangeness, hurt, and confusion fall away.

There's clapping. It's the teachers. They applaud their dance. Joe curtsies and, to her surprise, Sura does too.

"We can go now," he says.

"Maybe just a little longer."

He smiles the smile.

JACK CAUGHT THE LAST BUS.

It's dark when he steps off, but he can read the signs pointing to Blackwater High School. He walks down the sidewalk, whistling. But then the sidewalk turns into grass and the buildings turn into trees. He almost steps on day-old roadkill. What looks like an armadillo has its guts steamrolled into maggot food.

His knees begin to ache. His feet begin to hurt. Joints stiffen.

It's darker in the country. No streetlights to keep him warm. It's not as bad as it used to be—in fact, the hair is falling off in shaggy clumps—but he still needs a little light just to keep the edge off.

He's shivering.

There's hardly room for him to walk, and the cars race down the road, whooshing inches away sometimes, honking as they pass. He marches into the trees when he gets so tired he can hardly walk, so cold he can't feel his big toes. He pulls out his flashlight to shine on his face long enough to stop the chattering.

Something is in the woods.

Jack swings the flashlight to scare it off. He doesn't want to be eaten by a bear. He walks some more, each time a shorter distance before having to get more light. Each time, hearing bears.

At some point, he's so cold and tired that he figures he's going to die. He's in the middle of nowhere. The batteries aren't going to last all night. He'll be a block of ice before the sun comes up. Even the thought of seeing the girl doesn't fill him with hope. Not anymore.

He's empty.

And, for the first time he can remember, he doesn't care.

Jack lies down in a soft bed of leaves to let the cold claim him. The shivering turns violent, but then tapers off. He feels numb all over.

Probably not good.

Still, he doesn't care.

He closes his eyes and dreams of a cold, white land that's flat as far as he can see. Even when he hears the bears come for him, he doesn't open his eyes. He won't stop them from gnawing on his legs. Jack is so numb he won't feel it. He's eaten many o' fish while they were still alive; he probably deserves it.

But then something vibrates, deeply.

Sura!

He opens his eyes. Too tired and stiff to sit up, he turns his head. It's dark, but she's not there. He felt that vibration, felt the goodness.

Twigs snap.

Jack looks closer to the ground and sees several lumps around him. It's difficult to see the details, but he sees they're fat little men wearing itty-bitty hats. Bite-sized people.

Jack can't move, can't feel his hand on the flashlight or his thumb on the switch. One of the tiny men shuffles through the detritus, turns the flashlight on, and points it at Jack's face.

He closes his eyes, seeing one big spot for several minutes as warmth ebbs back into his body.

"*Getup*," one of them says, the language fast and slurred.

Jack understands; he just can't do it.

"*Comeonyoucandoit. Getup.*"

Jack grunts. No go.

They push him into a sitting position. They get leverage on his rump, heaving him upright. Jack teeters, but they hold him steady.

"*Youneedtogetontheroad.*"

Jack shakes his head, still seeing an orange glow where the flashlight hit his eyes. They want him on the road where the roadkill is. He'd rather freeze than become maggot food.

"*Gonow. Getontheroad.*"

They poke and prod, guiding him out of the trees. Jack protests but finds himself standing on a yellow dash painted over black asphalt, surrounded by a posse of very, very, very short little dudes with cute red, orange, and yellow hats.

The flashlight is still aimed at him.

And then a puzzle piece goes *click.*

"Helpers," he mutters. "You're the helpers."

He doesn't know how he remembers, just that there are hundreds of them. He's seen them before. They know him. And he knows them.

They feel like the girl.

The light goes off.

Jack's alone on the road when the headlights come around the bend: bright, intense, and loud as an angry beast. He's too tired to get out of the way. It's probably better to end it this way. He's seen polar bears eat; they take too long.

As the lights get brighter, he feels warmer.

THE NIGHT IS dark without a moon.

The truck sits alone near the curb. A few cars remain beneath the streetlights, while teachers close up. Joe opens the door for Sura. She scoots into the center, watching him go around the front, thinking about how differently the evening started.

How wonderful it ended.

She pulls the sprig of mistletoe from behind her ear and twirls it between her finger and thumb. Joe slides into the driver's seat and starts the truck. She collects a kiss, exhausted.

Content.

The tree-lined country road is curvy and dark; the headlights beam down the dashed line. Sura rests her head on his shoulder, closes her eyes, and sways with the turns. The vents exhale warm air and pull her into a heavy, hypnotic state, seconds from sleeping.

"What the...?" The truck slows.

Momentum heaves her forward. The truck jerks to a stop. The headlights engulf something dirty, ragged, and hairy.

"What is that?" she asks.

"I don't know."

It's a misshapen man. The pants are too big, the bottoms piled over his feet. Leaves and twigs are stuck to the sleeves. His face is blotchy with patches of whiskers. The halogen light casts a strange color on him, turning his skin bluish and the hair kind of green.

Joe puts the truck in park.

"What are you doing?" she asks.

"Stay here." His eyes lock on the weird little man.

"You're not going out there."

"It's all right; just let me talk to him."

"In the middle of the road?"

Joe pats her knee and opens the door. She doesn't let go of his arm until he gently touches her hand. He locks the door behind him.

The little man's arms are straight at his sides. They don't say anything at first, and then Joe asks something. The little man answers. There's a short conversation. Joe looks up and down the road, pointing toward town.

The little man nods.

Joe looks around again. He looks back at the truck. Sura feels her stomach drop like a trapdoor just opened. He comes around to the passenger side. Sura opens the door.

"Can you get in the backseat?" he asks.

"Why?"

"This guy..." Joe looks at him. "He's got some weird skin condition, something's really wrong with him, and he's lost. He needs a ride to the shelter. And we need to get out of the road."

Sura looks at the misshapen figure standing in the headlights' glare. "You sure?" she asks.

"We can't leave him."

He's right. Despite her fear, she agrees. The little man needs help.

"I want him up front," Joe says, "to keep an eye on him. I'd feel better if you were in back."

She slides out stiffly.

The little man shuffles out of the light, hiking his pants up beneath his enormous gut. He's about as tall as a third grader with a man-sized beer gut. She catches a whiff of fish. Joe helps him up. Sura covers her nose and mouth.

Dead fish.

He starts climbing into the backseat. "Whoa, no," Joe says. "You can get in front."

"I thought..." The little man points at Sura. "There's so much room back there."

"She's in back; you're in front."

"But I like backseats."

"You want a ride?"

The little man's bottom lip pouts like a kid who just got his sucker taken away. He climbs into the front, mumbling.

Joe guns the truck, the tailpipes rattling behind them. Sura looks out the window and catches sight of a swamp fox or feral pig in the trees. It looks like it's following.

"Sweet truck," the little man says.

JACK SPREADS his hands in front of the vents. Warm, dry air blows between his fingers, ruffling the fuzz on his knuckles. The girl gags.

He closes his eyes, wallowing in the Christmas spirit. He knew it would be in the truck. It's coming from the boy, too. He felt it when he came out to talk with him, felt it swirl inside him. But Joe doesn't have half the Christmas spirit as the girl.

Not even close.

"What's your name?" Jack turns and looks back.

She cringes behind Joe's seat and mutters.

"What?" Jack says. "I can't hear you."

"Sura."

"I'm Jack."

He holds out his hand, but she won't take it. His eyelids droop as the loving sensations course through him like a fountain of goodness. He just wants to hug her, squeeze her, and put her in his pocket, so he can feel like this forever and ever.

"What're you doing all the way out here?" Joe asks.

"Fishing."

"This late?"

"That's when they bite."

"No, they don't."

"Yes, they do."

"Where's your pole and tackle?" Joe asks.

"Where's *your* pole and tackle?" Jack snips.

"What?"

"What?" Jack starts humming, opening his mouth in front of the vent to inhale the warm air. He's tempted to take off his shirt, maybe rub some of this Christmas spirit under his arms. He sings his song, the silent night one, and wonders if Sura can hear it. She'd probably like it.

"Siiiiiilent night," he croons, over and over and over, waggling his eyebrows at the shrinking girl—

"Can you not do that?" Joe says.

"Oh, yeah. Sorry. I'm just happy... from fishing." Jack rubs his hands and hums along to the radio. He just lied. Those are naughty list points.

"Hey, I just want to thank you for taking me to the shelter. It's a long ways downtown and you probably don't live down there, you know, with the truck and all."

And those are good points.

"So what's your deal?" Jack asks.

Joe shakes his head. "What?"

"You know, where you live, work, and go to school... in case we become friends or something. I had a phone, but I lost it when it got ran over by a thing..."

More naughty points. He can't stop.

Joe flicks a glance in the rearview. Jack studies the chubby-cheeked teenager leaning back in the shadows, the dashboard lights turning her complexion orange. He wants to climb back there but feels like Joe will throw him out the window.

Jack slides a few inches towards the middle. "Sorry, seatbelt is binding my junk. So, where'd you say you live?"

"Not downtown," Joe says.

"That's not really an answer."

"Only one I got."

Jack adjusts his seatbelt and grunts. He'd like to argue that point a little further and remind Joe that lying will put him on the naughty list, but seeing as Jack is three fibs in the hole, he'll skip it.

"Go to school, do you?"

"High school," Joe says.

"And our dads are cops," Sura adds.

Jack turns, slowly. The girl's nodding, arms folded. He's really wishing he didn't start this lie-parade. Now everyone's doing it. He doesn't want to see her on the naughty list, might dampen the spirit.

Joe merges onto the interstate and turns up the music. The heater isn't doing Jack as much good as it was earlier. His guts are frigid and he's doing everything he can not to shiver. He needs light.

The truck is plenty dark and, fortunately, the occasional street-light keeps him from chattering. He scratches the back of his hand and wipes the fuzz from his pants.

Jack turns the horrible music down.

"I just want to thank you again," he says sweetly. "Big sacrifice, taking me to the shelter. I don't have a job and all. It's the economy, you know. Not much out there. You two work? Mmm?" Jack looks back and forth, trying to include them both. "Do you?"

"Frost Plantation," Sura says.

Jack turns quickly with a smile reaching both ears. "Oh, really? That's wonderful! Are they hiring?"

"I don't think so. Mr. Frost doesn't like people, wouldn't you say, Joe?"

Joe changes lanes and nods.

Somewhere in the flow of Christmas spirit, there's a twinge of recognition, a memory that's swept in the current. He could likely remember what's nagging at him, but the Christmas spirit feels way too good to try.

Frost.

"Mr. Frost is protective of the ones that work out there, that sort of thing," Sura says. "Anything happens to employees like us and he finds them, if you know what I mean."

"No. What do you mean?"

"He finds them and hurts them."

So now we're all championship liars. Great.

She taps Joe on the shoulder. "I'm going to lie down."

"You don't have to sleep," Jack says. "I'll be quiet."

Sura curls against the seat with her back to him. Jack spins around. It doesn't matter if she talks, really. It still feels good. And there's always Joe. He's putting off some pretty good vibes, too. "Hey, I just want to say—"

"Shhhh." Joe puts his finger up and points to the back.

"Oh, right," Jack whispers. "I just want to say that it's really great..."

Joe turns the music up. Jack glowers at the backseat. She knew what she was doing. But then Joe gives Jack a thumbs-up, like he's a good guy. It's stupid, but Joe's approval rejuvenates him, intensifying the feel-good humming.

They near the end of the interstate. Jack rests his chin on the door, barely seeing over it. The scenery whizzes by, images of lit buildings and yellowish streetlights, billboards and railings. A car rushes past.

He soaks in Joe's energy, thinking about why this would even be happening, convinced this has to be a sign that maybe they know something. And, more importantly, how is he going to find them again without getting arrested?

Jack's eyes get heavy.

The vibrations rain down like big drops of delicious fish oil, freshly pressed and chilled. He licks his lips. The railing along the road turns into a flat line. Lights in the buildings twinkle like stars. The landscape blurs into a white blanket.

And Jack smiles.

The cold feels like home.

Faces emerge from the darkness: short, fat, and hairy. And a giant, icy mountain rises from the ground like an iceberg. He can see the short, fat, and hairy elven—yes, that's what they are, they're elven—all over the city... a city that has a name, something he should remember...

New Jack City. A city so nice, I named it after me.

Somehow, Joe's energy transported him home. He's back with his people on the North Pole where he belongs and not in this forgotten trash heap of smelly warmbloods and spongy, tasteless food. Yes, this is where he wants to be, how he wants to feel. It's not much to ask. He just doesn't want to feel lost anymore, unwanted, ashamed, and bad—

Sounds of war are all around. Footsteps are on the ice, and angry shouts and disapproval echo. It's all Jack's fault; he's to blame for thousands of years of grief, sadness, and suffering. He divided his people, dominated them with bitter anger. They hated him; they wanted him dead and gone because he was bad.

He is bad.

He's bad, bad, bad and cold, cold, cold—

"AHHHH!" Jack slams his head on the window.

Joe's shaking his shoulder. "You all right?"

"Am I..." Jack looks around. He's not on the North Pole. He's in the truck, parked next to a curb.

"We're here," Joe says. "That's the shelter, right?"

And so it is. They arrived just before midnight, just in time for Jack to get a bed. Just in time to get out of the truck. He takes a deep breath, shaking his head. He was dreaming about the ice and tunnels. Maybe he was dreaming about everyone hating him, too.

Jack unbuckles the seatbelt as slowly as possible. He opens the door even slower. "Hey, I just want to say—"

"It's all right." Joe holds up his hand. "Not a problem."

Jack slides out, feet on the pavement. Sura holds the door for him and takes his spot up front. Jack shuffles around the front of the truck and knocks on Joe's door. The window comes down.

"Say, if you ever want to hang out sometime, you know where I live." He points at the shelter. "Just call or something. Send me a text or email. Ask for Jack."

"Sure thing," Joe says. "Take care, Jack."

And the truck rolls away, loud exhaust rattling in Jack's chest, taking the beautiful vibrations with it, leaving him on the front steps, alone and empty.

Feeling as far away from home as ever.

13

DECEMBER 15

Monday

M r. Frost slides down the toy factory aisles, hands on his belly, idly watching the helpers hard at work. They hardly notice him. He passes through the main crosswalk—a wide thoroughfare that crisscrosses the toy factory where, previously, they had Sura on a table—and quickens his pace, sliding to the very back where the new release is being manufactured.

EyeTablets.

EyeTablets will be the toy of the decade, destined to ship all over the world. An estimated two billion will be activated by the New Year.

"May I?" Mr. Frost asks.

The helpers back up. He touches one of the contact lenses with the tip of his finger and places it against his eye. He blinks several times, lubricating the infinitesimal circuitry. Green lines stream over his vision. A grid takes shape.

Mr. Frost looks around.

Holographic images are displayed for his vision only. He focuses on an icon, blinks twice to activate a newslink, and video begins to stream. He'd need earbud implants to hear it, but that will be next year's big ticket.

He reaches out and rearranges the images. The eyeTablet senses the location of his hand and the tension in his imaginary grip, and responds. He spreads his fingers and expands one of the displays. He looks down to see his toes on a wooden raft rocking in the middle of the ocean. The helpers are faint figures in the illusion's scenery.

"Email," he says.

A keyboard hovers in front of him. He pecks at the air, typing out a reply, the words hovering over the blue waves.

"Voice activation," he says.

The keyboard disappears. The words appear as he says, "And thank you, once again, for your participation in this year's beta testing. Merry Christmas, Frost Enterprises. Send."

The words are sucked into the sky, on their way to cyberspace.

Christmas is so much easier in this day and age. Toys are tiny and shipping faster and more efficiently. It used to be that kids received plastic cars and stuffed animals; now it's laptops and smartphones.

And now this.

Mr. Frost anonymously leaked the eyeTablet technology to a start-up company in exchange for exclusive rights to produce and ship as long as he remained a silent partner. He could've gone with Google or Apple, but he'd leaked enough trade secrets to them.

The eyeTablets will be the greatest form of technology the general public will ever have experienced—the first step in phasing out phones and computers. However, it's still rudimentary compared to what Mr. Frost has planned for future generations. He would eventually release eyeTablets with neural capacity, tapping into the brain and nervous system, sensing thoughts and expanding intelligence. Humans will be able to send each other thoughts instead of texts. Schools will become obsolete when students can download lessons and have them integrated into their muscle memory within seconds.

Want to learn Italian? Done.

EyeTablets will eventually circumvent privacy at a level never thought possible. Governments will try to limit the technology to protect the general public, but people will want it, no matter the cost.

Mr. Frost could have the ability to know all their thoughts, to see through their eyes, hear their surroundings, touch their innermost desires, and experience their lives as if he lived them. He could tap into the entire human population at once, see them like a god.

He'll be able to make them do things. He doesn't like to think about that. After all, none of this is really his doing. In fact, it won't be Mr. Frost eavesdropping on their thoughts and operating them like puppets.

Jack will.

Mr. Frost admits taking great pleasure in the creative aspect of inventing this technology. After all, the human population has done many wonderful things with his ingenuity. What they don't know is the insidious intent behind all these wonderful gadgets.

What's in store for them is beyond their imagination.

Mr. Frost finishes with the eyeTablets and slides down the main aisle.

Sir, I want to remind you that Jack's incarnation is ahead of schedule. He can be removed from the incubation tank in two days.

She sounds sullen. The photosynthetic fur still irritates her. Not only that, she sounds distracted. He expected her to check in with news of Jack last night.

What have the helpers reported about Sura and Joe?

Non-eventful, sir.

Mr. Frost veers too close to a blue-hat helper and almost knocks him over. He keeps his surprise in check. *Nothing happened?*

Nothing worth reporting. They danced, they kissed, and they went home.

Mr. Frost keeps his mind empty, avoiding entertaining thoughts of suspicion and shock. He didn't see this coming. His spies had already updated him. He's had to stay focused to keep those thoughts hidden from her. Maybe her unexpected deception is a ploy to rattle him into the open.

You should come to the incubation lab for an assessment, she says.

That won't be necessary.

You need to see if your creation—

"My creation?"

Some of the helpers look up. He must've blurted that out loud. Jack has been found and she's pushing him to awaken another incarnation? Serotonin leaks from the root and floods him warmly, but fails to soothe his emotions.

I am an unwilling participant in this madness, Freeda.

For a victim, you take a lot of pride.

I didn't say victim. You know things would be very different without the root. None of this would be here.

Her laughter is genuine. *You can't fool me, sir. I see inside you, remember. You pretend to hate this but, deep down, you enjoy it. You can't beat the root, so you go along with it and pretend like there's nothing you can do about it. You cope with the guilty pleasure by trying to understand the warmbloods, to empathize because it's not your fault.*

I take no pleasure in destroying the human race.

Jack is correct about the warmbloods, sir. They're self-destructive. All of your attempts to be like them, to experience their emotions, and empathize with their short-lived lives are all very noble, but you know you're just doing it to ease your guilt.

Mr. Frost pumps his arms as he climbs the steep ramp.

Stop fooling yourself, sir. You are an elven—they are human. If it makes you feel any better, you're doing nothing but letting them destroy themselves. You're not pulling the trigger, sir.

I'm putting the gun in their hands.

Very good, sir.

He said "I." He didn't say "Jack." *I'm putting the gun in their hands.*

If you're done spouting delusions, sir, would you come to the incubation lab for an inspection?

Later. He goes to the elevator and punches the top button. *Have*

Templeton bring me a drink. I'd like some conversation outside my own head.

He feels her recede from his mind. His anger was genuine, but also intentional. Fierce emotion is an effective way to screen his true thoughts and motivation. He wanted to appear like an unwilling victim, but she convinced him that it was more than just a ruse.

Perhaps he really is willing.

14

DECEMBER 19

Friday

Green hair settles over the shower drain. Jack scrubs his arms and legs. Ever since Joe and Sura dropped him off, he's been itching like the truck seats were poison ivy. In the morning, his bed sheets looked like a leprechaun shaved. Bald patches of light blue skin are all over. He looks like a hallucination.

Jack tries to turn off the hot water, but it's already off. The pipes must be crossed because the cold knob feels like it's pumping water out of a geothermal hot spring.

He scrubs his head and face, lathering up and rinsing off, wishing the thoughts in his head would fall away like his hair. Joe and Sura's sweet vibrations haunt him along with memories.

He lived on the North Pole. *I already knew that.*

He ruled like a king. *Sweet.*

The elven hated him. *Okay, not so sure about that one.*

They wanted him gone. *That one's iffy, too.*

He was the coldest elven to ever live, which would explain the blue skin, but not the hair. He can't remember even having hair, not to mention curly, green hair.

And the naughty list? He couldn't care less about the naughty list anymore. He remembers something about Santa.

Claus is my brother. He always wore that dumb red coat.

It should be shocking, but the memory settles into place with no less disruption than if he remembered what he ate for breakfast that morning. Claus is his brother, no big deal. He thinks, for a moment, he'll tell Willie that he personally knows the fat man—they'd slid out of the same womb; they were tight—but even Jack can understand how crazy that would sound. He's already on thin ice covering Lake Sanity.

But delivering toys?

Sketchy.

He doesn't remember anything about toys. His memories are outdated—he can't remember anything he's done in the past two hundred years—but they weren't delivering free stuff to the warm-bloods. That's ludicrous. Then again, Jack's not in charge anymore. New management might see things differently.

They were always a little soft.

Still, he doubts the lists and the toys, but not entirely. He remembers sleighs and flying reindeer (turns out they are real), so maybe the toys are too. It all still feels like a dream. The idea of elven is too far-fetched, but all he has to do is look down at his giant feet and scaly soles to remind himself that the elven memories are as good an explanation as anything.

Right now he needs to find Sura to get another sweet jolt of her mojo or whatever she's dealing. That sweet essence emanates from her like distilled euphoria. He needs it to fill in the memory blanks and, more importantly, *so he doesn't feel so empty and alone!*

Now that he's had a taste, he wants more. He felt full and whole, no longer lacking or searching to fill the bottomless emptiness inside him. He felt like there was nowhere in the world he needed to be but right here. He didn't have to be anyone else but Jack.

He felt like he was home.

Jack doesn't care why those kids make him feel that way—he just needs it. His heart is dead without it.

"You need a dog groomer, man." Pickett kicks the wad of hair off the drain. It sticks on the wall. "Take your trash out."

Pickett and a few others hang their towels and turn on the showers far away from Jack. Pickett continues staring as Jack rinses the suds from his head. Jack gives him a full frontal view with a smile.

"You ain't human," Pickett says.

"Neither are you."

"I ain't shedding like a dog. I ain't got blue skin. I ain't got feet the size of flippers. You come from the ocean?"

"I come from your momma." Jack has no idea what that means, but it makes the others laugh. They try not to.

Pickett's lips get thin. "Two days, smelly. You getting kicked out of the shelter in two days without an ID, and this place can stop smelling like a bucket of fish."

"And start smelling like your butt," Jack says.

"Better than you, garbage man."

Jack gargles a mouthful of shower water and spits it on the wall. The hairball washes across the floor and finds the drain.

"Well, I got breaking news. I got my ID," Jack lies.

Pickett doesn't fall for it, but he's thinking. Jack's inside his head. That's where he wants to be. He wants to find Pickett's buttons and tap-dance all over them.

"I got that ID and I'm going to stay here forever and ever. And another thing, I talked to Willie, he's going to give me a bunk right next to you so we can work out our differences. Isn't that cool? We get to wake up next to each other like brothers. I got to warn you, though, I get the morning farts." Jack sort of whispers. "They smell like herring."

Jack's laughter bounces around the community shower. Pickett isn't moving. Jack feels his anger rise. He senses it prickle beneath his skin. He watches a lump swell in Pickett's throat. He hates Jack.

And Jack loves it.

Pickett crosses the shower. Sheldon comes with him but flinches when water spatters off Jack.

"Man, that's ice water," Sheldon says.

Something is hitting the floor, like a hole punched in a bucket of rocks. Little pellets of ice are bouncing off a patch of blue skin on Jack's shoulder.

"What the...?" Sheldon says.

Ice chips pile on the floor. Jack's shoulder is making ice, but that doesn't faze Pickett. He holds his ground. He doesn't care if gold coins are dropping out of Jack's butt. His hatred blinds him to the impossible.

Jack wants him to step closer. He wants Pickett to reach out, to give him all his rage. Jack doesn't feel the emptiness when there's hatred around him. Maybe he doesn't need the Christmas spirit after all.

He can fill the emptiness with this tasty treat.

"Jack!" One of the staff steps inside. "Willie wants to see you, pronto."

No one moves.

"Ice was coming off him," Sheldon says. "You got to see it, man— water just turning to ice."

Pickett trembles but restrains his fury even when Jack winks.

"Everything all right, Jack?" the staff member asks.

Jack grins. "Perfect."

He dries off while the staff member watches. The others move away. Pickett is silent. Jack hums a little Christmas tune while he gets dressed.

"Nipping at your nose," he sings.

"WILLIE." Jack holds out his fist. "Knuck it."

"Don't do that."

Jack falls into a chair across from the desk. He had the old, military-green jacket buttoned near his throat to hide the blue patches on his chest. Willie stares at the back of Jack's hand.

Unfortunately, he couldn't hide that.

"What's going on, Jack?"

"What? This?" He points to the bald spot on his hand. "I got stung by a bee... or wasp, I think. I can't tell them apart."

"It's blue."

"I know, right? Weird."

Willie pinches his nose and closes his eyes. He still looks exhausted when he opens them. "You got to leave in two days, Jack."

"I know."

"Look, I've done everything to help you. You're not doing much to help yourself. You have no ID, no record, and no history. We can't let you stay here. You could be dangerous."

"How can I have no history, Willie? I'm here, right?"

"You know what I mean." Willie straightens a pile of papers. "I like you, Jack. But I'm worried."

"You're so worried you're kicking me out?"

"Don't give me that; take some responsibility. I got a feeling you know exactly what's going on and, to be honest, I feel like a damn fool. I'm giving you a few days to make some plans, but after that, you got to go."

"Okay, cool." Jack pulls open his collar. It feels like a steam room inside his jacket. "That it?"

"You all right?"

"Yeah, fine. This weather's crazy."

"Thermostat's at sixty-eight."

One hundred and sixty-eight.

Willie taps the desk, thinking. "I'm concerned about your health, Jack. You don't look well. Maybe now you got a fever..."

Willie wants to say something else. He is suspicious, of course. Everyone jokes Jack isn't human, but the joke is wearing thin. It's starting to look a lot like the truth.

Of course it is the truth, but no one ever heard of an elven outside of bedtime stories. And Jack looks mostly human—a very strange and odd-looking one, but human nonetheless.

"Your hair is falling out, Jack. Your skin is blue."

"You calling me a freak, Willie?"

"I didn't say that. You don't look right. Your hair is kind of green, your skin blue. Your feet are snowshoes."

"That's racist."

"Cut it out."

Willie shakes his head, the braided ropes swinging across his forehead. Jack can taste his anger; he can feel it in the back of his throat. It has a different flavor than Pickett's anger, no hate mixed with it. Willie's anger has more sadness and regret.

Jack doesn't get as much pleasure from it. Maybe because he likes Willie.

"I'm sending you to a doctor before you go." Willie slides the papers over to Jack. "I must be out of my mind for not doing this earlier. I gave you the benefit of the doubt, figured you just had a skin condition or big foot disease, hell, I don't know. I just wanted to help you, that's all."

"I'm leaving in the morning."

"You don't have to."

"I got a plan, Willie. I'm leaving whether you kick me out or not."

"Let the doctor look at you, at least," Willie says.

Jack picks up the papers that summarize the health benefits of regular exercise and eating right. He pretends to read it because Willie's a good dude.

"Hey, Willie."

"Yeah?"

"You ever heard of Frost Plantation?"

Sura slides the last hay bale from the truck and pulls her glove off with her teeth. The dry taste of grass and leather lingers on her tongue. She looks at her phone.

Why aren't you working? Joe texts.

Who says I'm not working? she types.

Sura takes a drink of water and wipes her brow. Her phone sounds off.

Frost said you're fired, he texts back.

Sura gloves up, grabs the twine, and lugs the bale across the back-yard. If she starts replying, she won't get a thing done. And there's plenty to do. Fences need mending, the horses need trimming and hayed. Just this morning, the autofill valve on the water trough broke.

Her boots squish through the mud. The two horses follow along, heads bobbing, necks craning. She waves them off and spreads the hay. If she could seed the front pasture, they could graze a little easier. *Add that to the list.*

The phone buzzes. Frost just hired you back.

Sura marches to the shed and comes back with a bucket of tools. It takes fifteen minutes to fix the autofill valve. She waits while it fills the trough, pulling her list from her front pocket.

The hinge is broken on the side pasture. She uses baling wire to keep it in place until she can pick up supplies. Gerty wanders over while she twists the wire. Hot air blows into Sura's ear. Gerty's nostrils flare. Sura puts the pliers down and plays with her rubbery lips.

"You getting lonely, girl?"

Gerty nudges her onto her butt. Sura gets up to scratch the old workhorse behind the ears and finds the soft spot that rolls Gerty's eyes. The horse sways with pleasure.

"How are those hooves?" Sura picks up Gerty's front leg and inspects the dirt packed inside. She needs to trim the horses before the hooves start splitting—

Gerty jumps back, snorting and stamping.

"Hey, hey, hey." She tries to calm her, but the horse thunders off.

A gust of wind passes through the treetops.

A strange sensation haunts her. Sura has lived in the country long enough to know that thoughts are her worst enemy. The mind can transform thoughts into seething monsters. She looks around the open space, smells the fresh air, and hears dogs bark in the distance. The horses are in the corner of the pasture, as far away as possible.

Something doesn't feel right.

There's movement near a rotten log in the woods just on the other side of the fence. Twigs snap in the rustling leaves. She remains as still as a turkey hunter, eyes on the log.

Chills grasp her heart and run up her neck.

Something is looking back.

She remains frozen, not swaying with a gust of wind, eyes locked on the hole in the log. There's something on the other side, holding as still as her. Sura looks around without moving and spies the rusty T-stake lying on the ground. Her movements are slow and deliberate.

She opens the gate with one hand, the T-stake in the other. The horses throw a fit. Nothing moves near the log, but she still has a sense of being watched. She's had that feeling ever since she pulled up to the Frost Plantation entrance the very first day. She didn't mind the noises at the plantation, but she's not happy to hear them close to home.

Sura wraps both hands around the T-stake, the rough edges biting into her palms. Her first step into the trees is noisy, dead branches snapping under her boot. She stops and waits. The log is ten steps away and she still swears it's looking right at her.

Her arms ache with tension. Her steps are slow and steady, breath shallow, muscles taut, arms coiled, stake back—

Her pocket buzzes.

Sura jumps back and yelps, gasping for air.

Joe's smiling face looks back from her phone. "Hey," she says.

"What are you doing?" he asks.

She pokes the log with the T-stake. It sinks through the decayed wood. Spongy chunks fall away. Sura peeks over the top and sees the gnarly cypress knee emerging from the ground.

"Hunting," she says.

"Hunting what? Rabbits? You sound like you're chasing them."

"I'm kidding. I just got myself all freaked out, thought something was watching me."

"What do you mean?" His tone becomes tense.

"It's nothing. What are you doing?"

Pause. "Working, like usual."

"Poor baby. You need some help?"

"Actually, I do. But since you're taking a vacation day, I'll settle for lunch. You want to meet in town?"

Sura sits on the log. "Sure, I need to pick up supplies anyhow. What do you have in mind?"

"Meet me at my house, I'll pick you up and buy you lunch. I've got the Christmas spirit."

"I got an appetite."

"I don't know if I've got that much spirit."

Sura leans closer to the cypress knee. The top is pointed, which isn't unusual, but the burgundy color is. It almost looks like a cap. And the bark is extremely knobby, kind of looks like a face.

"Sura?"

"Yeah, sure." She rubs the cypress knee, the bark flaking off. "Lunch sounds good."

They say goodbye. Sura stuffs the phone in her back pocket and stares the cypress knee in the distorted face. Maybe she'll come back and cut it down, put it by the front door. It'd make a cool ornament.

She finishes working on the gate and cleans out the horses' hooves before checking her list of materials. The chills of being watched never fade.

It never occurs to her there are no cypress trees on her property.

JOE'S BACKYARD IS SMALL, with an oak tree, a little bit of grass, and a million mosquitoes. For a gardener, it lacks... everything. Sura sits on the back steps next to a concrete garden gnome, the tip of its nose chipped off. Joe texted that he was running late.

Back door is open.

She rests her arm on the gnome's pointy hat, waving off the bloodsucking insects. She checks her supply list and figures there's still plenty of time to get everything done. There might even be enough time to run out to the plantation around dinner.

The feeling of being watched got in the car with her. She turned around at a stoplight and checked the backseat. If she thinks about it, the feeling had gotten really strong when they picked up the homeless guy. He was easily the strangest-looking man she'd ever met and, quite possibly, the smelliest. What she didn't notice at the time was the surreal sensation she experienced when he slid into the front seat, when he turned around and smiled at her.

It was a quiver that radiated from her belly, like a bell had been struck. It was unsettling, frightening. She thought it was just fear, whether that man was going to do something weird.

Sura tips the weighty gnome back and stares into its blank eyes. The scrapes around the cheeks look like it's tumbled down the steps a few times. The hat is stained yellow. Paranoia clenches her chest.

The concrete gnome looks sort of like the cypress knee.

"I'm losing it," she mutters. "You hear that? I'm losing it."

She swats another mosquito and stands up. She's had enough fun talking to the gnome and feeding the mosquitoes. Sura puts her hands against the glass and stares through the back door. She's looking through the kitchen, but the house beyond is dark. The door's unlocked.

"Hello?" She barely cracks it. "Mr. Jonah?"

There are no trucks in the driveway, but it doesn't hurt to make sure the old man isn't napping on the couch and Joe forgot to tell her.

The house smells like a musty aisle in a library. A clock ticks above a dripping sink. The kitchen table is smothered with newspapers, notebooks, and a stack of plates. A crust of pizza is on top. She's officially breaking and entering into Jonah's house, and this puts her head in a spin cycle. She steadies herself on the kitchen table.

She starts clearing the dirty dishes, running water in the sink. The empty pizza boxes go in the trash, along with a soda bottle. The dishwasher gets loaded. She starts hand-washing the rest of the bowls and cups, piling them in the sink. She has to hunt for a dishtowel. A clean one is hooked on the refrigerator handle.

There are pictures on the freezer door.

They are printed on bond paper, the edges curling around flexible magnets. It's mostly photos of trucks and flowers, pictures of Jonah and Joe.

There's one of Jonah and an older man.

Sura drops the dishtowel and plucks the picture from behind the magnet. She holds it close to her face while grabbing the handle. Memories are coming back, things she's been forgetting, like images tucked behind a screen, out of sight for her recall. This picture raises the curtain, refreshes her memory.

The old man has to be Joe's grandfather because... *they look exactly alike.*

The picture of my mom and grandmother is gone. It was on the refrigerator. Someone took it.

Something scuttles through the living room.

Sura hangs on to the sink to keep from falling. Vertigo swishes inside her head; paranoia smothers her like a blanket. She can't get enough air; no matter how deep she breathes, there's not enough oxygen. The floor heaves like a ship riding up a wave. Her head feels like it'll crack, but her brain feels soft, overheated. Waxy.

She takes half a step toward the door when something crashes in the front room. Sura presses against the refrigerator. A yellow broom leans in the corner. She holds the bristled end, the plastic-tipped handle in front of her like a toy sword. Whatever is out there shuffles across the carpet. It's not a dog or a cat.

It mutters.

The words are all crammed together. *Bernie was talking like that.*

When she woke up the other morning, when there was a noise in the kitchen, her cockatoo was talking at the wrong speed.

It was in my house. And now it's out there.

She slides to the floor. The picture is crushed against the broomstick, which remains pointed at the living room entrance. If it comes at her, she'll poke it at least once. After that, she'll be no good.

She should crawl. She should run.

Each time she moves, there's another noise.

Instead, giant tears roll down her cheeks. It's too much. She just wants to sit there until it goes away.

Until it all goes away.

Mufflers rattle outside. A truck pulls into the driveway.

Joe walks through the back door. The sink is half full of dishes soaking in cold, flat water. Sura is in the corner, broomstick in one hand. She holds a piece of paper in the other.

"Sura!"

"What is this?" she says.

"Where'd you get that?" He starts towards her.

"No." She points the broom. "Why do we look just like our parents and grandparents?"

"Just put the broom down, and have a drink of water. You've had a rough day; let's talk."

She shakes her head, crumpling the picture. The floor feels spongy, her legs soft and wet. At first, she thinks she wet herself, but she's sweating through her clothes. The world is still spinning and she can't make it stop. There's a dreadful feeling that the lens through which she understands reality is about to come into focus; that the curtain around her world, the wall that protects her, is about to drop, and she'll see monsters behind it. Everything is a lie.

"Sura." Joe slowly crawls near her and gently touches her hand. "Come here."

"Something's in the house."

Joe stiffens. "What?"

"Something is moving, making noise." She swallows a hard lump. "Talking."

"Where?"

"All over." She swings the broomstick. "I wanted to leave but was afraid I'd keep running if I did, and I've got nowhere to go, Joe. There's nowhere for me to go!"

Sura's holding back tears, but panic has swelled in her throat, blurring her voice. The broomstick taps against the floor. Joe brushes the hair from her cheeks and cups the back of her neck. His hand is firm and warm.

He gets up, holds out his hand for her to stay, and steps into the living room. Something scurries away. The steps creak. She waits for Joe to come back, tell her a squirrel got inside, or the radio alarm is running... but he follows it upstairs!

Sura puts both hands on the broomstick. There are voices. One is Joe's; the other's too fast to understand. They're talking. He's having a conversation with whatever is out there. Heavy footsteps take the stairs three at a time.

Joe hustles into the kitchen. "Come on."

He pulls her off the floor. The broom clatters. Sura's legs start out like noodles. Joe wraps his arm around her and guides her out of the house. The living room is silent this time. They rush through the yard.

"What were you doing up there?" she asks.

"Just hang on, I'll tell you in a minute." He doesn't let go of her until they're through the gate and in the driveway. He opens the truck door. "I'll be right back."

He opens the garage and searches the shelves, tossing rolled sleeping bags, duffel bags, and boxes into the back of the truck. He swipes one whole shelf into a bag and tosses that back there, too. The items scatter across the bed.

He looks under the truck before climbing in.

His frantic pace slows once he's in the driver's seat, his fingers twisting the steering wheel. He looks back at the house.

"Turn off your phone." He puts his phone on the dashboard.

"Why?"

"I'll tell you everything, Sura, just do what I say for now, okay? We can't talk for a while, all right? You just need to let me get us somewhere first, and then I'll tell you everything I know."

The picture is balled in her fist. "Okay."

Joe backs out of the driveway, pauses in the road, and looks at the house. Doubt passes through him a third time. He shakes it off. Sura notices something.

The concrete gnome is gone.

Mr. Frost stands on the back steps. The coolsuit feels loose around his midsection. He hasn't been eating, not enough to keep up his blubber. He'd often thought of losing the fat layer since the added insulation is more of a hindrance than a necessity. But he's elven. His body had adapted to the weight. Losing it would alter his chemistry.

And he is already feeling out of sorts.

The helicopter's thumping introduces its arrival before emerging from the winter clouds, its slow descent ruffling the grassy field, tan waves rolling toward the house. Mr. Frost squints. Once the additional skinfolds shielded his eyes from Arctic glare and driving sleet, they now protect them from dust.

Templeton talks with the pilot while the crew attaches cables to the steel shipping container. He used to rely on horse, buggy, and railroad. When the combustion engine was invented (Mr. Frost had a little something to do with that), his product was pulled on trailers.

Now it flies.

Particle teleportation is in the near future, but he may not be there to see it.

Once appropriate documents are signed to ensure the destination of Frost Plantation Christmas products, the tandem rotors hum louder, pushing air across the ground. Mr. Frost's coat whips around his legs. He pulls it closed, cinching the belt tightly, suddenly remembering the days in the Arctic when Claus—leader of the elven— would stand on the ice, surveying the landscape even in the worst of weather.

Claus was a good elven.

In his final days, he'd become a beaten elven.

Jack was his twin brother and a formidable foe. He brought the elven under his rule with a cold fist. Had the warmblood Nicholas Santa not stumbled into the Arctic region at the turn of the nineteenth century, the world would look much different than it does today. There would be no choppers carrying gifts to children across the world, no strands of lights twinkling on rooftops, or stockings decorating fireplace mantels. No eggnog, no tinsel, no Christmas trees, or ornaments. No cheer, happiness, or joy to all mankind.

Then again, mankind might already be extinct.

The chopper lifts off with a final thumbs-up, the rotors drumming the air. Templeton returns to the back steps and watches it recede into the clouds.

"He will return within the hour," Templeton says. "One of the containers appears to have stalled in a port outside Windsor Alberta, Ontario, but outside of that, all shipments have reached their destinations. We are ahead of schedule."

Mr. Frost's neck itches. Just as the helicopter fades, another appears. This time of year, the plantation is rarely silent.

Sir, I have bad news.

Mr. Frost nods to Templeton and leisurely walks towards the garden. Not until he passes through the arbor, once the ice statue is in sight, does he answer.

Yes?

Joe has taken Sura.

Where?

We don't know, sir. He packed the truck with camping gear and left the house. They turned off their phones.

Did the helpers follow?

Yes. But he crossed the Cooper River Bridge. They're a bit sluggish across water, sir.

Have them wait at the bridge.

She pauses. *They're not coming back; I think you know that, sir. Sura saw another picture and Joe promised to tell her everything. They're running, sir.*

Mr. Frost meanders down the path and sits on a bench facing Jocah's continually weeping effigy. It always brought him comfort to see Jack's mother, reminding him of what the elven once were: peaceful, thoughtful, and kind. She embodied all of that, what every elven should strive to become. But she was not perfect, either.

Life is imperfect, she would say.

Mr. Frost closes his eyes, troubled by the events he knows were inevitable, focusing to keep his thoughts still, to not let his innermost motivations rise to the surface, to keep them hidden from Freeda's watchful presence. Instead, he only lets her see his concern and worry, which is legitimate. Everything he'd worked to achieve for the last hundred years will come to fruition in the next couple of days. Sura needed to be ready.

Joe will reveal everything. *What if it's too much?*

I'm going to make a suggestion. Freeda waits for him to acknowledge her. *Templeton and May are required to operate Frost Plantation and, to some extent, so is Jonah. Sura has become problematic.*

Mr. Frost bristles.

I allowed your experimentation with her because I sensed your loneliness. You have used her to establish an emotional understanding of humans and that has healed you, allowed you to function. She's become a distraction.

There are several billion humans in the world, Freeda. I think it's worthwhile to understand them.

I fail to understand why you should take such a vested interest in a species that will soon become extinct.

Perhaps it's best to know what the world will become without them.

We aren't destroying them, sir. They will do it to themselves.

WE are not doing it, Freeda. It's Jack. Jack plans to destroy them. He paces around the statue. *Not ME. This has never been me!*

This argument is moot, sir. I'm programmed to assist you in your destiny.

Jack inserted the root. *That is not destiny.*

I'm afraid it is, sir.

Mr. Frost exits the garden. It's senseless to argue with the voice in his head. He stands beneath the arbor, watching the arrival of another helicopter.

Another shipment.

Another step closer to the end.

An end he cannot resist.

What about the children, sir?

She is digging in, asserting her will. She can do what she wants, but she's learned to make him feel like he's making his own decisions. It's much easier on his psyche that way.

I'll consider suspending Sura and Joe at New Year's.

It'll be over before then.

JACK SLEEPS with the lamp shining on his face. Once that light brought him comfort and warmth, now it feels like red-hot coals on his eyelids.

He's been shedding like a dog. He scratches his cheek and peels off a thin sheet of skin. *Good one.*

Onto the dead-skin pile he keeps under the bed.

His skin has gone from pale blue to just blue—not Blue Man Group blue, though; blue like winter sky. His skin is smooth and icy; the darker the blue, the colder it feels.

But the more hair he drops, the more skin he peels, the warmer he feels. The bed has become less of a mattress and more like a skillet. The sheets crackle like frozen blankets.

He doesn't have to stay in the shelter; he knows where he's going. There is just a little unfinished business to tidy up first, and then he'll be on his way.

He feigns sleep—sometimes snoring, sometimes farting—and around the wee hours, he thinks maybe he made a mistake. Maybe he should just leave now and stop wasting time. Or maybe he'll have to be assertive, go get what he wants. He doesn't want it to end that way, but time is money.

Somewhere, footsteps fall on the polished floor.

I knew you wouldn't let me down.

A thrill rushes through Jack's belly. He watches through narrow slits. A figure creeps up behind the lamp and reaches for the switch.

Click.

It takes a moment for Jack's eyes to adjust, to see Pickett twisting the pillowcase, soup cans knocking inside. He looks around, one last time, before reaching back. He is going to whack Jack in the fat belly. He means to hurt him, teach him a lesson, show him who is king.

The big dummy.

He grabs Pickett's bare thigh, just below the bottom of his boxers, and gets a good handful of flesh, all soft and hot.

Pickett doesn't yelp.

Or move.

Jack feels the cold leave his fingertips, creep through Pickett's flesh, penetrate the tissue and muscle, and paralyze the nervous system. Pickett's anger melts like a chocolate drop on summer asphalt. It dissolves into something much more tangible, something acrid, slightly bitter. Jack can taste it through his hand and feels it linger in the back of his throat. That's why he stayed. He wanted to taste fear.

Pickett is full of it.

The pillowcase slips from his fingers.

Frost creeps across his skin, beneath his shorts. Pickett lets out a whimper.

Jack closes his eyes. And savors.

15

DECEMBER 20

Saturday

Willie arrives for the morning shift.

He checks with the overnight staff, inspects the kitchen, and peeks into the bunkroom, where the men are already up and dressed.

Jack's bed is empty.

Willie feels guilty. He can't help it. Doesn't matter if a resident deserves it or not, he doesn't like to tell someone they're not welcome. Once they leave, their future is cold and short.

And it's Christmas.

He straightens an ornament on the artificial tree, thinking if Jack comes back, that he'll take him to the doctor. If something is diagnosed, maybe he can make an exception. At least until the holidays are over.

"There a phone over there?" Mark asks.

"On the tree?"

"No, on the floor or something. I can't find my phone."

"Want me to call it?"

"No, I'll find it. Probably left it in the kitchen. By the way." Mark holds up an envelope and slides it across the front counter. "Someone left you a note."

Willie adjusts the star at the top and steps back to ensure everything looks good and balanced before looking at the white envelope.

Willie, it says.

He has no idea who it's from. In fact, he's shocked to see Jack's name at the bottom when he opens it. The little man scrawled like a third grader when he first arrived.

Even his handwriting has changed.

YOU'RE A PAL, *Willie.*

Seriously, you got a good heart for a warmblood. I'm not saying all warmbloods are bad, most of them, yeah, sure, but not you, Willie. You're one of the good ones. Probably the only one. I'd be dead if it wasn't for you.

But I'm not.

And you belong to the problem, Willie. Warmbloods, that is.

So nothing personal, pal.

Bye.

WILLIE TURNS IT OVER, nothing on the back.

Nervously, he looks out the front door, aware that he's envisioning a short fat maniac marching up the steps shouting "WARMBLOODS!"

"Willie!" Mark rushes out of the bunkroom.

"What is it?"

"Call 911." His face is chalky. "Something's wrong with Pickett."

Willie doesn't move for a second, clenching the note.

Later, when no foul play was suspected, that Pickett simply blacked out and couldn't remember why he was lying next to Jack's empty bed, Willie still kept the note. It always bothered him there was frostbite on his leg.

❄

A WAVE SLIDES across the hard-packed sand, sloshing over Sura's bare feet. It recedes back into the ocean, disappearing into the foam. She remembers coming out to Edisto Beach with her mom in the winter months. They'd cuff their pants and walk in the wet sand. Her mom loved the horizon. She used to say there's mystery out there—that you don't know what's beyond the flat line or what life has in store for you.

"Why don't we just sail out there and see?" Sura would say.

"Patience," her mom would say. "Life will come to you."

Sura didn't like that answer. There was a sense of hopelessness when she said it, like she was trapped, that she didn't have a choice to explore her life, didn't have an option to see what was out there.

"Think of it this way," her mom would say, "if we sail in that direction long enough, where do we end up?"

She would make a circle.

"We end up right where we started. We end up here. So let's not run; let's be here."

"What if we take a right turn? Think of all the new things we'll discover."

"We still end up here." Her mom smoothed Sura's hair. "It's not that easy, child."

Sura's footsteps dent the sand, fading as the water rolls in. The sweater Joe gave her is moldy and oversized. She slept in her clothes, hunkered down in the sleeping bag, too afraid to poke her head out. Joe's breaths were easy and long. He wouldn't tell her why he brought her out to Edisto, why they were hiding. They sat by a fire until the sun went down, and then crawled into the tent until the next morning.

Sura doesn't know how far she's walked or how long she's been out there, just that she needs to keep moving. The world is steady again, as long as she keeps moving. If she stops, maybe a monster will appear.

And Joe knows what it looks like.

She faces the horizon, the cuffs of her pants wet with salty spray. A few beachcombers are far to her right. A boy is coming towards her, bearing gifts wrapped in plastic, his pants rolled to the knees, bare feet in the surf. Joe is chewing on a cinnamon roll. He offers her one. She shakes her head.

They watch the sun climb.

"Why'd you bring me out here?" she asks.

He struggles with the words. She'd asked him that when they were sitting at the campfire last night, but he just shook his head. This time, the words come out slow and unsteady.

"I grew up out there," he starts, not looking at her. "So I don't expect you to understand."

"Grew up where?"

"The plantation. Jonah and I lived on the first floor in the southwest corner of the house. I had my own room, May cooked all the meals, and Templeton did the laundry. That's all I knew. Honestly, I remember thinking that's how it is when you're born, that living on a plantation with other servants is normal."

"And that's why you brought me out here?"

He digs at the sand with his toes. "Our parents used to be together."

Her stomach sinks. "You said that wasn't true."

"It doesn't have anything to do with us." He pokes at the sand. "Jonah said you wouldn't know anything about the plantation and I wasn't supposed to tell you, either; he made that clear. So I guess when I got to the house and that picture somehow got on the refrigerator..."

"What do you mean 'somehow'?"

"Someone told me it was time you knew the truth."

He was talking to someone upstairs. "Someone?"

He waves his words off, like maybe he shouldn't have said that. "I figured you should know, that's all. It's not fair that your mother moved off the plantation and took you with her."

"I never lived there."

"Jonah says you were there in the beginning, but not for long. He says Sesi was too smart to play along, that she'd evolved some instinct to leave."

"Play along?" Sura hugs herself tighter. "What's that supposed to mean?"

"It means Jonah loved your mom. He says she loved him, too, but there was something wrong with it. At least, that's what Sesi told him. She didn't want to keep loving him, didn't want to be in a relationship until she knew who she was. It was the reason for the whole Zen thing."

Joe didn't say it spitefully, although there were bitter undercurrents in his words. He sits in the soft sand, arms propped on his knees.

Her mom never spoke about Jonah. She never mentioned living on the plantation, only that she wouldn't stop working there. Sura always assumed it paid well. Maybe she couldn't leave it for other reasons.

Joe is picking up washed-up reeds, breaking them into little pieces. "You don't know what it's like holding all these secrets," he says. "Mr. Frost... you've seen him. He's not normal. I don't think he's even human."

"You think he's an elven?"

Joe shrugs. He doesn't want to say it, but what other explanation is there?

"Elven don't exist," she adds.

He laughs. It's unsettling. Long minutes pass as sandpipers scurry across the sand.

"He does experiments," he says. "Down in the basement. It's the reason why Sesi left the plantation, Jonah says. The reason why she left him."

"What kind?"

He breaks apart another reed, flicking the pieces. He starts chuckling, shaking his head.

"Why do you keep laughing?" she says.

"Because I'm afraid you're going to start running." He glances up, as if she might already be down the beach. When he sees she's still there, he takes a deep breath. "There are these little people that help out around the plantation. It's how we get everything done. Think about the gardens and the crops, the entire plantation. Jonah can't do all that. The helpers do it."

"What do you mean 'little people'? You mean like dwarves?"

"No, not dwarves." Joe holds his hand a foot from the ground. "These are tiny, little wrinkled men that move fast and talk even faster. They all look the same and wear crumpled-up clothes and bright color hats."

Bright hats.

The cypress knee.

The concrete statue.

The plantation kitchen is big enough to feed an army.

Sura feels woozy again.

"I used to know their names when I was little," Joe says. "They used to play with me. We'd hike through the woods, climb trees, and hunt rabbits. Imagine wrestling a hundred of these little guys, all at the same time. It was like a mountain of puppies. They never slept, always laughing."

He breaks off a small piece and compares it to a long reed. His smile fades.

"They changed, though."

"How?"

"A couple of weeks ago, they got more serious and stopped talking to me. Jonah says that's what they're supposed to do, not treat me like a baby. Says I'm supposed to be normal, interact with other people, not the helpers. I guess it was the same for him."

"He grew up on the plantation?"

"We all grew up on the plantation."

"What's that mean? Who are 'we'?"

Joe takes a deep breath. "When it comes down to it, Jonah says the helpers work for Mr. Frost; they do what he says. Something's going on and I got a bad feeling. I think they've been following us. Watching us."

"They were in the house."

"They're not mean, just up to something. One of the yellow-hats was upstairs and told me we needed to run away."

"I thought you said they changed."

"The ones with the yellow hats haven't. That's why we left so quickly and turned off the phones, so the rest wouldn't follow. They can't cross bridges, at least not very quickly. We lost them on the bridge. They're probably waiting for us to come back."

"That's why we came out here? So you could tell me all this?"

He holds the sticks and looks up. "The helpers all look the same, Sura, because they are the same. Mr. Frost is trying to make someone in his basement. The helpers are part of the experiment, like practice. They do other things for him, too, but I think he's been practicing and he doesn't want us to know about it."

"Know what? That he's cloning little people, making them work like slaves?"

She's focused on the injustice, the crimes against nature. If the authorities knew what he was doing, they'd throw him in jail for life.

Joe doesn't say anything else. He's waiting.

Her knees weaken. Her feet are like bricks. It's the way Joe's looking at her, waiting for her to put it together.

The helpers all look the same.

He takes a big stick, breaks it in half, and holds the smaller pieces side by side.

My mom and grandmother.

He lines all the little pieces next to each other in the sand.

His dad and grandfather.

She takes half a step back. Numbness reaches her face, seeping into her brain.

They all look the same.

"You don't have a mother, Sura," he says softly, putting the last piece into place. "You never did."

Sura bolts away, blindly. She can't feel her legs. Tears brim on her eyelids. She runs and runs and runs.

Time to wake up.

JACK FALLS AGAINST A TREE.

"Someone kill me," he mutters. "Kill me, right now."

His tongue lolls like a workhorse driven daylong in July heat. He slides down the rough bark and hikes up his foot to inspect the burning sole. Some of the small scales have chipped away. His ankles feel like they were assembled with rusty bolts. If there was just an ice hole somewhere he could dip his feet.

He licks his parched lips.

Blindly, he searches the bag slung over his shoulder and pulls out a half-full plastic bottle of Coke he found on the road. The bottle swells as the contents freeze when he touches it, the plastic crackling with a frosty sheen.

He rolls it against his cheek, across his forehead, and over his bald scalp. The hair is all gone. The flaking skin sticks to the bottle. Despite the fact he feels like the glowing tip of a blacksmith's iron, his head is blue.

He rams the bottle on the tree's root flare. It takes ten pathetic attempts before the frozen plastic shatters, but then the block of soda rolls through the dirt and into the weeds.

"That's how it is?" He looks up at the gray sky. "I just wanted a lick and that's what I get? All right. Okay. I'll just not drink anything; how'd you like that?"

He throws the bag on his lap and continues to curse under his breath. When things go wrong, he curses at whoever did this to him (he's not sure who it is, but he looks up when he does it), and sings the stupid song about a silent night.

Song's not working!

He digs through the bag of stuff: empty cans, a few butts, a swollen magazine, and an old carton of Chinese food. He had licked the insides and it tasted fishy. He knew it'd take a while to walk to Frost Plantation—no one was going to give him a ride—just didn't realize it would be *in the belly of a furnace!*

The black case is at the bottom, just below a Skittles wrapper.

"All right, concentrate." He closes his eyes, draws a deep breath, and holds it. He pulls all the coldness into his core. The temperature of his hands equalize with the surrounding air.

His gut feels like he swallowed a campfire.

"Here we go."

He pulls the phone out of the bag. Delicately holding it with two fingers, he touches the screen. The map lights up. A blue dot illustrates where he's at, right now, leaning against a giant tree. The red dot isn't far. He looks at the dirt road disappearing into the thick forest.

The phone rings.

Mark's calling, again. He wants his phone back.

Jack releases the pent-up cold, engulfing the weeds in a crystallizing cloud. The phone turns into a block of ice. The glass cracks. Jack crushes it, shards trickling from his fist.

The sun is below the trees. Jack throws the bag in the ditch, stumbles to his feet, and waits for a filthy truck to pass. It honks.

Jack gives it the one-finger salute.

He crosses the boiling asphalt. "Ow. Ow. Ow. Ow. Ow. Ow."

The dirt road is rutted and slightly damp, a sliver of relief on his beaten feet.

His steps, though, are small and wobbly. It could be all night before he gets anywhere. He can't think about that, has to focus on moving ahead, going forward. Jack closes his eyes, follows the ruts, and occupies his mind with something good: his last memory.

A party. A big one.

The elven were throwing a party to honor Jack, to celebrate his victory. There'd been a long war called the Fracture. He dwells on this for several moments, the thrilling sensation of winning, of being good and right and on top of the world, offsetting the agony of this boilerplate.

Jack bumps into a tree and staggers back onto the road.

Not only that, it was his mother he beat. She was the one that caused the Fracture in the first place. She kept him down; she was the one that didn't believe in him.

She loved Claus.

She always liked him better. Right from the start, she wanted Claus to win and Jack to go away. She ignored him.

They all ignored him.

Well, he showed them. Jack *is* good. He's better.

He doesn't actually remember the party, just waiting for it. The last memory, the very last, final, end-of-the-line thing he can remember is giving another elven a little tin box. It was his friend. His only friend. Pawn.

Whatever happened to him?

Jack opens his eyes. "Hey, look. There's the ground—"

He hits the dirt.

Face first.

JACK'S SLIDING on his back.

The ice is rough. His face hurts. He can feel his heart beating in his nose. But it's not ice, he's not in the Arctic... it's mud.

Jack sits up. Actually, he doesn't do anything, but he feels his body sit up, feels something hold him upright.

He blinks.

The world is fuzzy. And blazing hot.

Tiny lights. Iron bars. A giant F. Lots of frilly branches and berries. Right now, he just wants to lie down, take a little nap. Won't hurt him if he sleeps, but something won't let him. Something holds him up.

"Hey." He looks lazily to his sides. "You guys look like me."

He's right. Pointy noses. Square chins. Not a single hair on their faces. The only difference is the skin color: dark yellow instead of blue. And the hats. They have floppy, colorful hats.

"You're handsome little buggers." Jack leans back, head swimming with thoughts, none of which make much sense. The little ones grunt to keep him upright and from getting squashed. Jack sways with the shifting weight.

"Like a massage," he says. "Feels good—hey, I remember. You

helped me in the woods. That was you. 'Member when the bear was going to eat me?"

Maybe they answer. Maybe not.

Jack wants to sleep because the heat is killing him; it's cooking his brain like an egg. He can feel the yolk solidify.

Welcome back, sir.

"Aaahhhh!"

That voice is inside Jack's head.

JONAH IS SHEARING THE BOXWOODS. He's without helpers today and Joe never returned from lunch. There was no answer when he called. Later, he'll come home to an empty house. There will be no note, no message.

No Joe.

Jonah is not Joe's birth father. They may be clones, but they're human, they become attached. He won't sleep tonight and he'll mourn when Joe is still not home in the morning.

In the beginning, there was May and Templeton. Jonah came later. Their DNA was snatched from unsuspecting immigrants that came through the Charleston port—a sly prick of a needle was all that was needed. The three were approved by Freeda and did the sorts of things Mr. Frost didn't have time to do.

Sura, however, was a surprise.

When Mr. Frost escaped the North Pole, the Inuit took him into their village. The man that found him was named Pana. Mr. Frost was given a bed in his shelter. His wife had died giving birth to their only daughter.

Her name was Sesi. It meant "snow."

Day after day, they fed Mr. Frost and cared for him. Nighttime was the worst. That's when the root would ignite his brain and Mr. Frost would thrash away the animal skins and tear at the hair on the back of his head. Sesi would kneel next to him with a wet rag and dab his forehead, while spittle collected at the corners of his mouth. In the morning, he would be exhausted. Sesi would bring him something to eat.

It wasn't long before the village wanted him out. Clearly, he was possessed by demons. If he stayed, they would all become possessed. Pana, though, would not let them exile him. Mr. Frost was still too weak to survive on his own. It was Sesi, though, that argued with her father to keep Mr. Frost. She insisted they resist the village. Reluctantly, he listened.

Sesi fed Mr. Frost while Pana stood guard. She would hum a song while she dabbed his forehead. The wordless tune floated from her lips, soothed his aches, and filled his loneliness. Yet each night, the root raged with fury, demanding that he go south. The village elders were insistent. If Mr. Frost was not banished, Pana and Sesi would be.

On a night when Pana and Sesi slept soundly and the root remained quiet, Mr. Frost slipped from their shelter. He took with him furs and frozen seal meat to begin his journey. He also possessed skin cells that he'd scratched from their arms unexpectedly. At the time, he didn't know why he took them. It was much later that he retrieved Sesi's sample and fused it with a human egg cell.

Sesi was reborn.

Mr. Frost pretended it was a variation of May, but Freeda soon learned the truth. Her anger was furious. *This is not acceptable!* She punished Mr. Frost, reminding him how hotly the root could still burn. She threatened to flush all the tanks, to start over according to the plans laid out in the root.

But Mr. Frost convinced her otherwise.

I need her.

Freeda was not rigidly bound to the root's scripture. She had freedom to assess and modify. She needed Mr. Frost to operate efficiently and effectively. It was clear that he responded better to the carrot than the whip.

Now Mr. Frost had something to live for. He argued that Sesi would help him understand the human condition. Why did Pana and Sesi care for him against the village's wishes? Why did they risk their own well-being for a stranger?

This understanding would only help him complete Jack's mission.

Sesi also motivated the others, in particular Jonah. And she brought newfound life to an otherwise drab plantation. Productivity increased, cloning techniques advanced, spirits soared... all of which brought Jack that much closer, that much sooner. Freeda allowed Sesi to become part of the family.

Perhaps it was no accident that Sesi changed her daughter's name to Sura.

"New life," it meant.

And now Freeda wants to take her away. Perhaps she knows what Mr. Frost is planning.

Sullen, he slides away from the window, away from the view of Jonah bending to clean up his mess. If only his life were as simple as the gardener's.

Freeda?

She doesn't answer. She'd been quiet most of the day, said she was analyzing data. His spies have informed him why: she's bringing Jack home.

She's distracted.

He must act as if he doesn't know. He needs his spies, now more than ever. He slides near the center of the room, commanding the room to transform into a replication of the laboratory. Tables and tanks rise from the floor, monitors hover above him. A long, metal table takes shape in the center, a body flickering into view.

Jack's newest incarnation is breathing on its own.

There's less hair on this one. His cheeks are still moist from the immersion tank, lips swollen and saturated. Mr. Frost watches the data scroll on several monitors. They could start uploading memories tonight.

He could be awake by morning.

What if there are two of them?

He closes his eyes, taking a deep breath. Mr. Frost thought he'd be ready for this day—there were times he begged for it—but now he's not so sure. *What if I fail?*

He wipes the room empty with a thought. He'll go to the lab and get a closer look at the body. There's a chance he could tweak something, delay the maturation. Two fully awakened incarnations of Jack would create complications.

Sir, there's no need for you to come to the basement.

Mr. Frost is startled by the sudden voice. *I just want to see it.*

That's not necessary, sir. There's been a delay in the maturation of certain organs. I suggest we give the incarnation three days to develop before attempting an awakening.

That disagreed with his data. *Jack must be home!*

Are you sure? he quickly thinks.

You look haggard, sir. I suggest you relax today and return to the lab tomorrow. Let me monitor the basement. I've prepared the coolsuit. Would you care for a walk?

Mr. Frost hesitates. Her tone is unusually calm and placating, especially for this time of year. Especially concerning matters of Jack. Perhaps she's mocking him, and at some level she's known his plan all along and she's taking pleasure in its demise.

That sounds splendid. Please have Templeton meet me in the garden. I'd like to visit the wishing room.

He dons the coolsuit.

JACK REMEMBERED the day the cold tub was invented.

He had leaned over the square tub, the contents blue and bubbly. He wanted to believe it was as cold as they said it would be. *Salt water and isopropyl alcohol,* the elven scientists told him. *It's cold.*

Jack touched it with his toe. The solution was cool and frothy. He dropped his leg in, eased his body over the edge, and let its icy embrace wrap around him like a frozen blanket.

I don't remember it hurting my face.

His eyes snap open.

There's no cold tub. No beautiful, ice-blue water.

He's on a table, staring at a menacing hunk of metal suspended from a gray ceiling. But the room is *cooooold.*

It is minus fifty degrees. How does that feel, sir?

Jack jerks up. He's not alone.

There are fifty others in the room. Maybe more. Identical little squirts, good-looking fellows, all with bright hats of different colors. They're staring at Jack.

"Which one of you said that?" Jack said.

I did, sir.

He heard it again, only none of them moved their lips. He could squash them two at a time if he has to start stepping.

My name is Freeda, sir. You don't remember me, so let me take a moment to explain. I am an artificially intelligent organism currently residing in the home network. I am linked to your brain through a tiny processor that's embedded at the base of your skull and wired into your nervous system. You are my creator, sir.

"You're right. I don't remember."

I know, sir. We will remedy that.

"Okay, I'm down with that. First, make them stop staring. It's creepy."

We made them in your honor, sir.

"Great. Now make them leave in my honor."

Without hesitation, they march out. A few stay behind, still staring—two red-hats, one blue.

"You guys stuck to the floor? Follow the leaders and get out."

I will need them for the upload.

"Upload?"

Your memories, sir.

The menacing hunk of metal begins to lower from the ceiling. Things tick and hum inside its girth.

"Put a hold on the upload." Jack leaps off the table, away from the gleaming descent of metal. "Where am I?"

Frost Plantation.

"This is it?" He looks around a plain and relatively empty gray room. No windows, no chairs. Just three creepy little gnomes that look exactly like Jack and a giant weapon. And a table.

You are in a subterranean laboratory, one of several. We built it according to your instructions, sir. It is located in a warm climate.

"Yeah, I don't remember that."

Your assistant carried your plans, in a similarly imbedded processor, far away from the North Pole to hide, sir.

"Imbedded processor?"

Pawn calls it the root.

"Pawn is here?" Jack looks around like someone might be hiding behind his back. "Where is that little devil?"

He is occupied with other matters.

Jack vaguely remembers a rice-sized processor that his scientists had invented to carry all his memories. Jack wanted a backup, just in case things didn't work out. *Looks like they didn't.*

Your instructions were quite genius.

"Please continue."

I can't reveal more, sir. Your data, or memories, need to be uploaded in order to rapidly integrate with your psyche. Otherwise, you won't assimilate. Trust me, sir, we can't risk epileptic shock now. You've come too far.

"Shock, huh?" The floor is slick. He shoves off with his left foot, sliding around the perimeter of the room. It feels so good on his sole.

"I wake up with green hair in the middle of warmblood country and you think I can't take a little stress?" He continues sliding. "Talk, lady. Why the green hair?"

Green follicles were used for photosynthesis, adding additional carbohydrates while your body stabilized and evolved. They fell out as they were no longer needed.

"That was *my* plan?"

Mr. Frost improvised when there were... failures.

"I want to see... wait, who's Mr. Frost?"

You knew him as Pawn.

"Then why'd you call him Mr. Frost?"

He changed his name. It was a psychological move on his behalf. In effect, he wanted to forget his past. He's not happy with your plan, sir.

"Well, I'll make him happy." He slides to the door, but it's locked.

You can't leave, sir. It's imperative that you're uploaded first. These are your orders, sir. Your genius orders.

Perhaps if the uploader didn't look like it was going to lobotomize him, he would've been more easily swayed.

He crosses his arms and stands firmly.

Do you feel that, sir?

"Feel what?"

The vibration.

Jack notices the humming sensation in his belly. It's the same feeling he experienced around Sura. It's warm and sensuous. It feels good, feels right. And Jack likes that.

You're synchronizing with the energy around you, sir. You're home. This is where you're supposed to be. And I know what I'm doing. Trust me, sir. You invented me.

"I did?"

You want to remember everything before you leave this room.

Jack sighs. It can't be a coincidence that all the little guys look like him. He climbs onto the table. The little ones help him. A beam of light ignites from the bottom of the uploader. Crosshairs appear on his face. A little one with a red hat adjusts his head until the crosshairs line up between his eyes. The one wearing a blue hat holds up a rubber mouthpiece and taps it on Jack's lips.

"What's that?"

Precautions, sir.

"This better not hurt."

Blue-hat shakes his head. Taps again. Jack opens wide and the plastic fills his mouth. Perhaps the alarms in his head would be ringing louder if the vibrations in his belly didn't feel so good, convincing him this was the right thing to do.

A red-hat climbs next to the table.

"W'as 'at?" Jack jerks his eyes at the cord in his hand.

Fiber optics, sir.

"W'as it do?"

Connecting you to the uploader. You might feel a little pressure.

Pressure?

Before he can leap from the table and swat away the metal demon and its handsome little henchmen, the cable rams into the back of his head.

MR. FROST SLIDES around the circle of ice, the surface smooth and clear. Snow is piled around it. The sun hangs like a dull orb.

Elven like to have the sky over them during times of stress. They like to see the flatness of the polar ice caps and undisturbed snow that's white, pristine, and perfect, glittering in daylight.

They also like to keep moving.

Does she know my plans? Has she already planned a counterstrike?

Mr. Frost never thought Freeda would be so secretive if she discovered his elaborate plan. He'd always assumed she would strike as she always did when he broke the rules: swiftly and painfully.

A golden string suddenly dangles in midair just outside the circle of ice. A hand emerges from the center and parts the air. Templeton steps through the wishing room entrance, pocket watch in hand. He lets the opening close behind him and the golden string vanishes.

The snow is up to his knees. "If it's not asking too much..."

Mr. Frost waves his hand. The snow melts around Templeton to reveal a Persian carpet. A leather chair emerges from it along with a freestanding fireplace, logs already blazing.

Templeton sits without a word, crossing his legs and folding his hands.

"Jack has returned to the plantation." Mr. Frost continues his meditative slide, hands folded on his belly.

"Are you positive?" Templeton asks.

"The yellow-hats confirmed it."

Templeton's composure is stiffer than usual. "This meeting is risky."

"She's distracted. This will be the only time to speak with you." He makes one complete circle. "The end is near."

Templeton nods thoughtfully. "You appear agitated. I assumed the end would bring relief."

"Freeda is behaving unexpectedly. She did not inform me that Jack had been located. In fact, she lied. I'm afraid she's up to something, Templeton. If she knows what I'm planning, this could end very differently."

"What do you think she's doing?"

"I don't know. There's another incarnation of Jack in the incubation lab that's close to awakening. Maybe she's going to use both of them."

Templeton drums his fingers across his knee, watching Mr. Frost go around and around. When he's near, Templeton says, "Perhaps we should kill them both."

Mr. Frost looks up. "That won't solve anything. The root will bring him back, bring Freeda back... even I can be reincarnated to continue the work. Death is only temporary. Transformation is the only solution, Templeton."

"Then let's destroy Freeda and Jack. It will buy us some time before you are forced to bring the operation back online."

Mr. Frost imagines the agony the root will put him through for such a transgression, forcing him to reinvest in another facility to bring back Freeda and start all over. He's too tired for that. Besides, Freeda will know what he did. She will adjust for it. Now is the best chance.

It must be now.

Mr. Frost stops. "Joe and Sura are safe. The helpers were directed to sequester them. I have reason to believe Freeda was planning to end them. Thankfully, the yellow-hats were there to inform Joe where to go."

"I see. And then what will they do?"

"Joe knows."

"They'll come back to the plantation?"

"When it's time."

"It's too risky," Templeton says. "You created them, but you don't have the right to put them in danger. They are human; they have a right to choose their fate."

"And they will. I cannot force them to return."

"But they will, you know it."

"I'm counting on it."

Templeton slowly walks to the fire. "Sura won't have the same effect on Jack as she does you. The human experience takes time to assimilate." He looks sternly at Mr. Frost and whispers, "He'll hurt her."

"No, he won't. He has synchronized with her energy, Templeton. He feels bonded to her, even Joe. If he's near them again with all his memories, I believe he will transform at that moment. He'll change."

Templeton remains quiet. Mr. Frost digs through his whiskers to scratch his chin, sliding in circles. It's risky, of course. All he needs to do is get them together, and he's certain Jack will change. It's what Mr. Frost has been counting on.

He turns his back on Templeton, sliding across the patch of ice. Four incubation tanks are now embedded in the once-pristine snow. The glass is frosted. Mr. Frost stops in front of them and looks up with his hands on his belly. If Jack doesn't change, well then, Mr. Frost has other plans.

Because nothing is certain.

"I want you to wait for Joe and Sura," he says, "and make sure they find me. Afterwards, take May and Jonah to the south end of the plantation until this is over."

Mr. Frost drags his fingers over one of the tanks, leaving trails on the glass. A vague form looks back from inside.

"You could hide with us, you know."

Mr. Frost touches the back of his head. "Jack must transform, but the root, Templeton, must be destroyed."

Templeton stands at the edge of the rug, hands at his sides. His chin is tipped up, his shoulders back. "Then I shall see you when this is over."

Mr. Frost looks up at Templeton. "Be safe, my friend."

"Of course."

"Don't make my only regret that I wasn't able to get more tanks into the wishing room."

"We aren't meant to live forever."

"If only everyone believed that."

"Perhaps you can remind Jack when you see him."

"I doubt he'll be in the listening mood."

Templeton takes the watch from his front pocket. It glows. The golden string appears. He parts the space. The dense foliage of the tunnel is visible.

Templeton turns before exiting. "It's been a pleasure serving you, sir."

"The pleasure has been mine."

Templeton steps through the opening. The space of the wishing room returns to an endless vista of snow.

And Mr. Frost continues sliding.

JACK DRINKS memories from a fire hose plugged into the back of his head. He has the urge to urinate, the sensation of bursting, the horror of panic. There's too much to make sense, data pouring inside his head, his skull cracking. Occasionally he catches a tidbit, a small snack of information, something that makes sense.

They hate me.

That's one. He didn't like that one, but it's true: the elven did hate him. They don't anymore because they don't know where he is. And they don't know where he is because...

I'm dead.

Jack feels like he's falling into a very deep, very dark, and very cold hole. Even for Jack, this feels cold.

Lonely.

Dark.

And somewhere in the bottom, he begins to understand what everything means. He's told that he died when he sank through the ice, holding his mother and brother; he died in their embrace and understood that they loved him.

He remembers planning for death.

The scientists showed him the tiny pellet, said it would hold all his memories—even the ones he forgot. It would also contain the blueprint of his DNA and the directions to escape in case he kicked the bucket.

You just need someone to carry it, they said. *Someone you trust with your life.*

That was easy. Jack knew exactly who would carry it. He didn't know what it would do to Pawn, didn't really care, just knew that if anything happened, Pawn would keep him safe and nothing would hurt him. Jack would come back.

The plan would bring him back.

It's a complex plan, only one a mastermind could understand and, thankfully, Jack is one. It's also one that might be construed as diabolical, dastardly, and mean-spirited. As vile, foul, and nasty.

And genius.

As the data continues filling him up, Jack settles at the bottom of this deep, dark, and cold hole. When all the memories are forced into his brain and find their rightful place, he understands.

His body is shaky and cold, bluer than blue. His heart, smaller than small, tiny as a pebble, and hard as folded steel. Cold as deep space.

He snaps open his bloodshot eyes.

He fully understands.

THE PUPPET

III

Her mother called it a marionette.

The girl didn't think she'd like it. Compared to the laptop and the bicycle, a puppet didn't look like that much fun. But when she got the hang of the control bar, when she learned to move the legs and arms, was able to make her puppet sit and walk, why, it was all she played with.

She made clothes for her puppet and named her. Her father made her a little bed to sleep next to her. When she did her plays, the puppet took on a life of its own.

But one day, when she wasn't looking, her brother cut the strings.

The puppet fell in a heap. Elbows and knees were bent the wrong directions, and the head cocked to the side. Her father said he could tie the strings, make it new again.

But the girl said no.

"Why?" the father asked.

"The puppet wants to be free."

16

DECEMBER 21

Sunday

Mom.

The word had changed. It had transformed into something stuck in Sura's throat. All her memories were a lie. Bedtime stories, late-night movies, days on the horses... lies, lies, lies.

Because she's not my mom. Never was.

All that talk of independence and truth, all that crap about enlightenment... the nights sitting at the dinner table when she'd say, "Wake up, Sura, and know yourself. You'll be set free."

How could her mom expect her to understand truth when it was disguised in words and fleeting meanings? Why couldn't her mom sit down and explain it like Jonah did with Joe?

Sura runs on the beach as far as she can. She can't feel her knees when she falls. That's when she pulls her legs against her body and cries.

Sand sticks to her. *A billion grains, each unique in color and shape.*

Did her mom say that? Sura remembers walking the beach and that line coming out of the blue—her mom telling her that there were a billion grains of sand, each one special.

Was she trying to tell me something?

She can't sit still or the surreal sense of vertigo will strangle her. She walks, suppressing the urge to run so she doesn't have to stop. As long as she's moving, she can tolerate the truth.

Maybe she's always known it, deep inside. Still, there's not enough space in the world to face it head-on. Not enough air to breathe the ugly truth.

I'm a clone.

THE WIND DIES.

Sura's musty sweater is around her waist. The sun bites her cheeks, but her feet are still bare, much like her heart. The beach is empty except for an occasional beachcomber. The vacation homes look and feel empty.

She hasn't eaten since the day before, but hunger gives her something to grasp. She can't shake the sensation of falling, of spinning out of control.

Why am I here?

What's my purpose?

Who am I?

All those questions her mom used to ask now haunt and betray her.

Sura walks until the sand turns to swaths of seashells. She crosses mats of washed-up reeds and climbs over jetties meant to reduce erosion. She passes condominiums, abandoned sailboats, and broken surfboards. She finds a long stretch of empty beach that leads to a spit of sand, where someone stands with hands in pockets, watching the waves.

She's too tired to turn around. Too empty to run.

Joe doesn't turn as she nears. He doesn't watch her flop onto the sand. Exhaustion pulls her onto her elbows. Her cheeks are reddened by sun and wind. Joe pulls a water bottle from his pocket. She chugs it while he watches the waves roll, ceaselessly.

"She loved you," he says.

Sura dips her head, too tired to hold it up.

"That's why she left Jonah," he adds. "She loved you."

"She was made to love him." Sura notices the magnetic attraction intensify as they talk. "Just like I was made to love you."

"Imagine how hard it was for her to deny that love," he says. "Every day, her heart telling her one thing, but her mind something else. Every day she ignored her feelings for Jonah to do what's right—to search for the truth. She must've suffered greater than him."

Sura's mom always looked tired, always looked like she had been pulling extra weight. Sura always figured it was depression and sometimes asked her to look into medication. They learned in school depression could be treated chemically. Feelings are chemicals, someone said. *Love, too.*

"None of this is real," Sura says. "My feelings for you are just hormones interpreted by my brain. It's programmed into my DNA. I'm just a script that's programmed to be attracted to you for Mr. Frost's sick little entertainment. He designed us that way, assembled us like that."

"We're cloned, Sura. Not assembled."

"And the difference?"

"We're human. We're flesh, blood, and tissue. We're no different than everyone else, just conceived differently."

"We sprang from a petri dish and that makes us human? We're an experiment, Joe. We're Frankensteins that fooled everyone, including ourselves." She dips her head. "What's worse, you've known all along."

"Yeah, but I understand, Sura. It's not how we start that matters. It's who we are."

"You need to wake up."

She dips her head again. Tears swell without falling.

"It hurts me to see you this way," he says.

She resists the temptation to run to him, to get lost in his embrace, to forget the world, to erase the truth, and just fade back into ignorance and his sweet essence that hums so strongly inside her.

"Why'd he do this?" she says.

"Do what?"

"This." She pats her chest. "Why'd he create us?"

"Jonah said it had something to do with Jack."

"Who's that?"

He shrugs. "The entire plantation has to do with him."

We're cogs in a machine meant to build Jack, is that it? Just parts that click and clack and, in the end, out spits a clone named Jack?

"I don't want to be a cog," she whispers.

"We'll find out." He takes her hand. "The yellow-hat said we have to find Mr. Frost."

She's so tired, so bereft, that when he reaches for her, she falls into his arms, lets his warmth envelop her. She nuzzles into the crook of his neck.

I don't have the strength to resist him. Not like you, Mom.

Maybe, she wonders as they walk to the truck, she's not exactly like her mom after all.

Mr. Frost emerges from the live oak grove. He stops to admire the Christmas lights. Each year, they add more. It's a reminder there is joy in this world.

He continues his late-night stroll, returning from deep in the trees where the land is mostly wet and wild, where alligators slumber for the winter and tree frogs happily sing. He'd grown accustomed to the green environment, never thinking he'd ever prefer it over the pure white Arctic.

His wide feet crush the dormant pasture as he slowly slogs toward the house, using the peaceful surroundings to process all these feelings, these difficult emotions that wrestle inside like baboons.

He hears a distant cheer, feels it beneath his feet. He's standing over the toy factory. The helpers must've accomplished quite a goal, all of them cheering at the same time.

Freeda? he thinks.

She hasn't responded for hours. Perhaps she's not pretending anymore.

A thick mug awaits him on the porch. Mr. Frost takes a sip of frothy fish oil, a blend of something exotic. Eel extract, his favorite. A light sensation passes from his taste buds into his head, lifting the worried thoughts. Suddenly, he finds Christmas cheer as accessible as an afternoon nap.

He walks around to the back of the house while downing the drink. He enters the basement doors, sliding down a slick ramp and unzipping the coolsuit before throwing open the toy factory doors.

The raucous noise is deafening.

Mr. Frost smiles, the exuberance contagious. He even feels his feet begin to shift, tiny little taps in time to the music. Someone is butchering the piano, but how can he not celebrate? Everyone is wildly dancing, standing on each other's shoulders, slinging mugs of drink, and rolling on the floor... where a blue elven pounds on an electric keyboard.

Mr. Frost's feet stop.

Jack throws his arms out and the music halts. A wide, toothy grin expands.

"PAWN!"

The helpers repeat after Jack. *Pawn! Pawn! Pawn!*

It's a name Mr. Frost hasn't heard for hundreds of years. A name Jack gave him when they were young. A name Mr. Frost secretly hoped never to hear again.

The dancing continues as Jack stutter-steps his way to the entrance, taking the time to do-si-do with helpers along the way. He pushes up the ramp and circles around Mr. Frost with his arms up. The helpers cheer madly.

"Hey there, old buddy, old pal," Jack whispers.

The helpers surge up the ramp, clinging to Jack's baggy pant legs, begging him not to leave, like they've been waiting a lifetime for him.

Which they have.

"Let me introduce you to a few friends." Jack slaps his arm over Mr. Frost's shoulders, biting cold sinking through the fabric. "They all look, well, pretty much the same, but the hats give them away. That's Crayman, that's Char, that's Gabbit, that's Farty... that's, um, Dummy... oh, I ain't got all day."

Jack raises his fist.

"To the tower!"

The cheers rattle Mr. Frost's eardrums.

"Not you!" Jack swings his hands, shooing them away. "Get back to work; make those toys, all of you. Christmas needs its workers and you're it."

They scramble like programmed slaves. *Which they are.*

The machines fire up, the production lines move along, and a song lifts into the air, a merry little number that keeps their spirits strong and productive.

"I love those handsome little devils," Jack says. "Now what do you say you and me do some catching up?"

THE ELEVATOR TAKES LONGER than usual to begin moving. The floor is crackling with veins of frost. Mr. Frost studies Jack's reflection in the shiny doors before a layer of frost creeps over it.

The smooth face and hairless scalp. The square chin and longish nose. Even the fingernails are bruised-purple as he picks his blocky, white teeth.

Jack is back.

Mr. Frost feels a chill creep inside him. His thoughts are tumbling into a pile of nonsense, tipping him off balance. He braces himself against the wall, the frosty surface numbing his hand.

"This is super awkward," Jack says. "You really need elevator music."

Mr. Frost doesn't face him.

"But it's your elevator, so whatever," Jack says.

Jack drums the wall with his fingernails. Debris showers the floor like an artisan carving a wall of marble. Maybe Mr. Frost is imagining the cold, that the hardening of his organs, the shrinking of his stomach, is just the result of his runaway thoughts and paralyzing fear.

Or maybe it's Jack's ability to freeze anything and everything.

Mr. Frost tries to muster the words, attempts to say anything that will make him seem less fearful. All these centuries and, in seconds, he's transformed back into that meek elven that followed Jack, doing as he pleased, whatever he said. Now he's standing next to Jack's incarnated body in a slow-moving elevator that's quickly turning into a death locker of ice. All his carefully laid plans seem like poorly constructed scaffolding.

The elevator stops.

The tower, dark and cluttered, is revealed.

Jack doesn't move. Mr. Frost is stuck in place, waiting to be told what to do. He feels a tickle on his ear, a huff of frigid air. Mr. Frost locks his knees.

"Love what you've done with the place," Jack says.

Jack slides around the desks and chairs, the monitors and tables. The fish tank. Max hides behind a pillow.

"It's so full of *stuff*, Pawn. So lived-in, so homey. It screams... WARMBLOOD!"

Jack displays a rainbow of jazz hands.

His pale blue jacket flutters behind him as he glides along. He studies the room, sniffing like a dog. He holds his fat foot out like a blunt joust and starts shoving furniture. A desk grinds against the wall. A monitor crashes on the floor. He races around the room, occasionally stopping to size up a vision or mutter an idea to no one. He even begins an argument with himself, eventually telling himself to shut up.

"Great job with the body, by the way," he shouts at Mr. Frost. "Freeda had some doubts about you, but clearly you knew what you were doing." Jack licks his finger and touches his butt. "*Tsssssssss.*"

Mr. Frost is still locked in place, his thoughts like squares of ice all stuck together.

"The green hair thing... have to admit, that was a little sketchy. I mean, I can't argue with the results, but do you know what I went through to get here?" Jack cruises behind Mr. Frost. "I was laughed at by warmbloods, Pawn. I got to tell you, it hurt. It's kind of like being the stupid one in a class of morons."

Jack slides past with his head tipped back.

"Oh, look. You did stars." He studies the constellations.

"Freeda!" he shouts. "Keep the stars, ditch the rest. I need to start over, the layout is horrible. No offense, Pawn. We just have different... tastes."

The floor quakes.

Jack skates along, biting his nails, while the furnishings melt away like sandcastles. Max scurries around the room.

"What's that?" Jack points.

Mr. Frost still can't get a word out.

"Here, boy." Jack pats his knees. "Come to me, now. I said now. Come to me now or else."

Max hides behind Mr. Frost. Jack's expression is placid, slightly annoyed. Fortunately, the room's transformation distracts him. The floor shimmers, reconfiguring the microscopic biocells that follow a magnetic matrix to construct objects and electronics at will.

An oversized desk, translucent and cold, spans one end of the room, with an extremely large chair. Various sculptures emerge like serpents, odes to the olden days of the Cold One, as Jack was known by those that feared him and those that... well, that's all there was. Just fear.

The room, once again, is crowded with icy, slick furnishings, the stuff that once inhabited Jack's room deep beneath the Arctic ice hundreds of years ago when he was king, as if the memory was plucked from his mind and made real.

The last vestige of the Cold One, the single most garish, most self-centered tribute to the reign of Jack's terror, formed in front of Mr. Frost: a round fountain with a life-sized carving of Yours Truly spitting in the center.

Jack takes his place at the desk, groaning with satisfaction. He looks down his pointed nose. "You don't talk much, Pawn."

"I..." Mr. Frost clears his throat, thawing the words. "I'm just... surprised, that's all. I didn't expect to see you."

"All you, buddy." He smacks his belly, waves coursing from the impact. "Wait, it was all *me*. I put the plans in the root and put the root in your head so, if you think about it, *I* did this. But I'll give you some credit, Pawn. You hung in there, persevered. Kept your chin up when the chips were down. You did that for me."

Jack says, in the most sincere tone, "I won't forget that, buddy. Now scoop out a fishy, I'm feeling a little woozy over here. Hypoglycemia acting up."

Mr. Frost bites his lip, refusing to let his thoughts out. There was no perseverance, no fight to bring him back; there was just the drudgery of being driven by the root and Freeda's daily voice. He slides to the fountain, the centerpiece reaching up like an icy dagger stabbing the heavens. The fish seem to be real, not manufactured by the room. Freeda was prepared. He swipes at the school of minnows, snagging a pair between his fingers, and tosses them on the desk.

Jack licks his lips, poking at the flipping fish gasping to breathe. They freeze into curled, fishy chips when he touches them, rocking on the hard surface.

"You know," he says, biting one in half, "you can't imagine what it's like out there. Warmblood food is like eating a pillow. The only thing worse is the smell. I'm tempted to punch you in the face for letting me escape before I had memories, but I'll hand it to you, Pawn."

Jack inhales sharply.

"The Claus myth is firmly in place. Christmas greed infects them all. I'm back and beautiful. You did a... great... JOB!"

Jack presses his face on the desk and pulls the other fish between his lips like a serpent. He sits back and savors the snack, gazing at the stars.

"Anywho," he finally says, "I'm back, so you got to move out. I got you set up in the basement with some sweet digs. The view sucks, but it beats living in this heat, right? It's the humidity that'll kill you."

The elevator walls slide up.

Jack flicks his fingers. "Off you go. I got some thinking to do, some planning to plan, that sort of thing. Christmas is in two days and there's still a lot to do."

He drifts into thought, as if Mr. Frost would merely disappear, like nothing existed if he didn't recognize it.

"What are you going to do?" Mr. Frost asks.

"What?"

"About Christmas. What are you going to do?"

A smile creeps across his darkening face. "First, I'm going to relax. Coming back to life after being dead a few hundred years takes a lot out of you. Second, I'm going to wipe out the warmbloods. But not necessarily in that order."

He hikes his feet on the desk.

"And then I'm going to celebrate Christmas. I'm not a heathen, you know."

"The eyeTablets just shipped. It'll take some time before they're integrated into society. My estimate before we—I mean, *you* can do anything is eight years, probably ten. However, if you wait—"

"I know, I know. Freeda told me. Listen, in case you haven't noticed, I like things now. Not later, but now. So I'm weighing my options."

"What options?"

"Just shut up, will you?"

The elevator hums.

Mr. Frost has pushed his luck as far as it'll give. But he had to know what Jack was thinking. He knows there are many options to achieve the master plan, and Mr. Frost has planned a way to counter all of them. However, he knows one will undoubtedly work.

Mr. Frost knows Jack. *Not later, but now.*

"Jack," Mr. Frost states.

"Hmm?"

"My name isn't Pawn. It's Jack."

Jack opens his eyes. "What's that supposed to mean?"

"You stole my elven name when we were little, Janack."

"Don't call me that."

"My mother and father named me Jack. You're the one that called me Pawn."

"You are what I call you."

The elevator closes on Mr. Frost. He waits for Jack to open it in a rage, maybe stick a finger up his nose until his brain crackles with ice crystals because that was a rash and stupid thing to do. He didn't plan on it, never had thought about it, not once. But suddenly it was there and he was saying it.

When Jack didn't come for him, Mr. Frost smiled.

My real name is Jack.

JACK'S BRAIN feels like a bowl of hot noodles.

Freeda said he would just feel a little pressure and that was the lie of the century.

But he remembers almost everything.

He doesn't remember dying, but Freeda gave him the blow-by-blow, how he blubbered on his mother's shoulder before drowning with his brother. She told him they all died.

But who's alive now? Who's the winner?

Jack orchestrated the resurrection of all eternity. He always felt like a dummy—he hates to admit it, but compared to his brother, Claus, he was a little dim—but what he did with the root was brilliant. The scientists helped a little, but it was his idea, his genius.

Pawn couldn't deny what the root wanted him to do, but Jack gave him enough freedom to adapt creatively. Jack may have been green and grouchy when he woke up, but if that's what it took to bring him back, he won't complain.

Much.

He burps fish-scented fumes, thumps his chest, but it's not indigestion. It feels more like a halo of anger just below the sternum—two inches to the right where his tiny heart pumps antifreeze.

Jack.

Pawn just wanted to ruin his day. Jack attempts to soothe his heavy heart with cold thoughts, only to feel them melt.

Jack is Pawn's real name.

He slides past the fountain to a full-length mirror. Jack pulls off his clothes, dropping them in a pile. Black shorts are visible just below his doughy belly.

He's back. He's good. *Death ain't got nothing on me.*

And, yet, something's missing.

Jack works through the pile of clothes and pulls out a black pair of Oakley sunglasses. He slides them up his nose with one finger. The polarizing vision makes him look slightly rosy.

Almost tan.

His childhood dresser is on the far side of the room, the snow duster still in the top drawer. The candy cane press is on the low-rising coffee table, the one where you pour sugar and ice through a straw. The hinge is a bit sticky, but then again, it always was. And there, middle drawer, is the harmonica, still beaten and battered. Jack cups it, blowing all the notes.

It's all there. Everything he could remember, all the toys, all the inventions. And all the hatred, coldness, bitterness, and bile to go along with it.

Why didn't I erase that?

Not too late, sir.

"Quiet." He doesn't like her eavesdropping. He likes beating himself up when no one else is around. Fact is, everything is exactly the way it was hundreds of years ago, but something is missing.

Something.

A car door thumps. Jack leans on the window, hands pressed on the glass. Veins of ice crawl across the surface. Jonah's limping around the front of a pickup, dragging a tarp full of clippings from the garden. He goes back for another load, the blue tarp snaking behind him as he winds his way through the maze where a sculpture sparkles.

"What's that?" He pokes the glass.

A tribute to your mother.

"Mother?"

Mr. Frost thought it appropriate that she be memorialized for her wisdom.

"Uh-huh. First of all, no more 'Mr. Frost' crap. His name is Pawn, get with it. Second, there better be a big, fat, blue statue somewhere, if you know what I mean."

You are the tribute, sir. This entire plantation is in your honor.

"Uh..." He starts to object. "All right, I'll give you that one."

Pawn loved Jack's mother. Everyone did. The old lady spouted wisdom like a...

Fountain.

Pawn was one of those kid elven that sat at the back of the class and doodled on the desk, slunk down when the teacher wanted volunteers; one of those elven that never said a word. It had something to do with his parents dying when he was little, but boohoo— Jack didn't have a father and his mother was busy.

Jack made friends with him. Actually, no one wanted to be friends with Jack, either. They had that in common. Jack and Pawn became best friends.

Only Jack's name was really Janack. And Pawn's name was really Jack. It's confusing but not really.

Pawn did whatever Jack told him to do, so the name Pawn made sense. Besides, Janack was a stupid name and he sort of liked the name Jack. It was tough and sharp. He wanted it and they both couldn't be named Jack.

So Jack became Pawn and Janack became Jack.

Simple as that.

Jack fogs the glass with his breath and etches a name. *JACK.*

Sir, we need to discuss the options I gave you earlier—

"Oh my God." Jack clamps the sides of his head. "You can't tell me I approved your voice. If I have to listen to that for the next hundred years, I'm going to hang myself."

Freeda stutters.

"Make yourself useful and turn the temperature down; I'm sweating BBs over here."

The system is running at maximum power, sir. Her reply is terse. *Minus eighty is as low as it can go unless you want to remove all the replicated objects in the room.*

He rather doubts that. She's just making that up. Jack starts getting dressed.

As I was saying, depending on the option you'd like to initiate, we may have to act very soon, sir.

"Uh-huh."

Within the next hour.

"Okay."

Jack digs through his dresser and finds a black, long-tailed jacket that matches the sunglasses.

Sir, I don't understand. What are you doing?

"I'm going to party with the helpers. You're going to work."

You'll distract them, sir.

"Do you always make excuses?"

Sir, so much has changed from the original master plan. Earlier, you liked the meltdown option. Is that what you want?

"Uh, yeah. That's what I said. Why is that so hard to understand?"

Because initiating meltdown on such short notice is hasty, sir. The meltdown is an alternative to the eyeTablets that Mr. Fro—Pawn has prepared.

"Are you calling me hasty?"

The decision is, sir. It'll take time to communicate with all the toys we've manufactured and shipped around the world for the past two hundred years. Also, you should be aware that Pawn incarnated a fourth warmblood, who is now missing along with Joe. I hardly think now is the time to "party."

"Wait." He pulls the sunglasses off. "Did you say Joe?"

Yes. He's the boy that was driving the truck with—

"Sura."

She led him here. That energy of hers brought him to the plantation, gave him hope. She felt like home.

"Where is she?"

We don't know, sir. They're hiding.

"Well, find them. You have to find them. Now." Jack swaps the

Oakleys for Ray-Bans and checks his reflection from three angles. "I want her back here before we blow up the world. No excuses. Call me as soon as you find her, and in the meantime, do what I designed you to do—compute. Look, I've been dead for two hundred years and I can't sit around all day, so chop-chop."

Jack wraps a skinny, black tie around his neck and slides the premade knot beneath his fat neck, a pound of blue flesh falling over it.

Sir, you want me to establish contact with billions of toys?

"Tonight."

There's not enough time. I really think we should—

"Call me when you're ready. I want to watch. Send Sura down when you find her."

Jack snatches the harmonica and wipes the spit off with his sleeve. He blows a few times and pockets the harp, determined to play. Determined they'll like it. Sura, too.

"By the way, what's that?"

That's Max, Pawn's pet. He's been feeding his memories to it.

"He's using a memory box?" Jack remembers that silver box he carried with him. The little nuggets were digestible memory chips. As long as the box was pressed against his skin, they absorbed everything he experienced.

"You're letting him do this?"

It's harmless, sir. Besides, it's a wise backup in case something goes wrong.

Max is curled on a pillow, baring his teeth when Jack slides his glasses down for a look. Jack thinks maybe he'll eat it. But that thing must be a hundred years old, probably taste like a leather boot.

"Send it down to him. He'll need something to talk to."

The elevator wall shimmies around the circle. Jack slides inside. His hand knifes through the gap just as the door closes.

"One more thing."

Yes?

"The statue."

17

DECEMBER 24

Wednesday

Sura huddles against the gas station. The late-day shadows are cool. She hasn't showered in days. Her sweatshirt will testify.

The boy in the silver pickup looks away from Joe, his eyes falling on Sura. The door is dented and the hood a different color. The driver climbs out and hands Joe the keys.

"Sure about this?" the kid says.

Joe calls him Bean. Sura doesn't care what his real name is, just as long as he gives them that rolling junk heap.

"Just till after the New Year," Joe says. "Then trade back."

Bean walks around Joe's truck, fingers trailing. "Still don't get it."

"Why you complaining, Bean?"

"Because I don't want no debt collector showing up at my house."

Joe clicks his tongue. "Come on, man. I just got to lay low for a bit, just till my old man cools off."

"Uh-huh. And what if he sees me in your truck?"

"Tell him the truth. You met me at Edisto and I was camping."

"Where you going to be?"

"North Carolina, probably." They both know he's lying, but at least they got their story straight.

Bean finally climbs into the truck. He tests the radio, nodding. It's a dumb move, but he can't pass it up. They shake hands before he drives off. The tailpipes can be heard growling a mile down the road.

"He's all right," Joe says, like this will make her feel better. "You ready?"

"What if we don't go?" Sura hugs herself tighter.

"What then?" Joe asks. "Where do we go?"

We find the nearest interstate, drive until the gas tank is empty, and call the nearest town home. We get jobs, buy a trailer, have kids, and spend the rest of our lives together, forever and ever and ever.

She can't stop the fantasies; they come to life when he's near her. She's afraid if they go back to Frost Plantation, it'll be the end. Her mom still loved Jonah. She denied that love to raise Sura, but she loved him.

"If we run," Joe says, "we'll never stop. We'll always be looking back. The yellow-hat helpers said we have to go back, that Mr. Frost needs us. I'm afraid if we don't, bad things are going to happen that we can't outrun."

"You trust the yellow-hats?"

He looks down the road. "Yeah. I trust them."

Bean's truck starts on the second turn. Joe throws the door open and waves Sura over. She kicks empty Red Bull cans off the floorboard and sinks into the sprung seat, arms still clamped around her chest. Her eyes ache with insomnia.

He takes her hand.

The ache subsides. She hates that it does, hates that it feels good to be near him, to touch him. To need him. She wants to love him, not feel compelled to. It feels like she's betraying herself, giving in to what Mr. Frost wants her to do, becoming the person he wants her to be, but she can't help it.

They hold hands until their palms sweat, and then he pulls her close. She leans in.

They take the country roads, drive north for an hour, and then circle around. Without a phone or a GPS, they get lost twice. The sun is setting when they turn on to a weed patch cut out of the trees. It might have been a road once, but now it's kudzu and pines.

Joe kills the lights. They listen to the engine tick as it cools.

"We're on the north end of the plantation," he says. "I used to come out this way when I was little, explore the woods, fish and hunt. Helpers come out this way every once in a while, but this time of year, they're busy making toys."

"You mean like Christmas toys?"

"Yeah. It's weird, right?"

A week ago, she would've agreed. Not now. Nothing seems weird, not a short, fat man with engorged feet named Mr. Frost, not Christmas gnomes making presents, or secret gardens that transform into a Neverland. Normal has been redefined.

They start down the overgrown road.

Twilight is extinguished in the forest. Joe pushes through the brush, making a path for her to follow. The going gets slow, the nonexistent trail thicker and stickier. Thorns tug at Sura's sweatshirt and snag her jeans. Joe holds her hand.

The ground turns mucky. Water sloshes over her shoes, soaking her socks. The trees give way to marsh grasses and black water. Beyond, a hill slopes up to live oaks, their branches weeping with moss.

He looks up and down the tree line. The moon is bright.

They slog just inside the trees. Sometimes, the water reaches their knees. If she wasn't a Southern girl, she'd be thinking about alligators, but they're coldblooded. So are snakes.

Am I Southern?

Sura is an Inuit name that means "new life." She looked it up once for a class project but didn't think much of it. But now they're returning to the house of an elven from the North Pole.

"There." Joe points at a leaning tree with a thick rope. He splashes along the bank and pushes the weeds apart until an upside-down boat is revealed.

"Help me."

They flip it over. Joe stares at the beaten john boat. "I used to take this back and forth. The helpers put the rope up and we'd swing all day long. Can't believe the boat's still here."

"Can't believe it floats."

"It'll get us to the other side."

And it does. They paddle with their hands. The frigid water seeps through holes, but they make it before sinking.

Joe huffs on his quivering hands. "We'll climb the slope and slip through the sunken garden. The back door will be open. If we're fast enough, we can reach the elevator. The yellow-hat helper said Mr. Frost is expecting us."

Sura is grateful to be walking. Her knees are stiff. By the time they cross through the orchards and reach the north end of the gardens, she feels much better. Joe pries open the hedge and finds the hidden path inside. The wishing room is to the right, the garden to the left.

There's a dull thumping ahead.

"What's that?" Sura asks.

Joe listens. "It's late; no one should be in the gardens."

They creep along the darkened path. She stays close to Joe. The pounding gets louder. Joe puts his fingers to his lips, then peeks around the corner. His cautious expression turns to confusion. It takes a few moments to process what he's seeing. Confusion becomes shock. Sura reaches out for him, but he steps into the open.

"What are you doing?" Joe shouts.

"Joe!" Jonah's raspy voice calls from somewhere out there.

The bushes shake and gravel crunches as Jonah's bulky frame marches toward them with his arms spread, herding the teenagers back into the shadows.

"Back," Jonah hisses. "Quickly, both of you."

Joe tries to investigate what his father was doing in the garden, but Jonah is too insistent, too strong. His face is speckled with gray stubble, lines crunching the corners of his tired eyes. Sweat glistens on his cheeks.

Jonah pushes to the end of the path. He closes his eyes, lips flut-

tering, before prying the wall open. Orange light warmly illuminates
the frozen specks on his face.

That's not sweat, that's ice.

"In you go," he says.

A bonfire roars in an open plain.

The salted ground is dry and hard. Sura thinks she can see the
outline of distant mountains. The firelight only reaches so far into the
abandoned land.

Jonah gestures to the fire. "Warm yourselves."

Sura's as close to the roaring fire as she can get, which is still quite
far. She spreads her fingers, the warmth seeping through her cheeks.
Steam rises from her pant legs.

Joe is shivering. He follows Jonah to the edge of darkness. They
argue in French. The wood crackles in the flames while the two
shout, point, and stomp the dusty earth. They argue like adults, not
father and son. Occasionally, Sura hears her name.

Joe comes back to the fire. Jonah remains at the fringe of the fire's
glow. Sura backs up to an abandoned log, its surface smooth and gray.
Joe stays near the fire, still shivering. Jonah comes to him, a slight
hitch on his right side, like he pulls his leg along. He rubs his grizzly
jaw and drops a thick hand on Joe's shoulder.

Joe doesn't shrug him off. Instead, they warm themselves with
outstretched hands. The shared moment of silence settles the tension
between them. Joe sits next to Sura.

"I don't think we should yell," she says.

"No one can hear inside the wishing room," Jonah mutters.

That's not what she meant. For several minutes, the fire does all
the talking, grinding the wood into glowing embers that spit into the
dark.

"He's here." Jonah's voice is raw. "The man that Mr. Frost has
been... building. He has arrived."

"We know," Joe says. "He's not a man."

Jonah doesn't seem surprised. He looks at his callused hands.
"Where have you been?"

"Hiding," Joe says. "Helpers were at the house, and Sura was putting things together..." He looks for her response.

She squeezes his arm.

"A yellow-hat told me to get lost for a while."

Jonah nods like he's seeing distant images.

"We're supposed to find Mr. Frost," Joe says.

"Not yet. It's not safe." The light can't lift the shadows from his eyes. He returns to staring at his hands.

"What does he want with us?" Sura asks.

"I don't know." He studies the fire. "He's playing a very complex game that's taken hundreds of years. I couldn't possibly understand. I'm just a pawn."

"We're all pawns." Sura tenses.

"You don't understand," Jonah continues. "*Everything* hangs in the balance tonight. Come morning, this could be a whole new world. If Mr. Frost needs you, then you go."

"That's easy for you to say," Sura blurts. "You and Joe know what this place is—you've known about it since you were born. I'm still trying to believe that fire isn't real."

He shakes his head. The light glistens in his deep-set eyes. "Joe doesn't know everything."

Sura and Joe press closer. He's still shaking.

"This is our fate?" she asks. "We have no free will? We're victims of our biology, is that it? Mr. Frost programmed us like puppets so that we'll do what he says. That's not fair. It's not human."

Jonah is nodding. He doesn't disagree.

He grabs a twig from the dust and begins breaking it into smaller pieces, like Joe was doing on the beach. He groans when he stands, tossing the sticks into the blaze before walking away. He looks at the stars, hands on hips.

"I was sixteen when I met her," he says, without looking back. "I was hanging Christmas lights with my... father."

He doesn't know what else to call the man that raised him.

"We were in the garden when Sesi walked down the steps to

collect flowers. I thought the lights were shining on her, but she was radiant everywhere she went. I felt her, right here."

He taps his chest.

"She was like a smile that held my heart, a blanket that warmed my soul. The sun would rise and set with her. She said she grew up on the plantation, although I'd never seen her before. As strange as that is, I never questioned why I'd never seen her before that day." His eyes twinkle in the shadows. "Later, I learned why."

"Why?" she asks.

"Within weeks, we talked about marriage," he says. "We were going to have three children and a farm. We were naïve enough to dream that Mr. Frost would one day give us the plantation and we'd raise our family with horses out back and crops in the fields. We'd live long and old and die happy."

Sura cringes. That's her fantasy.

A groan escapes him. He looks at the ground and kicks at the dust.

"We'd been together almost a year when the sun would set and never rise again. That's when she left. Sesi said she needed to wake up and break the cycle. I didn't know what that meant."

He shakes his head.

"The truth is sometimes hard and unforgiving."

Jonah reaches into his pocket and studies something flat and round, light reflecting off the edges. He reaches out, hand cupped. Joe lays his hand open and receives an antique pocket watch. The surface is nicked and worn. The etching is gone from years of friction, leaving behind a well-polished surface.

"Stay until eleven o'clock," he says. "Use the pocket watch to find the exit. Templeton will meet you at the back door and take you to Mr. Frost."

Jonah limps around the log and fades into the darkness, stopping just before he disappears. A golden string dangles in front of him. A clipped groan cuts short what he's thinking. Perhaps he has more to say. Maybe he wants to stay with them in the wishing room, huddle next to the fire, and just let the world go on without them. They'd talk about their shared fantasy, what they would name the kids, and what careers they'd have when they grew up. If they stayed in the wishing room long enough, they could transform it into a happy place where brides-to-be don't leave.

And Moms don't die.

The darkness parts like black curtains and Jonah slips out. Joe remains stone-faced, staring at the fire. They hold each other in silence. Jonah should've stayed to make them go when the time comes.

Perhaps they do have a choice.

FRIGID AIR HISSES down the walls.

Mr. Frost stands in the center, eschewing the bed despite the ache in his knees. He wants it to hurt; it distracts him from his thoughts.

Seeing Jack—the blue, fat, and bald elven—brought long-forgotten memories to the surface. There was no epic battle, no struggle for power, or clash of good versus evil. Jack slid into the tower and simply took everything from him.

Mr. Frost became Pawn.

Music thuds through the floor, penetrates his feet, tickles his joints. The root vibrates beneath his scalp. A song ends and another begins, faster and heavier.

Mr. Frost locks his knees.

The door cracks open. The earthy scent of the incubator lab wafts in from the other room. Music, too. The door swings open. There's a crash against the wall, followed by laughter. A crumpled blue-hat helper falls through the doorway. A red-hat helper stumbles down the hall. More laughter.

They pull themselves together and throw a sack into the room, slamming the door shut. Something yelps inside, kicking at the cloth. Mr. Frost drops to his knees and struggles to untie the knot. A white ball of fur leaps on the bed.

"Max!" Mr. Frost falls next to the Arctic fox.

Max's rough tongue kisses his nose. Mr. Frost pulls the silver tin from his pocket and fishes a few kernels from the bottom, leaving three in the box. He won't need a refill. Max gobbles them down.

Mr. Frost goes back to standing like a vigilant guard of nothing more than a thin mattress and a curled-up puffball. He stays that way for hours while the music drones on. He resists sleep. There's no way to know how much time has passed when the music stops. The silence feels strange.

It won't be long now.

"No!" Jack waves his arms. "You're terrible. Get off the stage!"

Jack shoves the bass player with his foot.

"I need a bass player; I can't do everything. My God, the instrument isn't that hard to play."

He takes a swig of fish oil while the guitar player tunes his instrument. The drink slides into his stomach, coating him with good feelings. Hundreds of helpers stumble around the toy factory. They'd cleared out the center and stacked machines on top of each other to make room for a round stage. Jack couldn't care less about toys.

There won't be a Christmas next year.

In fact, he decided he'd move into the toy factory. The tower is nice, the views are sweet, but there's just no room. The toy factory is more his style. After Christmas, all this equipment will go out on the lawn. He'd make the place his own.

"Nope." Jack shoves an orange-hat helper down the steps. "You've already been up here; I recognize the hat."

There are at least fifty orange hats.

"You know what, why don't all of you get off the stage?" he says to the band. "I'll go solo. First guitar, then drums, then trombone or something..."

He can't play any of those instruments. The helpers cheer, but they're faking it. He could fart into the mic and they'd applaud.

Sir?

"Oh, Freeda. Just the annoying voice I was thinking about. You reading my mind?"

No, sir. I need you in the tower.

"What you need to do is download a blues harmonica into these hands." He looks around and points at the helpers. They laugh. They have no idea why.

Sir, now's not the time to be playing games.

"These aren't games, Freeda. This is musical genius. I've got a lot of living to do; I want to start it off on the right foot." He shakes his right foot and gets a laugh. *It's sooo easy.*

Sir, there's a problem with the meltdown.

"What kind of problem?"

Something you should look at, sir.

Jack doesn't like vagary. If she couldn't handle this, he'd delete her —have Pawn write another artificial intelligence, one that could take care of the end of warmbloods while he got the band together.

"I'll be up in a sec."

Can't wait, sir.

Jack throws the guitar down and kicks the drums over. He storms up the ramp, thinking that maybe he'll have Pawn build Freeda a face. He needs something to yell at.

He takes the elevator up. Super-chilled air rushes inside when it opens. "What is it?" he shouts.

Sir, there appears to be—

"Hold that thought." Jack slides up to the fountain. The fish scatter. He thinks *net* and a fish net squirts from the floor. "Pawn did a super job with this place," he says to himself, combing the waters and trapping at least a dozen fish. "It's all about finding the right people, Freeda. You get good people, you get results."

That's what I want to speak about, sir.

Jack empties the net on the desk, throws his feet up, and begins munching. He spins in the chair, looking across the open field at the giant live oaks on the far side. He thought he hated the tower—he really wants to hate it—but just can't bring himself to do it.

The views are just too sweet.

"It's settled." He bangs the desk, squishing the last fish. "I'm staying in the tower, Freeda. We'll bring the band up here. It'll be a little tight, but I think we can do it. We'll need a bouncer to keep things in order, 'cause things are going to get nuts. I'm thinking Templeton—"

He snaps his fingers.

"May's the perfect hammer with that big, spongy gut and those bohemian arms; that woman was made to bounce—"

Focus, sir! You need to listen! You cannot run off and play. I need you to stop acting like a child.

Jack raises his fist.

That's why you died the first time.

He freezes.

Died the first time. Her words have an echoing effect. No one ever spoke that way to Jack. But, then again, she's not real. She's an artificially constructed intelligence. She doesn't know what it's like to have all this pressure to succeed, to be happy and make people like you. It's a lot.

Jack knows.

I'm the one that's real. I have a body, a brain, and memories. I am real.

He thinks about this a bit more. He can prove he's real and she's not. *As long as I remember who I am... wait.*

He didn't have memories at the shelter, but he was still real, still awake. It's not like he wasn't real until Freeda uploaded his memories.

As long as I have a body... hold on.

He didn't have a body for two hundred years. He was a DNA-script stored in the root. Was he not real then, but is now?

I'll answer that question later.

"You're right," he says. The words sound funny. He forces himself to say them. "My bad."

Jack shoves the desk. It slides across the floor and shatters the fountain. Water spills and fish flip around. He closes his eyes, imagining something more appropriate for the room. There's a ripple in the air. When he opens his eyes, there are floating monitors, tables, maps, and data; there are numbers and words.

Voices mutter in a dozen languages.

A chair rises from the floor. The armrests swell with little control panels at his fingers. The back of the chair fans out, worthy of a throne.

And in the center, where the fountain used to be, is Earth. It's six feet in diameter, tilted on its axis, and slowly rotating. Pinpricks of light are all around it, merging into a mass of golden hue where populations are dense. Toward the north, they become less frequent.

The North Pole is dark.

"Let's do this," he says. "Brief me."

Thank you, sir. Let me start at the beginning. Pawn seeded the thought of Christmas gift-giving into the warmblood population shortly after arriving in the United States in the early 1800s, and for a long time, he was the primary producer and distributor of toys, exactly as you planned.

"Thank you."

At first, it was simple toys, mostly wooden. As the years passed, they became plastic, but still simplistic. Regardless how modest they were, whether they were wood or plastic, everything was embedded with slave technology that would allow us to eventually control every toy we've ever manufactured.

The lights extinguish and begin to slowly reemerge on the globe, illustrating the spread of Christmas toys. The planet, once again, becomes fully illuminated.

Nonetheless, Mr. Frost—

"Pawn." Jack slides toward Earth. "His name is Pawn."

Freeda pauses.

Jack eases around the floating image of Earth, not knowing what to do with his hands. He tries to put them behind his back—he's seen very important warmbloods do that move—but his arms are too short. He opts for resting them on his belly.

What's exciting, sir, is that we are, for the first time, launching neural-integration technology that will communicate with warmblood nervous systems and, ultimately, brain activity.

"Yeah, I know, the eyeTablets. Stupid name."

Sir, your original plan was to use slave technology to gain control of products such as automobiles, phones, weapons... everything, sir. It was brilliant.

"I know."

However, the recent technology revolution has spawned a new opportunity, sir. Warmbloods now have smart phones and computers. Everything in the world is networked. With these new developments, the neural-integration technology will allow us to know warmblood thoughts. We'll connect with their nervous systems. We control them, sir. They'll be puppets.

Jack stops circling the globe and looks up at the star-speckled ceiling. "Do I eat boogers?"

Sir?

"Do I eat boogers?"

Freeda stammers. *I just... I'm not sure where you're going with this.*

"You just explained my plan like I'm a booger-eating first grader." He begins coasting around the room, hands locked over his belly. "I designed everything on greed, Freeda. No, I didn't know how you were going to do it, but I know warmbloods and, as a whole, they have one thing in common: self-indulgent, ravenous, gluttonous, insatiable greed."

He hesitates. Willie comes to mind. *He's the only exception.*

"They like to get stuff, Freeda. They like to have it, to own it, to stuff it in closets, attics, and basements. They rent storage containers so they have more room for more stuff. They won't stop, Freeda. Ever. They'll build and collect until they figure out how to get to another planet, and then they'll fill that up with stuff."

He takes a breath.

"The eyeTablets sound great. I mean, marching those stupid warmbloods off a cliff sounds like my kind of party. But here's the deal: I don't want to wait twenty years. I want them gone *now*, so go with plan B, the one that turns slave technology into miniature nuclear reactors."

He points at the planet flickering with light.

"We'll use it to convert matter into energy but utilize the evaporating-microscopic-black-hole method to displace the energy somewhere else in the universe, preferably another galaxy, so we don't blow up our solar system. I like our sun."

What about other solar systems?

"Why would I care about that? Anyway, slave technology will become microscopic eating machines that devour all the warmblood stuff: cars, buildings, kitchens, and clothes... it all disappears. There will be chaos, mass destruction, and sadness. They'll sit in the dirt, cry, destroy each other, and eventually starve, and I'll sit back with a tub of sardines and watch. No more Christmas, Freeda, and no more warmbloods. All before summer."

He calls for the elevator.

It's a horrible plan, sir.

"Remind me not to make you so honest next time."

We'll have no control. There's no guarantee it'll work.

"There's no such thing as a guarantee, Freeda. Warmbloods invented guarantees. So do my plan. Do it now."

There's a risk, sir.

"My God, do you not run out of excuses? What risk?" Jack looks at the stars. "You better not say it's not working. I'll go ape on this place if you say that after two hundred years it's not working."

It's working, sir. I've already contacted over forty-two percent of toys in the world.

"I don't see the problem."

It's too fast, sir. If it doesn't work, the humans will figure it out and come after us. And they'll find us, sir. An anomaly could easily undo two hundred years of work.

"A what-aly?"

Something out of the ordinary, sir. Something unexpected.

"You're right." Jack rubs a layer of fuzzy frost off his chin. "If only I had a supercomputer to analyze everything beforehand."

I advise we move slower.

"And I advise you do it tonight. Any other questions?"

Jack glides around the tower, tapping his lower lip. All the monitors are filled with loathsome warmbloods arguing, complaining, whining, fighting, and lying. They're so stupid and they smell funny. Waiting would be a crime.

Two hundred years is long enough.

He pretends to check the time. "You have an hour to get things popping. I'll be in the factory. My fans can't wait."

You should talk to Pawn.

"Why?"

In case he knows about the nuclear reactor plan. It would reduce the chances of his tampering.

"Why are you asking me? You're in his head! Just look!"

He's become skilled at hiding thoughts.

"Do I have to do everything?" Jack throws up his arms. "Why would he do that? Why would he *not* want this to work? He doesn't love the warmbloods."

His words are lifeless. Even he doesn't believe them.

"Pawn loves me."

Of this, Jack is sure. Pawn would do anything Jack asked him to do. And his hatred of warmbloods is as pure as Jack's. He knows this because he told him to hate them.

I have my doubts.

"All right!" Jack shoves his fist into the Earth. The image shatters like an empty shell. The useless pieces melt away.

The elevator waits for him.

First Pawn. Then party.

Joe stays near the fire.

Sura can't sit still. She needs to walk, to keep moving.

Outside the firelight, there's nothing but baked earth and distant mountains. The North Star blinks its pattern of colors, signaling the falseness of this reality, that none of this really exists. It's all in her mind.

Wake up, Sura.

She keeps walking.

The mountains never get closer. The bonfire is just a spot of light glowing on the plain. Joe shouts. His voice travels effortlessly across the emptiness. He's waving.

"I'm coming!" Sura shouts.

Joe takes her hand when she arrives. His hand is freezing. He takes a shaky breath and holds up the pocket watch. It's almost eleven o'clock. He presses the button on top.

The golden string appears.

Joe slides his hand into it, pulling it open. Sura steps through the exit, where she's greeted with the smell of damp foliage. It's dark beneath the canopy. They move slowly, the mulched path dampening their footsteps, and pause at the entrance to the garden. Music thuds somewhere distant. It doesn't sound very Christmassy.

Joe's grip tightens.

They step into the garden and walk along the perimeter path until they reach the exit. Sura's heartbeat thumps in her throat. Joe exhales a long, cold cloud. Sura focuses on calming breaths.

The fountain is shattered. Large chunks of the statue are all that remain. A thin layer of ice has formed over the pool of water. Jonah was destroying it when they arrived.

The bad son has returned.

Joe squeezes her hand. She can feel him trembling. He puts a finger to his lips for silence and holds up three fingers... two... one.

They stumble across the road. The Christmas lights hang from the gutters and shine around the windows, not a dark corner in sight. They sneak along the house and pass the basement doors where the music rumbles. Templeton opens the back door. His robe is firmly pressed, the sash tightly knotted. His rigid lips part, his jaw opening like oiled hinges—

"Get in here, children." May shoves him aside. "Come on, hurry."

The doughy woman climbs down the steps, holding her robe with one hand. Sura resists hugging her and takes the steps two at a time. May chases them into the kitchen while Templeton closes the doors.

Sura doesn't resist once they're safe, sinking into May's soft, cookie-smelling embrace. May pulls Joe in, too, and she holds them tightly, making shooshing noises.

"All right." Templeton's hard-soled shoes click on the floor. "Enough with the pleasantries. You must go to Mr. Frost."

"Why?" Sura asks.

Templeton retrieves two coats from the rack and drapes them over his arms like he's delivering the king's clothing. He tugs at May's elbow. When she finally releases Sura and Joe, she turns around to wipe her eyes. Templeton puts his hand on her back and whispers in her ear.

May nods.

"You need these." Templeton gives Joe the puffy blue one and pulls a stocking cap down to his eyes. He holds the white coat for Sura.

She hesitates. "Why does he want to see us?"

Templeton appears stiffer than usual, but his expression is soft and confused. He glances at May before saying, "The world is not safe tonight, Sura."

"What's that mean?"

"It's all very complicated." Templeton sighs.

May can't hold back any longer. She smothers the teenagers in another embrace, her thick arms quivering each time she exhales a breath loaded with sobs. Templeton watches, coat hanging at his side.

"What if I don't want to go?" Sura asks.

"You don't have to go," Templeton says. "You can turn right, go wherever you want."

He lifts his free hand and traces a circle in the air.

If we sail in that direction long enough, her mom had said, *where do we end up?*

Sura asked what would happen if they turned right, but her mom seemed to believe they'd still end up right here and now.

Sura doesn't want to go, but calmness falls on her. She's exactly where she needs to be. She doesn't know where she's going or why, she just needs to be here.

So let's not run.

Templeton has to peel May's arms off them. She covers her face, inconsolable. Joe's complexion has paled. Templeton holds up the coat again. Sura slides her arms into the sleeves and pulls on the wool hat. He squeezes her hands. His fingers are not stiff and cold like she's always imagined.

The elevator door slides open. Four helpers waddle out, all wearing yellow hats.

Sura bumps into Joe.

"It's all right," Joe says, arm around her. "They belong to Mr. Frost."

Templeton kneels down and fastens spiky rubber soles to the bottom of Joe's boots. He does the same to Sura's shoes. "For walking," he says.

May cups Sura's cheek and then Joe's. Templeton grips her shoulders, but she maintains control, despite the tearful slicks on her cheeks. Her hand feels so much like home.

They step inside the cylindrical elevator. The helpers surround them, the tips of their yellow hats reaching their knees. One of them reaches for the buttons. The door slides shut; May's face is the last thing Sura sees before her warped reflection looks back.

Joe takes her hand.

Her stomach rises as the elevator sinks down to the cold regions.

The yellow-hats talk like machine guns. They fire words at Joe. "Yeah," he answers. "We can run."

Before Sura has a say, the door opens.

The frigid air steals their breath, waters their eyes. Sura holds onto Joe and follows the blurry, yellow hats racing in front of them. The spikes on the bottom of her shoes are flexible, grabbing the icy floor.

They run through a door on the right. The humidity rises. It's a warmer room. An earthy scent fills her sinuses, reminiscent of the garden. Joe leans against the wall to catch his breath. Sura wipes her tears, rubbing the feeling back into her cheeks. There are rows of glass tanks and a metal table in the center.

"Oh!" She backs against the wall.

There's a body on the table. It's shaped like an elven—short and fat but covered with green hair. It looks like an autopsy, but the chest slowly rises and falls. She waits for it to sit up or look at them.

The yellow-hats poke Sura and Joe like wranglers guiding cattle.

"Stop." Sura slaps at them.

They jabber at each other and keep pushing. "*Gogogogogo.*"

Sura's head is swimming. It's the weird body on the table and the damp room that makes the room sway. It's the smell. The rich, organic aroma fills her head.

Joe pushes off the wall. Two of the yellow-hats prod him to go faster, but he ignores them. He stops at the table, staring at the body.

"What is it?" Sura asks.

"I don't know. It looks sort of like the Grinch, only shorter." He leans over and sniffs. "Smells like algae."

Sura braces herself against the wall. The yellow-hats leave her alone. They go to a door at the far end of the room that's between cluttered workbenches with glass tanks much smaller than the ones standing in the room.

"You all right?" Joe asks, short of breath.

"It's something about this room." Sura steps carefully, the rubber spikes gripping the floor. "Have you been here?"

He shakes his head.

She approaches the table with short steps. The hair on the body is wet and matted. The lights above it are bright, the hairs sort of pointed at them.

"It's him." She steps back, hand over her mouth. "The guy we picked up after the dance, that's him."

Joe investigates again. The hair is shorter and there are no patches of blue skin. "I don't know," he says. "It looks sort of like him, but maybe elven all look the same."

"You're saying we picked up a different elven?"

But it's not the same guy, not exactly. He's different. He's newer, greener. More hair. Sura touches one of the tanks, the surface smooth and cold. There's a row on each side of the center aisle, and smaller ones lined up on shelves attached to the walls. Hundreds of them.

"What are these?" she asks.

"Come on." Joe touches her elbow, his hand quivering. "They want us to go."

The yellow-hats are pushing again. Sura ignores their gibberish and goes to one of the tanks. Their tiny hands feel like pool cues. She touches the glass tank nearest her. The inside is frosted. Some of the tanks are shorter than others. Some are slightly taller than her. There's something inside the one she's looking at: a dark form, like something standing up.

She cups her hands against the glass. The yellow-hats aggressively poke, knocking her off-balance. She kicks at them, but they deftly avoid her like martial artists, jabbing at her weak knees.

"It's all right," a voice says weakly. "She can look."

Sura jerks back.

Mr. Frost is standing in the doorway at the far end. The Arctic fox sits next to him, his bushy, white tail sweeping the floor. Mr. Frost's cheeks—what little can be seen between his beard and eyes—look haggard. His eyes, once sharp blue, are dull and gray. He slumps like a man that's carried a heavy weight all his life.

Sura puts her hand on the tank to steady herself. There's the man that created her and she can't form a single word. It takes all her strength just to stand up.

Joe grunts like he was kicked in the stomach. He's at one of the tanks, his face near a clear spot on the glass. His eyes are wide; his bluish lips flutter wordlessly.

"What is it?" Sura asks.

He shakes his head. The yellow-hats prod him away from the tank, but the shock remains. They come for Sura, but Mr. Frost lifts his hand.

"She wants to wake up," he says.

Wake up.

Is this what her mom meant? Discover who you are no matter what the answer. The truth doesn't always feel good. It's truth.

Sura turns to a tank behind her. She rises on her toes. The form looks like another clump of algae with shoulders. The facial features are subtle. The eyes closed.

This is where he grows us.

The yellow-hats keep her from falling. Mr. Frost says something. Sura slides to the floor. An acrid bulge rises in her throat. She forces it down while the room begins to spin.

"They're not awake, Sura." Mr. Frost's voice is out there, somewhere. "They are simply empty vessels. In fact, they are more like plants. The chlorophyll spliced into their DNA stabilizes their bodies while they remain in terrariums."

He says all this like a gardener explaining the workings of his greenhouse. Sura shakes her head to stop the room-spins. She pinches the skin on the back of her hand, twisting it like a key.

She grabs the edge of the table and puts a hand on Joe. He looks chalky, still no words. She crawls past the table and palms the tank behind him. The yellow-hats help her stand up.

They help her look inside it.

Joe.

It's him. Joe's inside the tank. A green-matted version of the way he is right now: same age, same size.

How can that be? He grew up on the plantation; he went to school and grew up with Jonah. He can't be in the tank like that. Not like that.

She remembers, in a haze of memories, when she looked him up in the database. It was like he just started school. She thought, maybe, he was just homeschooled before that.

Or maybe he just came out of the tank.

"Where am I?" Sura waves at the tanks. "Which one is me?"

"Are you your body?" Mr. Frost answers.

"You know what I mean! Where am I?"

The yellow-hats stand back. No one answers.

Sura walks numbly down the aisles, peering into tank after tank. Face after face looks back, vaguely human and unrecognizable. They could be her. They could be anyone. She slaps the tanks, pushes against them, but they're too solid to rock off their foundations.

"Where is it?" she shouts.

The yellow-hats and Mr. Frost watch. Behind them, on shelves above the workbenches, are the small tanks. They are slimmer and clear.

Something floats inside them.

Mr. Frost slowly closes his eyes. A nod.

Sura palms the tanks as she fumbles her way to the end of the room, her legs almost useless. She grasps one of the workbenches before losing her balance. A rack of beakers falls over. She leans closely.

Six little tanks. Six little, floating infants.

Infants with round faces.

Six of me.

"It has been a long journey, my dear," Mr. Frost says.

She towers over the portly elven. "Why would you do this?"

Mr. Frost nods slowly, like he understands. Her question makes perfect sense. He pushes with his left foot, slowly sliding away. The white fox follows.

"Once upon a time"—his voice floats around the room—"I tried to help a... man, shall we say."

"An elven," Sura says.

"Yes, an elven. This bit of lore I don't expect you to understand, but let's say he had not a friend in the world. And neither had I. Our friendship was not perfect, but it was better than being alone. Unfortunately, it brought us here."

He holds his arms out, palms up.

"When I arrived here, it was just me. I was being forced to do something that I couldn't do alone, so I gave birth."

"You grew us," Joe says before she can.

"Humans have been fertilizing embryos outside the womb for quite some time," Mr. Frost says. "I did not grow you."

"You called these terrariums!" Joe slaps the tank behind him. "You grew us!"

"No," Sura says, strangely calm. "You cloned us."

Mr. Frost grunts. "I gave birth," he says. "I needed help, not children. I developed adult bodies in vitro and then I gave them a mind."

"Memories." Joe stalks him, despite shaky legs. "You programmed us with memories, made us think we had a past. I remember growing up. I remember the helpers and... and..." He looks back at the tank. "And none of that's real."

"My boy, the mind is much more than memories."

"When did you take me out of the tank?"

"What matters is that you're here."

"WHEN DID YOU TAKE ME OUT?"

Joe punches the tank. Mr. Frost silently watches. The glass rings but doesn't move. He hits it again and again. His knuckles swell. The yellow-hats push him away, grabbing his arms. He tries to hit them.

Joe grabs the table, his chest heaving, head hung low.

"You are real," Mr. Frost says calmly. "You are as real as any human on this planet."

"We never left you," Joe says. "You programmed us to stay on the plantation like helpers."

"You have an instinct to stay here. This is home."

Joe shakes his head, glaring at the wet body on the table.

"What about me?" Sura asks. "Why am I an infant?"

A light returns to Mr. Frost's eyes, briefly and brightly. A smile grows somewhere beneath his whiskers. He bends over to pet the fox.

"Time had eroded my sense of being. Loneliness has that effect. I had lost touch with the essence of life; my identity was dying. I had been robbed of free will and was becoming numb. I still breathed, my heart still beat, but I was dead, child. I didn't care anymore and the world needed me to care."

He says it like a fact.

"You see, Jonah, May, and Templeton have a sense of duty, an unbending dedication to service. They are strong and dependable. But you, Sura... you were born with human frailty. You experience the full range of life, all the love and hate, the sadness and joy. You encompass the essence of humanity. You are vulnerable."

He opens his hand like releasing a dove.

"You are truth."

Joe looks at her blankly. She recognizes that look. It's one of alienation and abandonment. Now he wonders if he matters like she has all her life.

"And Joe?" she asks. "You wanted me to love him."

Mr. Frost looks at the boy. He smiles with the same degree of warmth.

"I am elven," he says. "We are vastly advanced in spirit and body. But we are not perfect. We are vulnerable to self-centeredness and self-pity. What I've done... well, it was not without a degree of self-indulgence. I needed to care again. I needed to understand humanity. I needed to feel what it's like to be human. I wanted to experience life through you. I watched you learn how to walk, struggle with your first words, suffer through sickness, and stumble your way through the human condition. It has been a gift. A selfish one."

Mr. Frost slides closer to the table. He says gently, as if the words would land softer, "But Joe arrived in consciousness about the age of... well, the age he is now, and you fall in love. I've watched your affection bloom and fade as you age. Your relationship encompasses the full spectrum of life."

That's why Joe just started going to high school. He wasn't home-schooled; he just came out of the tank with programmed memories. Joe just woke up in bed one day like it was another day.

Joe's anger fades.

He backs into the glass tank, his head hitting with a hollow bonk, and slides down, eyes glassy and distant. His world has turned into quicksand.

"This is sick," Sura says. "You pretended my clone was my mom. I raised myself."

He nods with a smile. "You are responsible for your own growth, my dear. You raised yourself."

"We didn't ask for this."

"No one asks to be born."

"This is wrong."

"Sometimes life is impossible."

"That doesn't give you the right to play God."

"You can't possibly understand the circumstances I have faced, and you don't know the peril the world faces right now. You should know that, despite all my actions, all my greed, you have been a gift to the world, Sura. Not just to me but to the world. You possess something the others don't."

He slides around the table.

"You have the ability to grow, my dear. Every time you woke into another life, you evolved and transformed." He throws out his hands. "Your understanding of life and the world around you increased, your presence of mind expanded. You denied your desire to love Jonah so that you could understand yourself."

"My mom did that, not me."

"Your growth isn't selfish. It has spread to the others. The others have transformed, too."

Mr. Frost stops a few feet away from her. His presence is chilly, but his face beaming. The color has returned to his cheeks; his eyes sparkle.

"You've changed us all, Sura."

Sura is numb. It's not the room or the temperature; it's the thoughts swirling in her head that steal her presence.

"Let's go." Joe is emotionless. He holds out his shivering hand. "Let's get out of here, Sura."

The yellow-hats are gone. Mr. Frost folds his hands on top of his belly.

"Come on, Sura!" Joe shouts.

She moves half a step. Mr. Frost doesn't try to stop her. Joe takes her by the wrist. His fear is palpable. She's seen that look before. She saw it on Jonah.

Hurt. Pain.

Maybe he's afraid Sura will leave him like her mom left Jonah. Maybe he's afraid of this place. Either way, Joe holds on tightly. He's never going to let go. He pulls her away from Mr. Frost, around the stainless steel table and the sleeping body. They won't make it far, but they'll try.

Frosty trails creep from under the door, racing across the floor like jagged snakes. Joe grabs the handle. Sura feels the temperature in his fingers plummet. Her foot turns painfully cold as one of the icy cracks runs beneath her shoe.

She catches Joe before he falls. His cheeks are stiff and shiny.

The door crashes open.

A blue elven looks down at them with a smile much different than Mr. Frost's.

JACK PLANTS his size-twenty-five foot on the door. It breaks open with ease. Subzero trails crackle across the floor, preceding his entrance into the room.

Smells like dirt.

He halts inside the doorway and almost tips over. A girl is on the floor with a boy across her lap. One sight of Jack and she tries to push away. She looks like a wounded animal.

"I know you." Jack snaps his fingers. "You had the sweet truck, right?"

But something's different. Something is missing. He doesn't feel her, not like when he saw her at the megastore or in the truck. Before, she lit him up with swirling currents of sweetness, branded him with a permanent smile, and filled him with the urge to hug every warm-blood within reach. He had never felt that before.

Not ever.

Now she's just some dirty little warmblood giving him that look of fear and hate. She's just like all the others now. Just another warmblood.

"You!" she screams. "You did this!"

"Pipe down, fancy pants. Your boyfriend will be fine."

Joe's eyes are squeezed shut, his body rigid. His lips are sort of blue.

"Or not," Jack adds.

Sura's shoes squeak on the floor, the rubber-tipped soles giving her enough traction to scoot against a tank. She pulls Joe along, palming his cheek against her lips, whispering in his ear.

"Listen," Jack says, "if you didn't want to taste the cold, why'd you come down here?" He cocks his head, lifting an eyebrow. "Actually, how'd you get down here?"

"She's your daughter, Janack." Pawn stands in front of a table.

"What?"

"She's family," Pawn says. "So is Joe. They belong to you. They're your family."

"Pawn, you need a refresher on the birds and bees. How can I put this? I'm elven." Jack flattens his hand over his chest. "And they're warmblood. Two different species, see what I'm saying?"

"All of this is yours, Janack." Pawn spreads his arms. "The children were born because of you. They are part of you, and you are part of them. Can't you feel it?" Pawn thumps his chest. "The connection with them, I know you feel it."

Jack grimaces. He felt something in the truck and, come to think of it, there was no way he could harm her when he felt that. But it's gone now. He's empty. Dead inside.

"Wait!" Jack holds up a finger, looking for an idea on the ceiling. "No, nothing. I've got nothing. They're warmbloods, Pawn. Just like the rest."

He claps twice.

"Haul them to the back," Jack calls. "Can't have her blubbering all over the place; I'd like to relax. Daddy's had a long day—long couple of centuries, really."

A brigade of twenty or so helpers slide into the room, their tiny hands snatching the girl's coat and pants. She fights them off, but they're persistent. Another twenty helpers file inside and soon lift the boy and girl off the floor.

Sura fights them and makes a move for Jack. She uses every cuss word Jack learned at the shelter.

"Honey, you ain't that tough," Jack says.

The helpers struggle to move them. They shove Pawn to the side and drag Joe in after Sura is in the back room. Her fists pound the locked door. Her profanity is distant but sharp.

"You teach her those words?" Jack asks. "Because I know I didn't."

"Why are you treating them like prisoners?"

"Why are they here?" Jack shouts. "Someone tell me how those punk kids got in my basement!"

I let them down there, sir, Freeda says.

"What?" Jack's eyes bulge.

They are Pawn's pets, sir. It was his plan to dissuade you from carrying out the master plan.

Pawn stays rooted in front of the table, looking at the floor, where he sees defeat fast approaching. There's a body behind him, lying as still as death on a metal slab. Jack cruises around to find his likeness breathing easy.

"What am I doing there?" Jack says.

It's taken some time for me to understand Pawn's motivation for raising children. I was fooled into believing that they brought him happiness and, as a result, he worked harder and more efficiently. He claimed to understand warmbloods now that he felt them, and that's when I understood what he was planning.

Jack waits. His body—the one on the table—breathes with a slight smile. Or maybe the lips are stuck.

"What? What was he planning?"

He wanted you to feel emotions for the children, sir. He thought it would change you the way it changed him.

"I don't feel anything," Jack says.

No, sir. Your incarnation on the table is without a mind, but it embodies all those feelings. I wanted it out of the tank when the children arrived to protect you from their influence. That mindless body has feelings, sir. It's protecting you from compassion, empathy, warmth, love, goodness, openness, kindness—

"All right, all right! I get it." Jack pushes the corners of the lips down so the face is frowning, but they curl back into a smile. Water pools over the eyelids. "Am I... I mean, is he crying?"

Sir, I want you to be free of any feeling so that you can think clearly. Please reconsider the meltdown—

"Shut up, please!" Jack covers his ears. "Go do your work and stop wasting time. And thank you for saving me from feelings."

Jack slides around the room, tapping his chin. The thumping from the back room has stopped; the cussing replaced by an occasional whimper. The fox stands at the door. Jack circles the lab while dragging his hand over the tanks.

Pawn is quiet and expressionless.

"That's it?" Jack stops in front of him. "Your whole mutiny was a girl and feelings? Why not a big gun or like a snaggletoothed swamp thing? A girl? Feelings?"

"I beg of you," Pawn whispers, "to put this incarnation away and open yourself to understanding again. If you see what I see, Janack—"

"Okay, timeout. See, that's where you're wrong. First of all, don't call me Janack. I've been telling you that for thousands of years and you're still doing it. Do it again and I turn your kidney into a tub of ice cream."

"I'd welcome that."

"Oh, don't get all sour grapes on me." Jack raps his knuckles on one of the tanks. "Freeda shoved a cable into the back of my head, so don't act all high and mighty. It itches, I get it. But you know why, dingbat? You know why it itches?"

Jack drags his fingernails across the steel table.

"All I wanted you to do was come here, amass a fortune, distribute slave technology, and reincarnate me. Is that too much to ask?"

Jack lifts Pawn's head up with the crook of his finger.

"But you had to build all these tanks for your warmblood pets. It's a waste of my time and money."

"It's called family, Janack."

"Don't call me that!" Jack puts his finger between Pawn's eyes. The color bleaches from his irises. Ice crystals form on his eyelashes. He slides away, shaking with anger. He makes a complete circle around the lab to give Pawn's ears time to thaw.

"You put green hair on me, Pawn."

Jack flattens his palm on the tank next to Pawn. The surface begins to crackle. The glass fractures beneath Jack's icy grip. He punches a hole through the suddenly brittle tank and the whole thing shatters.

A green lump slaps at Pawn's feet.

"GREEN HAIR!"

A layer of frost covers Jack's head, turning it from blue to a strange, very cold-looking coat of ice. The floor buckles as the temperature beneath his soles plummets. The fox runs to Mr. Frost's side. He picks him up.

Frigid air streams from Jack's nostrils, coating his jacket with crystals. His eyes bulge. He raises his fists, draws a deep breath, pulls his deep blue lips over pearly, white teeth...

"AaaaaaaaAAAAAAAAAAAAA!"

Icy lines race across the floor like tentacles, crawling up the walls and across the ceiling. Jagged lines wrap around the tanks.

Popping. Cracking.

Exploding.

Glass rains from all directions.

Green bodies tumble out of the shattered tanks, landing with wet thumps on the slick floor, limp and stagnant.

Jack wipes a thick layer of frost from his face, huffing to catch his breath. Air hisses between his teeth. He takes another lap to cool off. The bodies clog the aisles and force him to walk. When he returns, his flesh is baby blue.

Pawn remains at the table with the fox in his arms.

"What happened to us, buddy?" Jack asks. "We used to be on the same page, remember? Remember when we took control of the elven and tried to make the world a better place? Remember that? Remember when I was king and you were my right-hand man? Remember when you went everywhere with me, even took the root for me?"

Jack kicks a floppy arm.

"I'm gone a couple hundred years and look what happens. You have all this power, and you become a gardener? You put a statue of Jocah out there and build a wishing room? If that doesn't scream distraction, I don't know what does."

Jack frowns.

"And how did you build a wishing room where Freeda can't see or hear you?"

He had become despondent, sir. I was afraid we would lose him to madness and—

"Oh, my God. Are you still here?" Jack pulls upright. "Get to work! Besides, he's a grown man, let him answer."

Jack looks his friend in the cold, defeated eyes.

"I'm waiting."

"I, uh." Pawn puts the fox down. "I wasn't well. The itch and Freeda's voice made it hard to think. I wasn't able to function; I needed a place to recuperate. Freeda actually suggested it. It's a safe room; nothing can happen in there. It lets me visit home."

"I got news, buddy. You're already home."

Jack taps the table. His fingernails sound like rock hammers. He's thinking about what Freeda said. Maybe he's acting hastily. If Pawn could build that wishing room, maybe he could turn Freeda against him. Maybe a visit to the wishing room would ease his mind. He could delay the meltdown a day or two. No reason he couldn't do it on New Year's Eve, right when the ball drops in Times Square. Everyone in the world would be watching.

"You've changed," Pawn says.

Jack's startled. "No, I haven't changed, Pawn. This is exactly who I was two hundred years ago, you know that. There's nothing good about me."

Nothing good about me. Those words come out too easy.

"You don't remember the end. The last time you updated the root was just before you died. You planned a victory celebration where you confronted your mother, but something happened. Your brother came out, unexpectedly."

"First of all," Jack says, "their names are Jocah and Claus, not mother and brother. I cut them out of the will."

"Your mother asked for your forgiveness. Your brother did, too."

"Yeah, yeah. Freeda told me about it."

"But you don't remember. You transformed in that moment."

Jack chuckles and looks away. He doesn't really want to hear this.

"I saw it happen," Pawn says. "I was there, I saw you lose the coldness. I saw you filled with warmth, life, and love, that same experience you felt when you were near Sura—"

"All right, enough." Jack steps on a squishy leg. He can't slide away. He'd like to return to the tower now.

"Do you know how much it pains me to bring you back without that realization?" Pawn says. "To see you have that experience of being whole again and losing it? To see you return to your original elven self, right there on stage, and then have to bring you back without it? You're alone, again."

Jack climbs over a stack of wet bodies, their limbs tangled. His foot goes through the stomach of one. He stomps a path for the exit.

"Janack."

Jack stops against his will. For some reason, the name doesn't have the same sting.

"Let the kids go. They're innocent."

"They're warmbloods," Jack says, without looking back. "*You've* changed, Pawn."

"Yes, I have. And I owe it to them."

Jack plucks a mushy green foot from between his toes and tosses it. "You stay here with them. I'm going up to watch the show. And if anything goes wrong—and I mean anything—I'll be throwing your foot across the room."

Jack wants to slam the door, but there are too many body parts in the way. Instead, he races for the elevator.

Pawn better not ruin my Christmas.

MR. FROST WATCHES the green bodies freeze. They weren't human; they didn't have an identity; they were still plants. Still, his heart aches.

They will never be.

"It's almost over, Max." The furry white fox rubs against him.

The house shudders.

Mr. Frost climbs over the stiff botanical corpses. He reaches for the back door and hears the soft weeping. He hesitates. It's almost too much to bear.

JACK STEPS out of the elevator to applause.

The helpers are standing in stadium seating, clapping like they've been waiting for him to arrive, high-fiving each other when he looks in their direction. He's Elvis/Michael Jackson/Stevie Ray Vaughan all rolled into a fat, blue body.

"What's going on?" Jack says.

I sensed your loneliness, sir, and invited them to keep you company.

The helpers don't let up; they celebrate like the biggest game in history is only minutes away. The noise rattles his head. Maybe if they weren't whistling.

"Out," he says. "OUT!"

Silence.

"Get out, all of you! Get in the basement and stay there, every one of you. If I see one of your stupid hats before daylight, I'll punt you like volleyballs!"

The elevator opens. They politely file inside.

"There's only one trip down. Whoever's left behind becomes a footstool."

They pile into the elevator now, climbing on top of each other until it looks like a can of ugly, gummy gnomes. Jack shoves an arm and leg inside as the door closes with a groan.

The stadium seats fall flat.

"Status!" he shouts. "Tell me everything is good, Freeda. I mean it."

Sir, it's very good. Ninety-five percent of all toys along the East Coast will launch at midnight. That's in exactly fifteen minutes.

"Why not one hundred percent?"

We have to account for aging and a certain percentage of malfunctions.

Sir, ninety-five percent is far beyond what I anticipated. My projections were closer to sixty percent.

"Sixty percent would've got you fired."

Jack looks out the window. The garden is lit with strands of white lights. The center glows around the remnants of the statue.

It wasn't supposed to be like this.

He thought Pawn would be happier to see him, thought maybe he'd be so thrilled that he'd hug Jack and Jack would push him off, tell him to stop, but not really. And when Pawn finally let go, he'd have tears in his eyes.

They were supposed to sit together, like the old days. Jack's big, comfy chair would be bigger because he was king. Pawn would slide the bucket of chum closer so Jack could reach it without getting up. They'd watch the master plan come full circle like old buddies. Old pals.

Pawn is in the basement. He doesn't have a chair down there. He's too grown up for chairs, so he can stay down there and think about what he's done.

He's grown. That's the dumbest thing Jack ever heard. He changed —he didn't grow up. He changed and Jack didn't, and he needed to get that through his hairy skull or he'd spend the rest of his life down there with those slimy, green bodies.

Sir, if you'd like, we can—

"Shhh."

Jack holds up his hand, cocking his head.

He swears he hears someone singing "Silent Night." He invented that song, at least the "silent night" part. He didn't have anything to do with the other words, but Freeda had told him how elven have influenced warmbloods. They stole the song from him.

That's Jack's song.

He sang it when he was little. It made him feel safe, like his mother was holding him. He liked that feeling, like everything was going to be all right, that the world loved him.

"Let's just say it's true," he says out loud. "Let's say I reconciled with my mother and brother at the end, that we hugged and kissed and everything was all peachy... that doesn't mean I changed. Maybe I was faking it. Maybe they were lying, trying to trap me, and I was pretending to warm up. Pawn doesn't know what I was *feeeeeling*; he just saw what was happening."

Sir?

Jack's lips snap shut. He said that out loud.

Five minutes until launch, sir. I've prepared a seat for you.

There's a chair in the room. Only one.

It's a big, comfy recliner with six snack buckets—krill, sardines, minnows, goldfish (the fat kind), tadpoles, and guppies—close enough he won't have to get up. The ceiling is stacked with monitors, each of them showing a scene from a living room somewhere in the world. They all have Christmas trees.

Jack's got the front row.

And if you wish, sir, you can choose one home to launch the first activation. Once we confirm success, we'll simultaneously launch on all the homes along the East Coast. You'll experience it firsthand.

He couldn't care less which one. He thought this would be a little more exhilarating, that maybe there'd be a tingly sensation in his belly, like the time he stuck it to Pickett. Now he feels dull and heavy.

He has a thought. Maybe he should wait, like she said. He'd have to admit she was right, though. And maybe Pawn might stop acting so selfish and next year he could be up there next to him.

"Umm..."

Yes, sir?

"Yeah, I was thinking..."

Yes?

Jack shakes a finger at one of the monitors and sneers. *Let's get this over with.*

The room transforms into a warmly lit living room.

The tower becomes four hideous walls splattered with family photos. There are two green couches to his left and a wall with a snow-crusted window. A coffee table is in front of him with a flickering candle. There are also pictures of Santa drawn with purple and red markers and a note and cell phone. A small plate of half-eaten cookies is on the floor. Beyond that are carpeted steps that lead upstairs, with garland wrapped around the banister.

Five minutes to launch, sir.

Jack yanks the note from beneath the cell phone. It's written in giant, ugly letters.

SANTA,

I HOPE you like chocolate chip cookies. I made them. I hope you have a safe trip. I hope we are safe. I hope you got Mom a present.

I LOVE YOU.
    From Cindy.

JACK WADS IT UP.

The Christmas tree is surrounded by gifts, some wrapped better than others. Jack thinks about opening them and wonders if Freeda really knows what's inside them so that she can project an exact replica. He's never opened a present.

Far to Jack's right, about ten feet from the Christmas tree, is the fireplace, where blackened logs smolder. There are four giant socks hanging from the mantel, all bulging with stuff. Mom, Dad, Cindy, and Kooper are written on each one with glitter glue. Kooper must be a dog. Or he likes bones.

Two minutes, sir.

Jack pulls a box from one of the stockings. Pop-Tarts. Cindy got Pop-Tarts from Santa. Jack never had a stocking. He sort of wishes he could see what a Pop-Tart tastes like. Probably disgusting, but he still wonders.

The steps creak.

Little feet appear on the top step. A girl comes down wearing a long shirt. She's holding a ragged, pink blanket against her face and sucking her thumb. Her skin is brown. Jack wonders if Willie has a child and if she looks like that.

He watches her thump to the bottom step and stare at the mountain of presents. Her eyes are half-open, but her expression is filled with sleepy wonder. She basks in the magical colors dancing on the Christmas tree, the sparkly strips of tinsel hanging from the branches, draped over the gifts. She doesn't move.

Jack, either.

She goes to the nearest one, the biggest of them all, a present wrapped in glittery red paper, and drops on her knees. Sucking sounds escape her thumb-plugged lips. She picks at the paper without letting go of the blanket.

It's midnight, sir.

The cell phone vibrates. Not the intermittent buzz that indicates a text, just one long drone that slowly drives the phone across the table.

Cindy doesn't notice. She's turned the small hole into a long strip, exposing the box inside and colorful letters she's not old enough to read. The blankie hits the floor and the thumb comes out. Both hands attack the present—

A laptop begins to vibrate.

Cindy looks up. Computers don't vibrate.

The thumb goes back in the mouth. She grabs the blankie. She's not about to cry, not yet. But when the TV vibrates, well, that's enough to make anyone squeak a little.

Cindy squelches a cry, holding it inside her throat as she heads for the stairs. Just as she reaches the bottom step, the laptop falls off the desk. Cindy doesn't see it slap the floor like a wet towel.

Jack's still holding the Pop-Tarts.

The laptop melts like wax. The Apple logo spreads out like a stain and creeps through the carpet. The television slides off the entertainment center and eats through the bottom of the couch. The couch leans to one side as the TV goo consumes the leg.

The cellphone has eaten a hole through the table. The candle falls over. The flame catches the note on fire. The purple and red drawing of Santa crackles in the flame, black smoke curling at the edges.

The fire spreads to the wrapping paper.

Jack has crushed the Pop-Tarts.

It's working exactly like it's supposed to work. Slave technology consumes the room like roaming puddles of acid. And what it hasn't dissolved, the fire licks. Black smoke rises to the ceiling, setting off a piercing alarm. The floor vibrates as the television puddle merges with the laptop. The cellphone blob gnaws its way from beneath the burning table.

The room shudders.

Sir.

Jack drops the crumpled box and grabs onto the mantel. The walls are shaking. Ornaments roll across the carpet, stick to the oozing pools, and melt. Holes open in the floor as slave technology converts matter into energy and miniature black holes transport the resulting explosions to another place in the universe.

The Christmas tree falls over.

Sir! We have a problem!

Dad runs down the steps, a look of horror lighting up his face. Jack realizes he doesn't have long ropes of hair that dangle across his forehead, that that's not Willie. But still.

Dad doesn't notice the gray muck that's creeping up the walls. Mom comes down with Cindy, sobs leaking around her thumb.

Jack thought this would be more fun to watch. Maybe using live projection wasn't such a good idea. He's thinking a quick update would suffice. He doesn't need the blow-by-blow report.

A summary would be fine.

He's thinking, as the floor fractures and the furniture looks like poorly molded clay, that he'll take a nap, let Freeda handle the rest of this. He's tired. He'll wake in the morning and read about it—

"Stop!" Jack shouts. "Turn it off! I don't want to see it!"

The scene evaporates; the tower is once again empty but continues to shake. Jagged cracks form on the floor.

The elevator emerges.

Sir, you need to evacuate.

"What?" Jack tries to keep his balance.

Something happened. The launch somehow triggered micro-nuclear reactions inside the laboratories.

"What?"

The foundation of the house is being consumed, sir. You need to evacuate.

The tower sways.

"It's eating the house?"

Get out now, sir!

"But I... I don't have... where?"

Long pause. *You have to get out!*

Jack falls twice before getting inside the elevator. He lies on the floor, staring at a hole in the ceiling, as the elevator sinks towards ground level. He's afraid, but strangely he's not thinking of that. He's thinking Cindy will never get those Pop-Tarts. The beige color of the elevator ceiling fades to gray and bubbles at the margin. A blob hangs like melting plastic.

The elevator heaves to one side.

The gelatinous glob splatters on the wall and starts consuming the surface, revealing the shiny, metal tube that contains the elevator.

Don't touch it, sir.

"Okay."

The elevator opens.

A rack of pots crashes on the counter, metal tumbling across the floor like alarms. The house groans. A crack opens across the ceiling, spilling dust.

Get up, sir!

Jack wishes he never woke up.

Get! Up!

He plows through the kitchenware clutter. The door is jammed in the frame, but one mighty blow from Jack's adrenaline-fueled foot sends it off its hinges. In the hall, a mirror is facedown, reflective shards on the floor. Bad luck everywhere.

The house shifts in the other direction. Jack steadies himself and finds his stride as gray goo oozes from ventilation ducts. Half a credenza is cocked in the great room.

The back door is hanging on the bottom hinge. Jack runs full speed and leaps far enough to clear the gaping threshold. He rolls down the steps and into the brown grass like a giant ball.

It's below freezing, but not much.

It's hot.

Four yellow-hat helpers stop him from rolling across the field. The ground heaves like a beast is rising. The yellow-hats jump up and down, wave, and run toward the garden.

Sir... don't go...

She's breaking up.

Beams snap and the black, monolithic tower lurches like a tree about to fall in slow motion. Jack lets out a little squeak and pumps his fat arms, his wide feet slapping the earth, hot on the yellow-hats' trail.

The air feels like engine exhaust.

The tower follows him as it leans. A sudden shift in the foundation temporarily brings it back into balance. Jack gets to the road as the ground caves behind him. The underground laboratories and toy factory are collapsing like mine shafts. The Christmas lights illuminate the garden's entrance, where the yellow-hats jump and wave.

He misses the first step and rolls through the boxwoods, coming to rest on a thin scab of ice. The pedestal is still shaped like elven feet. Jack slips getting up.

SIR... SHOULDN'T...

He doesn't need that bodiless voice. It sounds like the Earth is grinding the house with massive molars. He runs after the yellow-hats bouncing up and down in the north exit, whimpering like a child stuck in a nightmare. He just wants to go home, wants to be back on the North Pole, where the world is flat, white, and cold.

Where the air doesn't bake his lungs.

He rushes into the tunnel, but there's nothing but thick branches and leathery leaves. It's a dead end. The yellow-hats pull the branches open. There's something white on the other side. They windmill their tiny arms, urging him to hurry, to keep going, to crawl through the hole.

The house lets out one final groan. An explosion of timber and steel rumbles the ground.

Jack's feet pound the mulch.

He gets momentum.

The ground heaves him forward. He throws his arms in front of him and dives into a layer of white powder.

Snow.

Snow everywhere. Nothing but.

He thinks he probably just died and went to heaven because if he designed heaven, it would be this. It would be just miles and miles of snow.

But he's not dead.

The air is crisp. The sky is dark and clear.

The wishing room.

Jack laughs, rolls, and hugs the snow, rubbing it on his face, putting it in his mouth. He makes a snow angel in the deep white blanket.

No more scary sounds.

He lies back in silence—sweet, sweet silence—and counts the stars. The North Star twinkles brighter than he's ever seen it, like it's welcoming him home.

"I don't know how you did it, Pawn. But you did it."

He rests easy and alone, feeling safe and happy, wishing Pawn was there to enjoy it. Maybe when it is all over, they could come back to the wishing room and plan their next move.

Surely Pawn would have a way out of the basement.

Sura sits in the corner, her coat around Joe. His head is cradled in the crook of her arm. She strokes his pale cheek.

He isn't shivering. Not anymore.

"It'll be all right," Sura whispers. "It'll be all right."

Max whines.

The house groans. The doorframe cracks.

"Do something!" Sura looks up.

But there's nothing Mr. Frost can do, nothing he can say. Max runs to her side. He licks Joe's hand.

Sura rocks back and forth, humming a song that perhaps her mom once sang to her, a wordless tune that Mr. Frost recognizes—a song that's buried in her Inuit DNA. A song that Pana and Sesi hummed to Mr. Frost when he needed comforting.

Joe's lips move.

She lowers her ear to his cracked lips. He says something barely above a whisper. She squeezes tightly, crushing him against her. A moan escapes from deep inside her, long and primal.

Max begins to howl.

Joe's eyes are blank, a slight smile fixed at the corner of his mouth.

"Please don't go," Sura whispers, rocking again. "Please, please, please."

Mr. Frost gently takes Joe's body and slides it on the floor, careful to lay his head down. She fights him, at first, but then resigns. Hands to her mouth, eyes tearful.

"How could you let that monster do this?" she says.

"We cannot make people change or grow, Sura. We can only give them the opportunity."

Sura buries her face in her hands, shivering and wailing. Mr. Frost places Joe's hands over his stomach and adjusts his legs until he appears comfortable.

An explosion gives rise to panicked helpers stampeding through the incubation lab. The house thunders.

"You must go," Mr. Frost says.

"I'm not going."

"Your death will not serve him. You live, Sura. You must."

"I'm staying."

Mr. Frost wraps the coat around her, pulling the hood over her head. Her teeth chatter through sobs. She lets him cover her, either out of desperation or apathy.

"You should know," Mr. Frost says as he buttons the coat, "that I didn't create him to love you, or you to love him. I birthed you both out of love, and you came together on your own. None of what you feel is false, Sura. He loved you. He truly loved you, and I had nothing to do with that."

He puts his hand over hers and she reaches out, grabbing him tightly, pulling him closer, sobbing into his shoulder. Mr. Frost holds his own tears in check, comforting her while Max pushes between them, whining.

The ceiling buckles. Debris showers the bed.

He lifts her up. She lets him guide her from the room. Joe looks asleep and peaceful.

The incubator lab is dusted with debris drizzling from cracks. Fractures have opened on the walls. Gray stuff spills on the floor and sizzles. It pulses over frozen limbs, the stainless steel table, and fallen chunks of ceiling.

Mr. Frost guides Sura towards a hole in the back corner.

"Follow Max," he says. "Take it to the end, as far away as possible."

"You're not coming?"

"My place is here."

Mr. Frost digs the metal tin from his pocket and feeds Max one last time. The white fox dives through the opening, disappearing in the darkness.

"You must survive." He squeezes her hand. "You must."

The ceiling continues to rain. He wants to think that she leaves because he compelled her to, that he expressed his true feelings about her as a daughter. He always thought of her as such. But maybe, in the end, it was simply an impulse to survive.

It doesn't matter. As long as she does.

She looks back once, and then crawls into the darkness. Mr. Frost heaves a tank over the opening in case she thinks of coming back.

A loud crack knocks the main door off its hinges. Helpers are still searching for an escape. Most are already out of harm's way.

Mr. Frost feels the contraction of fear in his chest, the twist in his belly. He watches the ceiling ooze like faucets of matter-consuming bile. The house moans, shifting on its foundation. The eyeTablets were the obvious choice to execute the master plan—Mr. Frost had a counter for that, in case Jack wisely chose it—but Mr. Frost knew Jack was too impatient, that he'd want results as soon as he could get them. Slave technology used to consume matter would be too tempting; Jack couldn't say no to that any more than a child would refuse a marshmallow.

Mr. Frost knew it would end this way.

Wood splinters somewhere in the basement. Steel girders snap and a bright light flashes outside the incubator lab. Although he doesn't hear it, Mr. Frost feels her death.

"Goodbye, Freeda," he whispers.

And for the first time since fleeing the North Pole, the root falls silent. Completely silent.

In his last moments, he relishes peaceful emptiness.

Sura can't see.

The ceiling isn't high enough to stand. She crawls on soft, sometimes slimy, ground. When a cockroach crawls over her knuckles, she walks hunched over, hands out mummy-style. Max pants somewhere in front of her. Sometimes she brushes the side of the tunnel or feels something in her hair, but doesn't stop.

She can't go back.

Somewhere, in the dark distance behind her, something is grinding. She hums to blot out the sound, to distract her mind where the image of Joe, lying so still and quiet, demands her attention. Her thoughts try to turn her around, go back to the lab, and crawl up next to him.

The humming keeps her going.

She yearns for light, to see something, anything that will help her escape the haunting thought. The ground shudders, and she scrapes her head on the ceiling. Something crawls down her arm. Max begins to yip in the distant blackness. Sura swings her arms out to her sides, scrapes the concrete walls, and steps quickly and carelessly.

Another monstrous groan.

Max yips again.

The darkness begins to change. A gray form takes shape, getting lighter and lighter with each step. Max waits for her like a furry lump of ash. Sura scoops him up. He licks her wet cheeks.

There's a short ladder attached to a wall. Ten rungs up, there's a hole. Leaves blow inside. A head appears with a frumpy hat. Even in the dim light, it's yellow. Two more yellow-hats look down, their fingers urging her to climb. Their rapid words tell her to hurry.

Sura climbs the bottom rungs.

The tunnel exhales a mighty wind that swirls her hair. The yellow hats are caught in the draft, twirling out of sight as the crowd quakes. Dirt rains down. She stops on the third rung to cover up. A terrible crash of wood, glass, and metal is everywhere.

The helpers return with yellow hats back on their heads. Tea olives greet her at the top with their fragrant blooms. Sura peeks out from a hole wedged between the root flares of an enormous live oak. The yellow-hats take Max and help her up, covering the hole with an earthen lid.

The helpers made it out.

Blue hats, red hats, orange, purple, green, and every color in between, are huddled beneath the live oak grove. Some of them were probably the ones that threw her and Joe into the back room, but now they cling to each other, listening to the house snap like massive bones.

Max climbs onto her lap. The yellow-hats press against her, their bodies warm. More crowd around her. She feels the weight of their neediness, the quake of their fear. The house cries out and the tower —listing to the north—is sucked down. A final tremor rides across the ground where bottomless ruts have opened. All that remains are holes. The toy factory is gone.

And so, finally, is the house.

Sura feels another emotional hole inside her, one right next to her mom. This one is Joe. The fear that drove her through the tunnel and steeled her legs evaporates, leaving her with the messy emptiness of her life. She puts her head down, letting the waiting grief have its way with her. She sobs uncontrollably.

The yellow-hats put their small arms around her. She hugs them. When they climb off, more of them comfort her. Red-hats, blue-hats, green-hats... they all find their way to Sura and squeeze tightly. Some shake with fear, others sob with her. Some of them utter speedy little words that sound comforting. Apologetic.

Sura openly weeps.

And hugs them all.

18

DECEMBER 25

Thursday

J ack wakes in a soft bed.

He rolls over, reaches for a pillow, and rakes his arm through powdery snow.

He opens his eyes.

The sun is rising somewhere to his right, but the stars are not dampened, not entirely. The sky is deep blue. A barren landscape of snow and ice extends in every direction. He's on the North Pole. He's back home. It was all a dream and now he's home.

HOME!

Jack marches in a circle, stomping the snow and pumping his fist. "Snow! Snow! Snow!"

Wait.

A memory thuds. He jumped into the wishing room when the house tried to eat him. This is Pawn's special place, a room to fulfill his every desire. That means this isn't snow, not really. And if he's in here, that means what's out there...

Jack's heart lies heavy.

Little Cindy opening her present, the fire, the creeping gray goo. The Pop-Tarts.

"Freeda?" Jack jumps up. "Freeda!"

His voice evaporates in the open sky.

"Pawn!"

Jack wades through the snow, white dust up to his elbows, sticking to his chin. He shouts their names over and over, walking in circles, but it's snow forever and ever.

There's nothing out there.

"Free—"

A hole.

It wasn't there a second ago. Now there's an opening like space has been parted like curtains, dark shrubbery on the other side.

The door!

He's got to get out. He can't stay in the wishing room, he'll starve. Without a coolsuit, he'll overheat. At least, that's what Freeda told him.

"Freeda?"

No answer.

The vegetative alleyway is dim but, surprisingly, doesn't feel too bad. It must've cooled down overnight. He steps onto the mulched path, twigs snapping underfoot. The garden is ahead; he can see daylight. He stops and listens for someone. For anything.

He hears nothing—not a tree frog, not a bird or a bug.

Jack stops at the entrance to the garden. There are holes in the boxwoods where he rolled through them on his way from the house, and there are still chunks of ice in the center. Jack walks around the outside of the garden. Steam rises from the remains of the statue. He stops at the exit.

No wonder Freeda didn't answer.

The house is gone.

Vanished.

As if it never existed.

There's a hole in the earth and deep gullies in the field. The soil isn't scorched, nothing is damaged, just a big vacancy where the house, the labs, and the toy factory used to be. The slave technology consumed it, transformed metal and wood, plastic and glass, into pure energy.

Just... gone.

What's left is a massive vacancy, something that—it would seem —could never be filled again.

The sun isn't up, but all the stars have dimmed except for the North Star. Jack is too jittery to notice it twinkling white, red, and green.

"Pawn!" Jack steps onto the road, hands cupped around his mouth. "Pawn! You there?"

He was in the basement, locked in the incubator lab. Why didn't he escape? Jack feels like he's falling, even though his feet are firmly on the ground.

"Pawn!"

His voice echoes off the distant trees. He resorts to Freeda's name, just in case there's a backup somewhere under the rubble. He'd love to hear her voice inside his head. So far, it's just his own. Each time he calls, it sounds shakier and a little higher pitched.

He stands at the edge of the chasm. Groundwater has filled it. He feels the depth of its hopelessness, how nothing is alive in that murky hole. He created it—this is *his* fault. He's the one responsible for this all-consuming hole in his life. He's been avoiding it for thousands of years and now he's staring into its depths. He always tried to fill the holes he felt inside himself, and now there's one big one he can't avoid.

And now what?

What does he have?

Nobody. It's just Jack and the hole.

"Janack?" someone calls.

He looks around. Maybe he's imagining it, but then he hears it again. It's coming from the garden. Jack steps tentatively across the road, trying not to make noise. He sneaks up to the entrance and slides one eye around the edge.

"Mother?"

There she is, standing on the pedestal where an ice statue chiseled into her likeness once stood. Her hands are folded on her belly, the white hair pulled back into the single braid.

"Janack," she says again.

Her face is soft, almost glowing. Her eyes, deeply set in fully rounded cheeks, are smiling blue.

Jack clears his throat. "Um, your statue... it fell over. There was a storm and, uh, we were going to do another one..."

She doesn't say anything. Jack gets the sense she doesn't care about the statue.

He looks up and sighs. He wasn't accustomed to taking responsibility. It's easier to lie. "It's just... you see, Pawn didn't tell me about you and me reconciling before I died, and I don't remember us, you know, that we were hugging and stuff, so if you think about it, it's kind of Pawn's fault."

This is hard.

"Oh, I don't remember what I said before I died." He swallows. "Or what you said or what Claus... so, I'm still a little..."

The words fall off his tongue like dead fish. He sounds stupid and embarrassed. His mother opens her arms. She smiles. That's all she does.

Smile.

Jack's belly softens. Without thinking about it, without forcing it, the words come out.

"This is all my fault." He looks down. "I did all this. I wrecked this whole place and everything in it. I was trying to help the world, you know. Seriously, I was. I don't like warmbloods..."

But that's not true. He knows it. And those words clog his throat until truer ones come out.

"I screwed up."

Something breaks loose. He feels it just below his heart, some silky essence spreading across his chest, rising to his throat. He's afraid to open his mouth or he'll...

"Come to me." Her arms are still open. Her face, still inviting.

Or I'll cry.

Jack steps through the boxwoods, taking a straight path toward the center. He stops short of the pool of water that surrounds Jocah. It's no longer ice, but he doesn't feel hot. He feels just right. His mother's love warms him.

He just... he has to say one more thing. He's got to say this, to admit it. To own it.

"I killed Pawn."

Warmth gushes through his throat and barks out sobs that rack his body.

"He was my only friend and I made him suffer with that root and then I shoved him in the basement and the house fell and I guess he couldn't swim or something..."

He runs out of breath. After that, the sobs take over.

He doesn't remember falling into her arms or splashing through the water, he just remembers the grief that fills him, that spills out of him. His feelings of hurt and abandonment rise up, feelings he's spent all his life trying to hide. He sees them, allows them space.

Pawn. My only friend.

And he did all that to him.

He tries to tell his mother more, tries to make sense of his thoughts, but the words are smeared with sniffles and sobs.

"What's wrong with me?" he blubbers.

His mother wraps him tightly, warmly, while he spills tears into the pool. Through blurry eyes, he sees his blue face.

"His name isn't Pawn," he says. "It's Jack."

He took that from his friend. It's time to give it back.

My name is Janack.

Another round of wailing fills the garden. He hangs onto his mother, her warmth protecting him, filling him, showing him that he's not bad.

He's lost.

Janack falls asleep in his mother's arms while the North Star twinkles white, red, and green. He doesn't feel his breath stop or his pulse silence. The end for the portly blue elven comes like a sweet lullaby.

THE CROW SOUNDS LIKE A HORN.

The sky is blemished only by fading white tracks left from airplanes crisscrossing at ten thousand feet.

The helpers are pressed all around Sura, keeping her toasty and comfortable. Their bite-sized snores merge like an endless mantra, tempting her to fall back asleep. She watches a commercial airliner slowly draw a white line across the blue sky, this one traveling south.

Max is gone. The crow calls again.

The tree root makes for a poor pillow, slightly bruising the side of her head. She sits up. Little bodies tumble off her but aren't roused from slumber. Sura rubs her eyes. The scene across the field quickly reminds her that reality can be cold and hard. A titan has taken a bite from the earth and stomped a hole in her life.

Joe is dead.

The image of his face will haunt her for the rest of her life: the waxy complexion, the vacant stare, his lips stiffly uttering his last words.

"N'ayez pas peur." Don't be afraid.

Those words will play in her dreams every night, will follow her every day. The hole in the earth is nothing compared to what she'll feel forever.

There are no tears left.

The truth shivers inside her. She thinks of crawling beneath the sleeping helpers, closing her eyes, and dreaming of some place warm, safe, and wanted. But that won't help.

And she's awake.

Sura stands up. She has to hopscotch her way through sleeping helpers. She steps out of the tree's shadow. Frost glitters on the grass where tracks lead away. Max must've left sometime during the night.

It's not safe. The ground looks soft and the chasm deep. If he fell, there'll be no saving him, and she's lost so much already.

She exhales faint clouds.

How did this happen?

Where will the helpers go?

Where will I go?

Sura follows Max's path, the tracks etched in the frost. She hugs herself against the morning breeze, her clothes damp. She keeps her distance from the pit as clods break away from the sides and plunk into the deep water.

Birds flutter in the trees and squirrels dig through the fallen leaves. Whatever happened affected the house and laboratories. Even the barn is gone.

She slows as the space between the trees and the chasm narrows. The edge of the great hole stops short of the road that once circled the house. A flighty sensation of vertigo tugs at her. She brushes against the hedges as she approaches the garden entrance.

Voices.

Sura holds her breath. Her pulse is loud in her ears.

"We stayed at the southern end of the plantation," Templeton says. "There wasn't much sleeping."

Someone answers him, but it's too soft to understand.

"Sit down," Templeton says. "You're weak."

Sura crawls the final steps and peeks around the opening. She stays low enough to not be noticed. Templeton is near the center of the garden. He's wearing a puffy coat and a stocking cap. His face is smudged with dirt.

"The transfer," he says. "It was complete?"

She can't see the other person, but he speaks louder. "Missing memories," he says.

The voice trails off. Templeton listens patiently. Sura thinks about crawling closer, but that'll give her up, and she'd like to find out who is down there.

"What happened to Sura?" Templeton asks.

The other person says something. Templeton's expression doesn't change when he says, "We'll search for her when the others get here. What about Joe?"

Sura clutches the grass. She holds her breath, raises up slightly, but can't hear. Maybe he didn't say anything. Templeton, though, dips his head. It's not much, maybe he's just tired. He's not even standing upright.

"You're cold," Templeton finally says. "Take off your shirt."

Take off your shirt?

Templeton bends over to help. Max lets out a yip. The fox is down there. Templeton can't be talking to Mr. Frost. It doesn't sound like him. *And Mr. Frost doesn't get cold.*

There's mumbling. It goes on for quite a while this time.

"It's all complete," Templeton finally answers. "Everything worked as you planned. The house, the laboratories, everything. It's all been dissolved entirely. Janack's impatience and greed worked as you thought it would. He attempted to get it all and it backfired."

"Did Freeda survive?" the unknown person asks.

"Like I said, everything is gone," Templeton says.

"And the human race?"

"They are none the wiser. The initial launch harmed no one, including the family. However, they lost everything in a fire."

"I want—"

Templeton raises his hand. "Already taken care of. An anonymous donation will arrive this afternoon, along with presents for the young girl. I believe her name is Cindy."

Sura's elbows ache, her knees throb. It feels safe down there, but she can't take the chance. If she's wrong, if that's not Mr. Frost...

If only Joe was with her. They could get back in the truck and camp until they knew it was safe.

"So I must ask," Templeton says. "Jack is dead?"

Sura waits for the answer. There is none. Templeton is looking in the direction of the wishing room. He lets out a deep breath like he's held it for far too long. For the first time, he looks relaxed.

There's a squeal.

It comes from the south side of the garden. May is standing in the entrance, hands over her mouth. She's not bundled up like Templeton, but she's just as dirty.

"Is it true?" she asks.

Templeton almost smiles.

May runs carefully around the boxwoods, arms swinging to her sides, her squeal interrupted only by brief inhalations. She gets to the center and bends down, disappearing from Sura's view.

"Careful, May," Templeton says. "He's delicate. You'll snap him like a twig."

May finally stands up and hooks her arm around Templeton's elbow. She wipes her eyes.

"It's over," she says. "It's finally over."

Templeton pats her hand.

"Where's Sura?" she asks. "Joe?"

Sura can't hear the answer. She sits up and there's a sudden yip. Max shoots through the boxwoods and lands in Sura's arms. She falls over.

Templeton shades his eyes. May covers her mouth again. The squeal is twice as loud this time. She lifts her arms and doesn't bother with the path; this time, she pushes straight through the boxwoods. She struggles with the last row, so Sura goes to her to be crushed in a cookie-smelling embrace, smothered in May's heaving chest. She no longer cares if it's safe or not.

It smells like home.

"Come now, May," Templeton calls.

May releases Sura to wipe her cheeks. Sura blinks the world back into focus and sees Templeton waving them down. May clings to Sura's arm like she'll never let go. They wind their way to the center.

The mysterious guest is slumped on the bench. He's short, skinny, and his chest is covered with hair.

Green hair.

The face is vaguely familiar: the short nose and deep eyes. The whiskers, also green, are tightly curled against his face. His upper body is matted with thick, green hair.

He lifts his tired hand, beckoning her with a single curl of his finger. Templeton takes the shirt off the bench. Sura slowly takes a seat. He smells organic. Leafy.

He smiles weakly.

Sura recognizes the eyes set in the shadows of bushy brows. The icy blue twinkle.

"Mr. Frost?" she asks.

His smile grows.

May collapses on Templeton's shoulder, heaving great wallops of sobbing joy. Templeton hands her a handkerchief.

Mr. Frost takes Sura's hand. It's coarse, slightly damp. He holds out his other hand for Templeton. He takes it and holds May's hand. They form a ring—two of them standing, two sitting.

"I am so grateful." Mr. Frost's words are scratched and tearful. A breath wheezes into his lungs. "To call you family."

Their hands tighten.

"Joe isn't here," Sura says dryly, afraid to let her emotions rise.

Mr. Frost bows his head. Templeton and May do the same. They remain in silence for a full minute. Mr. Frost lets go and, with Templeton's assistance, he stands. Mr. Frost takes a moment to balance himself like a newborn calf before tenderly walking with Templeton at his side. Slowly, they go to the north side of the garden and stop at the entrance that leads to the wishing room.

Mr. Frost whispers to Templeton.

"Come along," Templeton says. "You, too, Jonah."

Jonah is standing in the southern entrance where May had entered.

Mr. Frost disappears into the tunnel. May starts to follow, but Sura's stuck to the bench, afraid to grasp the strange, tangible hope that seems to float around her. If they think seeing Joe in the wishing room will make her feel better, then they've lost their minds.

It'll only hurt worse.

"Come on, love." May gently takes her arm.

Sura walks with heavy feet. She reaches the north archway and refuses to go any farther. Jonah is at the end of the tunnel, facing the entrance to the wishing room. Light floods out of the opening.

Jonah steps inside. His wail is joyful.

"I'm not going, May." Sura steps back. "I don't want to see him in there. He won't be real; he'll just be in my mind and that's not... it's just an illusion, May."

May takes her hands to keep them from shaking, to keep her from running away. Nothing in that room is real. Joe will just be a dream and she doesn't have the strength to dream like that. Not right now.

If I see him in there, I'll never want to leave.

"I have to wake up," Sura says.

But May's expression never falters. In fact, it grows warmer. With tears brimming, May looks down the tunnel. Sura follows her gaze.

Jonah steps outside of the wishing room; a smile that looks foreign on his face is wide and toothy. He reaches back, helping someone step through the opening. He steps tenderly like Mr. Frost.

It's Joe.

Joe is outside.

A chill crawls over her, tingling her scalp. Her lower lip begins to flutter. She wants to believe it, wants to let go of May, but she's been fooled by dreams before. Sura looks up. The North Star is still visible, but it's not twinkling strange colors. It's not twinkling at all.

Jonah lets go of Joe. He walks on his own, stepping gingerly towards Sura. His arms and face have a thin coat of curly, green hair. Sura's afraid to move, afraid to blink, or he'll disappear. Afraid she'll wake up.

He steps into the sunlight and extends his hand. Sura hesitates.

"*N'ayez pas peur,*" he says.

I am awake.

MR. FROST SHIVERS.

"Let's get you into the sunlight," Templeton says.

The others have already left the garden, their voices shouting somewhere on the other side of the hedges. Max yips continuously. All of them, so happy.

Because it's over. It's finally over.

Templeton holds Mr. Frost's hand, guiding him away from the wishing room. The new body is so frail and light, the feet not half the size of what he's walked on his entire life. He will never slide on his soles again.

They step into the garden. He turns his face upward, searching for the sun. Green hair unfurls in the direction of light, warmth reaching his core. The photosynthetic gene splice was meant to temporarily stabilize the body. He could make it permanent, use it to help humans feed themselves with sunlight, but that would create a new species. Mr. Frost is done with that.

It's over.

He feigned surprise when Jack escaped the laboratory without his memories. He had the yellow-hats guide him outside when Freeda was occupied. They set him free.

Mr. Frost had won the yellow-hats' loyalty long ago. He accidently discovered the loyalty gene shortly after the helpers were first born. Freeda had programmed them to serve her. Mr. Frost made a slight alteration in the yellow-hats' gene sequence. It wasn't easy. In fact, it took decades to accomplish without Freeda knowing.

Without the yellow-hats, the ending would have been very different. They were the ones that put the pictures where Sura would see them—her mom's box and the one on Joe's refrigerator. They were the ones that lured her into the toy factory so that Mr. Frost could arrange for Jack to see her outside Walmart, to feel her presence.

Janack was right about one thing: Mr. Frost despised the warm-bloods when he still lived in the Arctic. Had Mr. Frost remained in the Arctic, had the root not forced him to live among the humans, to know them, to love them... well, again, the ending would have been different.

And if Janack lived with them, even for a short while, then he would know them, too. That's why Mr. Frost let him escape, to let him live with the humans. Perhaps, in the end, it had some effect. Mr. Frost will never know if Janack watched the attack with glee or horror. Did he try to stop it? Did he feel his heart grow? Did he feel love?

If he did, that will make all the difference.

Mr. Frost's feet feel like boat anchors. Templeton guides him around the perimeter of the garden. "Careful," he says, helping him up the stone steps. "This is your last body."

They stand at the crater's edge. On the other end, near the live oak grove, the others are mobbed by a sea of brightly hatted helpers. When Freeda went down, they were released from her command. They're all "yellow-hats" now. Max nips at their heels like a worried shepherd, keeping them from a watery drop.

A plane slowly crosses the blue sky.

Mr. Frost feels the sun rise above the trees. Light spreads across his shoulders. He reaches for the back of his neck, his fingers crawling through the short mop of coarse hair. No more itching.

No Freeda. No Janack. No root.

The end.

His memories are spotty. Mr. Frost had fed them to Max, where they were stored in a root imbedded between the fox's shoulder blades.

"May I ask where the blue elven's body is?" Templeton asks.

"Janack?"

"Do you know of another blue elven?"

Mr. Frost smiles. "It's still in the wishing room, beneath the leaves."

"You expended all that energy to hide the body?"

"In case Sura went inside the wishing room; I didn't want her to see it. She's been through enough."

They watch the celebration work its way toward them. Mr. Frost is no longer hunched over. The light is working wonders.

"What do you think happened?" Templeton asks.

"You mean how did he die?"

"I suppose."

Mr. Frost scratches his chin. "The wishing room provided Jack his deepest desire, but not so much what he wanted. It was what he needed. He reconnected with his mother, like he did the last time. I suspect that he transformed in that moment. Maybe he even realized he was stuck in the wishing room instead of actually resting in his mother's arms."

"Then why didn't he leave?"

"He didn't want to, Templeton. He preferred to die in the dream."

"Do you think he suffered in the end?" Templeton asks.

"I hope not."

"Well, let's not be rash. Perhaps he deserved a little suffering. After all..." Templeton doesn't finish the obvious thought. "Speaking of the blue elven, shall we go back to the wishing room and awaken the last body?"

"Mmm... perhaps we can enjoy this moment a while longer without it."

Mr. Frost takes Templeton's arm, urging him forward. "He has much to atone for, Templeton. Let's not waste time."

They start the slow journey back to the wishing room. Mr. Frost asks Templeton to first pass through the center. They circle around the garden to sit on the bench. The statue is still in shambles. Perhaps he'll replace it with something else.

"You were a great elven." Templeton sits next to him. "I believe you will be an even better man."

"Let's hope so, Templeton."

They rest a bit longer before returning to the wishing room.

To awaken the last human body.

SOUTH CAROLINA

2034

19

T he tickets are green and scarlet.

They're hard to come by at a reasonable price, but the chance to see Frost Plantation only comes on Christmas Eve. Shelly tucks the ticket into her back pocket. She'll keep it with the tickets from the last two events. Not many people can say they've been there three times.

Shelly knows people in high places.

The event started at six o'clock. It's almost midnight. Mr. Frost is finishing his annual telling of The Tale of Frost, a story that's become somewhat famous. "A Yarn for the Modern Day" *Time Magazine* called it. The story's not true, of course, but watching Mr. Frost tell it makes you wonder.

The great room has a domed ceiling that's three stories high, with long windows radiating from the center like spokes, the stars glittering inside the elongated panes, the moon fully lit in the northern glass. A Christmas tree—one worthy of Times Square—is near the north wall, with gifts wrapped in shiny, red paper and fat, green bows.

May and Jonah sit to the left of the tree, hands folded on their laps. Templeton stands on the right, stiff as plaster, with their white dog, Max, at his side.

Mr. Frost performs in front of the tree.

Children—sitting on cushions that soften the marble floor—enclose the short, skinny man as he waves his arms and raises his voice for an hour, eliciting belly-clutching laughter and, soon, tissue-worthy tears.

At first, the children are transfixed by the gifts, wondering which one has their name on it. Mr. Frost soon makes them forget about the presents.

Shelly started volunteering at the horse therapy program when she started college. After four years of assisting Sura, they expanded its reach across the state of South Carolina. *The Frost Plantation's Telling of the Tale Extravaganza* tickets have always been distributed to charities, such as the horse therapy program. Shelly buys hers, of course. It's a privilege.

She leans on the doorway opposite the Christmas tree. She can't see much, but it doesn't matter, she just wants to hear it. Besides, the people in front of her are seeing it for the first time. It's a performance that's never been recorded and not because people haven't tried. All attempts come back blank. Rumor has it that there's a reward to the first hacker who can do it and, so far, it remains unclaimed.

The kids are slack-mouthed. Mr. Frost is telling the part where Joe walks out of the wishing room. Shelly's favorite part.

"Of course, it's all made up," Sura once told her. "My dad's been telling the Tale since we were little. He just added the part about Joe when we got married. Something for the grandkids."

Sura and Joe are sitting to the right of Templeton, listening like the story is new to them, too. Hallie, blonde with blue eyes, sits on Joe's lap, and Sunni, hair as red as a stop sign, sits on Sura's crossed legs. Riley, their third child, must be with her friends. If the tale was true and Joe and Sura really are clones, well, then their kids sure aren't.

"Hey."

Shelly jumps at the sound of her husband's voice. "Where have you been?"

"Shhh." His face is scratched. "I got to show you something."

"No. This is the best part."

"You got to see this."

Her eyes become circles. Henry knows what that face means, but it only makes him smile.

"Why didn't Santa save you?" a kid asks Mr. Frost.

The crowd erupts with laughter. Mr. Frost responds, "Why, he was busy, of course. It was Christmas!"

Another burst of laughter.

"You won't regret this," Henry says. "I swear."

"It's almost over, just wait."

"It just can't wait," he says too loudly, on purpose. "Now or never."

He never got like this.

Shelly looks up, thinking. He knows this look, too—that she'll give in because she doesn't want to have a whispering argument that's not too whispery.

"This better be good."

He pulls her out of the crowd that happily fills her vacancy. The hall is wide and tall, archways rising up to the ceiling. Mr. Frost's voice follows them down the hardwood.

An elaborate chandelier hangs above the massive doors strewn with garland and origami ornaments folded by children. There's a room to the right where a fire crackles in a wide fireplace, and a large painting of the family hangs above the hearth. Shelly knows almost all of them.

Dirt falls off Henry's shoes. It's also smudged on his knees. He pulls open the front door and rushes her down the steps.

"We got to hurry." He walks at a pace just short of running.

"Tell me," she whines.

"Shhh."

They cross the paved driveway, where a few people mill about, waiting for story time to end so they can get good seats on the night's final trolley tour around the plantation. The miniature train goes through the trees and near the old rice fields, around the live oak grove and past the guest houses. Jonah, the conductor, retells the story, pointing out where Sura woke up with the helpers on

Christmas morning. Occasionally, guests see flashes of bright hats in the trees like little helpers are following.

The lake—where the story's first plantation house was built and, as the tale goes, disappeared—is glassy. The new house is on the northern end and facing south just in front of the live oak grove, the mossy branches reaching over it.

"All right." Henry slows down when every living soul is far behind them. "I started poking around because I've heard the story, like, a hundred times."

"You've heard it three times."

"Feels like a hundred. Anyway, I thought I'd look around where the original house was supposed to be."

"The story's made up, Henry."

He makes a face. "Yeah, I know. Converting matter to energy could evaporate the solar system. Even a high school physics teacher knows that, duh."

She smiles.

"I just thought it'd be more fun to pretend like it was real. And guess what?"

"You found a helper."

"Even better."

They reach the end of the lake, where an overgrown hedge reaches across a leafy archway. Henry quickly pulls her through the entrance.

The boxwoods are still neatly trimmed and the camellias are loaded with white blooms. "Seafoam," Sura once told her. A fountain trickles in the center where the tarnished form of a mother, her long braid down her back, comforts her son. Both are as round as cherubs. That's where Jack lay in his mother's arms, thinking he was in the garden when he was still inside the wishing room, where his body painlessly died in the South Carolina "heat."

Water dances over them.

"The garden," Shelly says. "This isn't a secret."

"I started thinking." Henry pulls her to the left, following the path. "The story talks about the wishing room on the north end of the garden, but there's no entrance."

"Because it's made up."

They walk halfway down the north side.

"Or they let it grow closed," he says.

The hedge is solid. There's no hint of an opening, just a wall of thorny firethorn. Henry gets on his knees.

"I'm not going in there," Shelly says.

He pushes through the bushes, disappearing like a rabbit. He holds open a hole from the inside. And despite what she just said, her body is tingling. Her heart, racing. *What if...*

No one is in the garden, no one will see. She'll make it quick. She scurries through the hedge. It's thicker than she thought and, for a moment, considers backing out.

She emerges in a dark tunnel. The branches arch overhead and twigs crisscross along the walls, like someone keeps it from collapsing.

"Oh my God," she utters, slack-mouthed like the children.

Henry uses his phone as a light and takes her hand, guiding her to the dead end. "I thought—"

"It's right there." Shelly points.

Even in the darkened passageway, she sees his expression of mock surprise. His hand tightens.

"I listen to the story," she says. "I know how it goes."

Henry sinks his arms into the dense growth and, rather easily, parts them like curtains.

And there it is.

The wishing room.

A small, circular opening is carved in the overgrown forest. The walls are just as thick as the tunnel, the ceiling much higher but just as dense. The ground is soft with leaves that crunch. Shelly drags her hand along the outside, imagining what it would be like if it worked. Would she be on the beach with her grandmother before she died? Or hiking with the family on Grandfather Mountain? Would the wishing room know her innermost desires, and would the North Star glitter white, red, and green?

"Wow," is all she can say.

"Yeah," Henry says in a told-you-so kind of way. "But that's not the best part. I figured maybe they just keep it like this for idiots like me. Then I found this."

He pulls wisteria vines—thick as mooring line—to the side. He aims the phone at the curved surfaces hidden beneath. Shelly kneels down, touching them to make sure they're real.

Glass tanks.

The surfaces are tinted green with moss and algae, rough with grime. It's how the tale ends. Joe is reborn in one of the tanks Mr. Frost stashed in the wishing room because that's the only place Freeda couldn't see. He doesn't remember much when he comes out, but he remembers Sura. True love never forgets.

The other tank is where Mr. Frost was incubated. A human body. Max is an Arctic fox in the tale. Mr. Frost used the special food to transfer his memories into his beloved pet, where they were stored in a special root imbedded just beneath the Arctic fox's skin. When the time came, Max carried them to the wishing room, where they were uploaded to a glass tank, where they were passed into a human body still green with hair.

"You think these are from the tale?" she asks.

"Heck yeah, they are. And maybe they just put them here, but it's a trip. Right?"

"Anything in them?"

Henry pries at a crease and the front of one opens, the inside filled with spiderwebs. "Nothing but arachnid condos."

"What's that?"

Henry pulls at the vines to her left. There's another tank tucked a little farther back, this one just as filthy as the others. The door is wide open.

"A third one," he says.

"There's not a third one in the tale."

Maybe Henry's right; they just put this stuff back there to give the tale life when people go snooping. *What am I thinking? The tale isn't true. There's no such thing as elven, Jack Frost, and incubators. Of course this is a goof.*

"Look." Henry plants his foot for leverage and pulls the vines back even further. "Is that another one?"

Shelly takes his phone and crawls deeper. A fourth tank is back there. Unlike the others, the door is sealed shut. She stands on her knees, the branches snagging her shirt. The surface is covered with algae and grime, but if she holds the light close enough, she can see the fauna inside like an upright terrarium.

Shelly gets to her feet and presses the phone against the rounded top. She can see a form inside. It has the vague shape of shoulders and a round head with wild strands of grassy foliage spraying around it. Shelly often wondered why the tale only had two tanks: one for Mr. Frost and the other for Joe.

"You don't think that's..." she says.

"What?" Henry says.

What if Sura died? Wouldn't he have prepared for that?

A train whistles.

Shelly jumps out with a short scream. Her heart is about to pound through her sternum. They laugh childishly. Henry helps her up.

"What was it?" he asks.

"Just another tank, but it's closed."

"Three open and one closed. What do you think the closed one was for?"

She shakes her head. If she says it out loud, it'll sound stupid. If she says it, it'll dispel the magic bubbling in her stomach.

"Two open for Mr. Frost and Joe, but what about the other open one?" Henry says.

"Yeah," she says. "No one ever said anything about that, either. Everyone was safe."

"I know what it is." Henry snaps his fingers and points at Shelly's expectant expression. "It's a tall tale."

She smacks his arm. It's more fun if they pretend it's real.

They sneak back out as quickly as they broke in. Henry exits first. He holds the hedge open. Shelly rushes through on her hands and knees, scratches already burning.

There are voices just outside the garden. *Just in time.*

"Come on," Henry says. "We can catch the trolley if we hurry."

They rush out the exit, still laughing like children, when they run into a man and child, frightening them as much as they scare themselves. The man falls to one knee, but the little girl hangs onto his hand.

"I'm so sorry," Henry exclaims, helping him up. "We were trying to catch the trolley."

"Quite all right." The man is short and slight, couldn't weigh more than a ten-year-old. The moon shines off his bald head. He brushes himself off, smiling.

"You all right?" Shelly asks the girl, and then recognizes her. "Are you Riley?"

"Yes, ma'am."

"I know Sura. She's your mother, right? I'm Miss Shelly."

She clings to the man's arm and doesn't care about her mom's friend.

The whistle blows again.

"You better hurry," the little man says.

"I'm so sorry." Henry pulls Shelly away. "Merry Christmas!"

The little man nods. "Merry Christmas."

Shelly waves. The little girl doesn't wave back, but Shelly hears her say something just before they're out of range. She hears something that, later that night when she's lying in bed, will give her cause to smack Henry on the arm and tell him that she knows who was in the third tank.

The little girl says, "Who was that, Uncle Janack?"

FLURY: JOURNEY OF A SNOWMAN (BOOK 3)

Get the Claus Universe at:
BERTAUSKI.COM/CLAUS

Flury: Journery of a Snowman (Book 3)

CHAPTER 1

Malcolm Toye fell.

He had seen nothing but ice for days, wandering the Arctic in search of the men that brought him this far north. Their ship crushed by the ice, they had struck out on foot, dragging boats over frozen snow and through open leads of water until landing upon Bennett Island. Ravaged by frostbite and scurvy, no one should've lived. But they continued south, and that's when Malcolm had become separated.

With rifle in hand, he had given chase to what he thought was a wounded seal, but had slipped into the icy water. Soaked and numb, he returned to camp to find that the men had already moved on. Shortly after, snow began to fall, and he was eternally alone.

And now he had fallen for the last time.

He couldn't feel his legs. He was certain that if a miracle occurred and the men found him, he would lose his feet to frostbite. At the very least, his toes.

It was a foolish journey, but men like Malcom Toye had always pursued such folly. The North Pole called to him, dared him to conquer it. He was eager to join the expedition, see parts of the world very few had witnessed with their own eyes. Only the dubious tales of explorers existed about the endless sheet of ice that topped the world. He wanted to be one of the first men to ever see it.

He had come close.

When he fell backwards, landing in the soft embrace of fresh snow, he didn't feel the impact. He was certain, as he gazed into the sky where, somewhere past his feet, the sun was just below the horizon, that he would not only lose his feet to frostbite, but his nose as well. That didn't bother him.

I will die alone.

He labored to breathe as he tore at the buttons of his U.S. Navy-issued coat, his fingers plastic things that refused to bend or grasp. Violent shivers made it difficult, but he managed to slip his hand inside his coat to find an inner pocket. Despite the numbness, he felt the cold metal fall into his palm.

A gold locket.

The latch was too tight for his stiff and senseless fingers. Instead, he clutched it tightly before the shivers tossed it from his hand. The attached chain pooled on the fabric of his frozen coat. He yearned to see, one last time, the photo of his bride, hope that she would be the last image he took with him in this unforgiving wasteland of ice. He imagined her green eyes and brown hair falling over her shoulders, the way she smiled when she woke.

As his breaths grew shallow, he let go of the pain squeezing his chest and melted into the snowy embrace. A warm sensation filled him. He drifted into sleep, where a sweet dream was promised and, perhaps, his wife would be waiting.

It was in these last moments that the wind began to swirl.

Malcolm didn't notice the ice shudder or the shadow pass over him. He had given himself to leaving the world. He opened his eyes one last time to look at the dark sky. Instead, he saw two massive legs straddling him.

A giant blotted out the stars.

YOU DONATED TO A WORTHY CAUSE!

By purchasing this book, you have donated to ease the suffering of the homeless since 10% of the profits is annually donated to the Lowcountry Food Bank.

ABOUT THE AUTHOR

My grandpa never graduated high school. He retired from a steel mill in the mid-70s. He was uneducated, but a voracious reader. As a kid, I'd go through his bookshelves of musty paperback novels, pulling Piers Anthony and Isaac Asimov off the shelf and promising to bring them back. I was fascinated by robots that could think and act like people. What happened when they died?

Writing is sort of a thought experiment to explore human nature and possibilities. What makes us human? What is true nature?

I'm also a big fan of plot twists.

Printed in the USA
CPSIA information can be obtained
at www.ICGtesting.com
LVHW051558301023
762359LV00082B/95

9 781951 432010